FORGET ME NOT

By Allison Blanchard

Martin Sisters Publishing

Published by

Mudfoot Books, a division of Martin Sisters Publishing, LLC

www. martinsisterspublishing. com

Copyright © 2012 Allison Blanchard

The unauthorized reproduction or distribution of this copyrighted work is illegal. Criminal copyright infringement, including infringement without by monetary gain, is investigated by the Federal Bureau of Investigation and is punishable by up to 5 (five) years in federal prison and a fine of $250,000.

Names, characters and incidents depicted in this book are products of the author's imagination or are used fictitiously. Any resemblance to actual events, locales, organizations, or persons, living or dead, is entirely coincidental and beyond the intent of the author or publisher.

No part of this book may be reproduced or transmitted in any form or by any means, electronic or mechanical, including photocopying, recording, or by any information storage and retrieval system, without permission in writing from the publisher.

All rights reserved. Published in the United States by Mudfoot Books, an imprint of Martin Sisters Publishing, LLC, Kentucky.

ISBN: 978-1-937273-70-5
Young Adult/Romance/Fantasy
Printed in the United States of America
Martin Sisters Publishing, LLC

"Every good and perfect gift comes from above."
~ James 1:17

DEDICATION

In honor of my Daddy, Preston Kelley Blanchard.
I will always be your little girl.

ACKNOWLEGEMENTS

My joy and thanks are to my Lord Jesus Christ first and foremost.
All the glory goes to Him alone.

An imprint of Martin Sisters Publishing, LLC

PART I

"But when a young lady is to be a heroine, the perverseness of forty surrounding families cannot prevent her. Something must and will happen to throw a hero in her way."

~ Jane Austen, Northanger Abbey

ALLISON BLANCHARD

PROLOGUE

Life is tragic, an ongoing river, a rough current that yanks you around until you have nothing left. It's a dangerous thing to mess with the flow, with the cycle of life. To try to change the course is not only hard but also stupid. No one can change destiny, the set path before us.

Life is beautifully tragic. Giving it up isn't the hard part; it's the living part that everyone struggles with.

ALLISON BLANCHARD

Chapter One

I almost lost my breath when he walked through the door. Here, in the small town of Great Falls, Montana stood an angel in the front of my geometry class. His very presence gave the whitewashed room a certain glow. His skin was a dark, rusty copper. His onyx hair stopped at his neck, curled, and hung close to his face. I finally looked into his clear, blue eyes, but found them looking down to his feet. He was standing awkwardly at the front of the class, never meeting anyone's eye as Mr. Holman read his note from the office. He was very tall, about 6'2", with long legs that couldn't seem to stay still as he swayed side to side.

Something about him caught my attention the moment he walked through the door. Like some magnetic pull. Nothing I could possibly explain, not even to myself. He looked strong, but seemed so unsure, nervous. But that wasn't the only reason it took so much self-control to look away.

It couldn't be that he was from the Indian reservation. Plenty of students had transferred from the reservation school. Although, most of them had transferred back for one reason or another. I never cared enough to take much notice.

I've never really taken much notice to any of the other students that attended my high school for that matter. That might be one of the reasons no one took any notice of me, either.

I was never the most social person in my grade. I didn't see the point of befriending people when in two years we would lose all contact because we were thousands of miles away trying to figure out what we were going to do with our lives. It seemed kind of pointless.

I heard Mr. Holman mutter something about finding a seat. The beautiful boy kept silent and sat down quickly, avoiding eye contact with everyone.

The thought flew across my mind about trying to befriend him, showing him around the school. But the thought left as quickly as it came. There was no way I could show him, whoever he was, around. I barely had any confidence left to take myself to class. And that was thanks to Lily.

One of my first, and very few, friends was Lily Shelton. We had been best friends all the way through middle school. But when we started high school, Lily changed. Suddenly, boys and the desire to be accepted were more important than me, than our friendship. Ever since our friendship crumbled into oblivion, I have kept to myself. Out of both pride and self-preservation.

I glanced to my left, simply curious to see how he was holding up. He turned at the same moment and our eyes locked. I instantly looked away, completely mortified, keeping my eyes glued to either the board or my book. However, I could not shake the feeling that he was still staring.

Thankfully, the bell rang. I stood up, shoving my books into my bag. I began to leave the room when a deep, rustic voice stopped me.

"Excuse me, but can you tell me where I can find room 102?"

I looked over my shoulder, and time seemed to stand still.

"Uh, it's down the hall," I replied awkwardly, vaguely pointing out the door.

"I could show you! I know this school like the back of my hand!" Interrupted Sasha, her fire red hair framing her striking, magazine worthy face.

I saw the triumph in her eyes and cringed internally. There was no denying she was beautiful.

I decided to end my embarrassment and leave the room. Sasha would show the new boy around. I was sure he had already forgotten the small, average girl he had asked where to find his next class.

Once I made it to the hallway, I could finally take a deep breath and steady my pulse. I wasn't sure why this particular boy was suddenly making me feel and act the way I was. The boy and this strange connection to him was unfamiliar territory. And being the coward I was, I was going to run from change. Not allow it to grow or continue to have any more influence on my life. So all I had to do was avoid him like the plague and life would hopefully return to normal. It wasn't too hard to avoid people, especially when half the school didn't even know your name. I was almost to my history room when I felt a warm hand grab my shoulder.

"Um, excuse me," the same voice politely began.

I glanced over my shoulder, completely dumbfounded. What was he doing?

"Hello," I replied still unsure. "Can I help you?"

"Oh," His eyes wavered from mine. He dropped his hand from my shoulder, his smile fading. "I was just wondering if you could help me find room 102? I'm completely lost."

Now I was completely lost.

"Well, I thought Sasha was going to help you."

His face fell in confusion. Obviously he had no idea who I was talking about.

"You know, the girl back in geometry? The tall red head?" I tried to trigger his memory. He couldn't have possibly forgotten Sasha, the essence of shallow beauty and every high school boy's dream.

"Oh, her?" His face expressed glimmers of past annoyance. "She wasn't very helpful…"

If I wasn't confused before, then I was surely bewildered now. Who was this guy? And why did he chase me down the hall just to ask where the history room was? I'm sure there were plenty of other friendly students who would have been only too happy to help.

"Well, I have history next. I could show you if you want.…" I responded, already walking toward the room.

His face broke out into a huge smile, "Thank you! I'd really appreciate it."

"Uh huh," I muttered as we made our way to history before the bell rang.

I sat down at my usual table in the back, always a little happy about getting the whole table to myself. There were perks to being socially unacceptable. However, my happiness disintegrated when the new boy took the seat beside me.

"I'm sorry, but I don't believe I caught your name."

I stopped unpacking my books and looked into his unfamiliar blue eyes.

"Adeline," I whispered as a blush covered my cheeks. Now I was completely annoyed with myself.

"That's beautiful," he said while getting out his note from the office and beginning to walk over to Mr. Jackson.

"What?" I asked flabbergasted.

"Your name. It's beautiful," he whispered shyly. He then walked past me and over to Mr. Jackson.

My legs suddenly felt like they were made of jelly and about to give out, so I quickly sat down and opened up my notes. He slid into the seat beside me, and it took every ounce of self-control to not stare at him like an idiot.

Why did he feel the need to sit beside me anyway? I saw how many available seats there were.

Mr. Jackson quickly began class and announced that we would be doing a project. Luckily (or unluckily considering it was me), the new boy was my partner. I glanced to my right and found him staring at me. I looked back to the front of the room, too embarrassed to say or do anything.

So my plan for avoiding the new boy had suddenly disappeared into thin air. Wonderful.

Mr. Jackson gave each table a sheet of paper with directions. We were assigned a major historical event. We were to write a paper and present a slideshow to the class.

I jumped when I felt my new partner take the piece of paper. He carefully read it over, his forehead creased in thought.

"So, what's our project?" I asked, trying to sound nonchalant. If we were going to have to work together, I was going to make the most of it, and hopefully after it was over, I could move on with my life.

"Reconstruction in the South after the Civil War," he replied handing me the sheet.

I nodded, not sure how to continue the conversation. I glanced back down to my notes,

"So, I never caught your name."

"Cole Dyami," he replied pulling out his history book.

"So, Cole," his name felt like fire on my tongue, "what brings you to Great Falls, Montana?"

He mused to himself before answering, "I live on the Little Shell Reservation. It's about ten miles from here."

His answer didn't really surprise me. Many Native Americans lived, worked, and went to school here. However, over the recent years, more and more Natives have transferred back to the school on the reservation. Now my school mostly contained Caucasians with the exception of some of our Korean seniors.

"Really? Why don't you go to school there?" I asked trying not to sound too curious. "Why don't you go back?"

"My family and I decided this was where I should go. It's what's best for our tribe," he answered carefully, embarrassed even. Almost as if he was afraid of giving away too much information.

I glanced around the room, avoiding everyone's gaze, especially Cole's. We then began discussing how we were going to do our project. Cole said his dad had plenty of materials we could use. I let him make most of the decisions, since he knew more about the subject. Soon, we had outlined most of our plans and were waiting for the bell to ring. The rest of the class was still complaining to Mr. Jackson about the deadline, hoping it would be due in two weeks instead of one.

"So, how long have you lived here?"

I glanced to my right and found Cole looking at me, his blue eyes captivating; almost hiding behind the black veil of his bangs.

"Um, my whole life," I stuttered like an idiot.

His lips turned upward into a smile, "Me too."

I smiled with him, finding his expression contagious.

"So, do you like our school?" I asked while doodling on my notebook.

"It's all right. The schoolwork is easy enough. It's definitely different," he replied, smirking.

"Different how?" I asked, confused yet again.

"Well, I've never met anyone like you," Cole answered, seeming embarrassed. He looked down to his hands, which were neatly folded on top of the lab table.

"Same here," I whispered, not trusting my voice.

He sighed heavily, tilting his head toward me, as if he was going to say something, but decided against it.

I looked at him questionably. There was no denying he was mysterious, that was for sure.

The bell rang, ending the period. I stood up, grabbing my bag and books. It wasn't until I was half way to the cafeteria did I notice Cole was following me.

I became aware of him walking beside me as I went through the lunch line, paid for my meal, and sat down at my usual table in the corner of the room, next to a window.

"What are you doing?" I asked, suddenly self-conscious of all the eyes looking at the new boy and me. This was the last thing I needed.

"Eating lunch," he said quietly as he sat across the table from me.

My cheeks flushed at my stupid question and at the fact that people were still staring.

"But why with me?"

"Why not you?" he countered, smiling a smile that would make anyone's heart melt, including mine. Stupid boy.

"I...I don't know," I stuttered. "I'm not very interesting."

He rolled his eyes. "You have no idea how truly interesting you are."

"Not as much as you," I replied. "Everyone's looking at you."

"I believe you are the one holding their attention," he smiled again.

"Please," I scoffed. "Don't make me laugh."

He looked around the cafeteria carefully, his eyes wary.

"What's wrong?" I questioned while following his gaze.

"Huh?" he asked, looking back at me.

"What are you looking for?"

"Oh, nothing."

He was lying. I could tell by the way his eyes wavered from mine then to the window. I didn't call him out though. I hardly knew him.

"Okay," I replied looking down at my soup unenthusiastically. I had lost my appetite about two periods ago.

I then noticed that he wasn't touching his food either. It just sat there on his tray.

"Are you going to eat?" I inquired.

"Are you?"

"Not hungry."

"Neither am I."

I looked to him again and found him staring at me, curiosity evident in his blue orbs. I was used to people staring, but his stare wasn't unkind. It was like he was taking me in. Memorizing every dip and curve of my face. I looked back down to my food trying to control myself.

"You do that a lot," he chuckled.

"Do what?"

"Blush. It's quite entertaining," he replied smiling.

"Thanks. I'll put that on my college transcript," I rolled my eyes.

He laughed, the skin around his eyes creasing in amusement. My gaze shifted to two figures that were coming toward us. I internally groaned. What could they possibly want?

Cole noticed the change in my demeanor. He looked over his shoulder just in time to see Matt Robinson and Brittany Ryan walk up to the table. They were, of course, a couple, but with the way Brittany was eyeing Cole, I would say Matt had some trouble in the works.

"Hey. I don't think we've been properly introduced. I'm Matt, and this is my girlfriend, Brittany," Matt greeted Cole, ignoring me.

"Hello," Cole said sounding shy, but hospitable. "I'm Cole and this is my friend, Adeline."

I was shocked when Cole brought me into the conversation.

Matt paid me a glance, "Hey," but then gave all of his attention back to Cole.

Brittany didn't even look my way.

"So, me and my friends were wondering if you would like to hang with us after school," Matt continued.

A mixture of emotions flooded me all at once. On one hand, I was beyond relieved that someone, anyone, would be able to avert Cole's attention from me. But on the other hand, the sting of rejection was beginning to burn again. The same wound of rejection Lily had first inflicted when she stopped being my friend.

"Sounds tempting, but I don't think I will be able to. But thanks anyway," Cole answered kindly, turning his attention back to my surprised face.

Matt and Brittany recoiled at the denial, the rejection. I wondered if either of them had ever not gotten what they wanted. I watched as Matt and Brittany awkwardly turned to leave. I looked to Cole's face and found him grinning ear to ear.

"Why did you turn them down?" I asked, still shocked.

"They are not very pleased, are they?" he ignored my question.

"Why did you turn them down?" I persisted.

"Like I said. I have other stuff to do later," he replied, looking into my eyes. "And I think one good friend is enough for one day, don't you?"

I almost choked on my food, "So, we're friends now? You don't even know me."

"Then I'll get to know you. That's what I'm doing right now, isn't it?"

"I suppose...." However, life would be much easier if he left now.

Our conversation drifted from one topic to another. Mainly shallow things, like the weather, what classes we liked, our favorite bands. And I had to say, Cole had excellent taste in music.

"Last song you listened to on your iPod?" he inquired seriously.

I thought for a moment. The last time I listened to my iPod was this morning on the bus, but I was having trouble thinking of the name of the song.

I was about to reply when I noticed Cole was no longer engaged in our conversation or even looking at me.

His smile had faded slightly, like he was focusing on something behind me. I turned my head and found Chandler Phalcon on the other side of the cafeteria, leaning against a wall. He was the only other Native American that attended our school. Funny, I could have sworn that he had moved months ago.

The bell rang, signaling the end of lunch and the beginning of our afternoon courses. I stood quickly, and Cole followed me to the trash bin where I threw my food away. He did the same and followed me to my locker.

As soon as I put my books away, I heard Cole whisper, "I need to go. Tell anyone who asks that I felt sick."

Confusion and suspicion hit me all at once.

"Where are you going?"

He looked at me warily and sighed, "It's complicated."

"Why?" I asked again, confused, but determined.

"I can't say," he finally replied, sounding somewhat ashamed, embarrassed again.

I nodded and then turned to walk away when I felt a warm hand grab my shoulder.

"I'm sorry, but I have to go."

"Well, go," I countered, still baffled and unsure about whom Cole Dyami really was.

He turned to leave, but glanced to me one last time before walking away, confusing me even further. People walked by, bumping into me, but I didn't care. I'm not sure what happened exactly, but as he walked away I felt something strange.

There was something different about this boy. Something I couldn't fully grasp or comprehend. It was the unfamiliar territory again. The idea that something new, something I had no way of understanding quite yet was on the horizon. The thunderclouds of a storm were brewing, threatening the life I knew, the life I was comfortable with. The life, up until that point, I was relatively satisfied with.

*

I was so consumed with making dinner that I almost didn't hear Emma walk through the door, her heels making a clicking sound as she walked into the kitchen.

Emma was my senseless, protective older sister that raised me ever since our parents died. Although she was a bit eccentric, she had a heart the size of Montana. She was my best friend. And the only person I was absolutely sure of.

"Hey kid. How was your day?" she asked, looking through the mail.

"All right I guess. How was yours?" I shrugged my shoulders while cutting the chicken.

She nodded, dropping the mail onto the table.

"I've had better," Emma sighed as she began scrounging around in the fridge.

I turned my attention back to dinner but didn't really pay much focus to what I was doing.

"Is Henry coming?" I asked, secretly hoping he was too busy. It was not that I did not like Henry. He made Emma happy, so for the time being I would tolerate his presence, so long as he was what she wanted.

"Not tonight," she sighed dejectedly. "He has papers to grade."

"That's too bad," I tried to hide my smile.

"Oh, I know your heart is just broken!" Emma laughed as she playfully pushed me.

We giggled and continued talking as we finished cooking dinner. We were half way through eating dinner when Emma brought up school again.

"I told you," I replied as I took another sip of water. "It was fine."

The laughter and silliness left Emma's eyes, "Did you talk to Lily at all?"

I gulped, swallowing the rest of my dinner. Emma knew that I hadn't spoken to Lily in years. She knew that it wasn't my favorite topic of conversation.

"No, not today."

Emma sighed, "You know, it wouldn't hurt to try to work things out."

I stood up, taking our dishes to the sink. I continued to clean as Emma stood and finished clearing the table.

"Just try calling her one day," Emma wouldn't stop. "She might want to have lunch or see a movie…"

"Have you ever thought that maybe I like being alone?" I snapped almost breaking the dish I was cleaning. "That maybe I am comfortable with my life right now? That I am happy?"

The last three words came out in a whisper, doubtful, like I was trying to convince myself more than my own sister. Emma nodded, ending the conversation, but I saw the skepticism in her eyes, acknowledging that the truth was that I was far from happy.

The next morning was as normal as always. I was listening to my iPod while looking out the window of the bus, trying to drown out the people around me. The bus ride was bearable, but slow as usual. After everyone cleared out, I followed slowly, taking my time while gathering my books. The bus driver seemed impatient, but I was too tired to care.

After I walked off the bus, I heard the doors slam behind me. I ignored it and walked toward the locker building, mentally preparing myself for another day and for him. I sighed as I walked to my locker and tried to pull it open. But, naturally, it was stuck.

I dropped my bag and books to the floor while I fought with my locker. I grunted, frustrated at my lack of strength.

Someone chuckled behind me, causing me to whip around and almost causing my iPod to fall to the ground. My eyes widened in surprise when I found Cole Dyami, the one I had been trying to forget, standing behind me smirking.

"Need some help?" he asked, cocking his right eyebrow in amusement.

"No, but thanks," I replied, trying to ignore him. I turned my attention back to my locker, trying even harder to force it open.

"Here, let me try," Cole said, gently pushing me to the side. He easily opened it.

"You have to push it in first, then pull," he said picking up my books for me.

"Thanks," I mumbled, while taking my books from him.

We stood awkwardly for a couple of minutes. He opened his mouth to say something, but changed his mind. Finally, he shook his head. At me or at himself, I wasn't sure.

"We're going to be late for class," he finally said, turning and walking away.

I was surprised to find Cole waiting for me after French. He just stood there, leaning against my locker, his forehead creased in thought.

"Hi."

He looked up immediately, his face softening when he saw me. I opened my locker and took out my geometry books.

"Hey," he smiled. "How are you?"

I turned to look at him.

"Fine. You?"

"I'm fine. Listen, I just want to apologize about what happened yesterday. It was sort of an emergency," Cole said running his hand through his black, silky hair. I wondered if it was as soft as it looked...

"It's fine. I hope everything is okay."

We walked to the geometry room and sat down in the back.

"Me too," he whispered as class began. I think he was talking to himself more than to me.

Geometry went by fairly quickly, but I didn't catch much of the lesson. It was becoming increasingly harder to focus on anything.

Before I knew it, he was walking me through the lunch line. The day seemed to have flown by. Whether it was our conversation or my wishing the day would end so I could be alone, I wasn't sure. Cole was full of surprises, especially when he pulled my chair out for me. I blushed and sat down staring at my food.

"Thanks," I replied as he sat down.

"You're welcome," he replied sweetly. "My father always taught me to treat ladies with respect."

I nodded, "Your dad is a smart man. Your mom is lucky."

His smile faded, coughing uncomfortably, "My mom is dead."

I looked up to him horrified, "I'm so sorry. I had no idea."

"Don't worry about it. I didn't even know her."

I looked down to my tray, mentally beating myself up. I was an idiot.

"What about your family?"

I looked up and found genuine curiosity in his eyes.

"My parents died in a car accident when I was five. My older sister, Emma, raised me ever since."

Cole was about to say something. Probably apologize, but he stopped himself.

"What about you? Do you have any siblings?"

"I have an older brother and sister. They are my half siblings through my father."

"What are their names?" I asked, taking a sip from my soda.

"Chenoa and Elsu."

I looked up to him, surprised. They were names I had never heard of.

He chuckled, enjoying my confusion.

"They are Native names. Chenoa means 'dove' and Elsu means 'flying falcon.'" Cole explained.

I nodded, intrigued with where the conversation was heading.

"Tell me more."

"About what?" Confusion clouded his eyes.

"About your tribe," I explained, suddenly excited.

He gulped and licked his lips nervously. Obviously, he wasn't comfortable talking about it. I immediately took back my question.

"Never mind. Forget I said anything."

He sighed heavily, and I continued to stare at my sandwich, disgusted. My stomach was in a million knots.

"I would love to tell you about my tribe, but…"

"But?"

I looked up to him and found him torn. He truly wanted to tell me, but something was holding him back.

"I can't," he whispered, shamefully. He turned his head to look out the window. I watched him carefully, taking him in again. His lips were in a tight line, and his forehead was creased.

"Okay. I understand," I mumbled quietly. I didn't even think he heard me.

He turned quickly to look at me, "What?"

"I understand," I repeated. "It's none of my business."

He leaned his head closer, his warm scent flooding my senses. My heart hammered, and I could hear my pulse in my ears.

He squinted his eyes, frustration sneaking its way onto his face. He sighed defeated.

"You are a strange person," he finally said, leaning back into his chair again.

I was taken back. Who was he calling strange?

"Oh really?" I questioned critically. "I'm not the one who ditches on their first day of school."

He laughed, immediately causing the knots in my stomach to become even tighter.

"Touché," he replied, smiling.

"So, why am I so strange?" I asked, exaggerating the word. He shook his head, fighting back another smile.

"I just meant that you aren't like anyone I have ever met."

"Is that good or bad?"

He thought for a minute, looking me over again. I shifted uncomfortably under his intense gaze.

"I don't know yet."

His answer startled me. He sounded worried and possibly troubled.

The bell rang, ending lunch and our conversation. Cole stood, and I followed suit. We threw our trays away, and he walked me to my locker.

"Staying today?" I enquired jokingly, trying to get my locker open.

Cole didn't answer but opened my locker for me again. I sighed defeated.

"Yes, I plan on staying," he said, looking around. His face was hard and intent. He wasn't just glancing around. He was searching for something.

"Looking for someone?"

His eyes rested on me, softening.

"No," he replied, smiling. For some reason I thought he had lied. There was a hidden meaning behind his scan across the hallway. He was keeping something from me, but I didn't dare call it out. I hardly knew him after all.

The final bell of the day rang, causing everyone to sigh with relief. I headed toward the parking lot, where my smelly, uncomfortable ride home would be waiting. It wasn't till my third scan of the parking lot that I realized the bus had already left. They forgot me. Again.

I sighed, rolling my eyes into the back of my head. I then felt raindrops gently land on my cheeks and eyelids. It was lightly raining, but with every second it rained harder. I groaned.

"Do you need a ride?"

I turned around, surprised to find Cole standing behind me, his keys in hand. It was hard to read his expression through the rain, as to whether he really meant it or just felt sorry for me. But as I felt the water soaking into my shoes, I was grateful for the offer, even if it was out of pity.

I stared dumbly and nodded. It looked like he smiled, but I couldn't tell through the rain. He led me to a massive, black, GMC truck. It looked new, the paint job shinning even in the rain.

"Wow," I breathed as I took in the immense truck.

Cole quickly opened the passenger door for me, and I hopped in. Well, that was my intention, but clumsy me slipped and fell backwards. I was about to land on the hard asphalt when a pair of warm, rusty-colored arms caught me and held me close. My breathing stopped altogether as I could feel his heart beating. My head became dizzy, the picture fading in and out.

"Let me help," he whispered, as he gently lifted me into the truck.

The door quickly closed behind me, and I scrambled to put my seatbelt on before he got in. Cole gracefully jumped into his truck and was able to start it and close the door at the same time. He drove out of the parking lot, speeding down the highway.

"Before I take you home, I need to run by my house. Is that okay?" he asked politely.

I stuttered, "Yeah, sure. Thanks for the ride by the way."

He laughed, making the truck feel lighter.

"Anytime."

We were quiet for a time. Cole played a CD to fill the silence. It was one of my favorite bands. I remember telling him about them at lunch the other day. He had said he had never heard of them, to my shock and dismay.

"I thought you never heard of this band," I said accusingly while pointing to the CD player.

He smiled, "I haven't, but when you told me about them, I went out and bought the CD. You're right. They are really good."

I chewed the inside of my lips nervously while glancing out the window. What was he doing? Trying to impress me?

"You don't have to do this," I whispered while staring at my hands.

"Do what?" His face fell into confusion.

"Be nice to me like this. I can take care of myself. You don't have to feel sorry for me," I replied, my voice shaking.

"Why would you think that I feel sorry for you?" he asked, his voice sharp, as if he was offended.

"I'm used to being ignored. You don't have to feel obligated to help the poor, invisible girl," I explained. I could hear my sarcasm seep through my words along with self-pity.

We drove in silence, except for the music, for a few minutes. He slowed down, and I knew we were near his house.

He pulled into his driveway and parked the car. Neither of us made an attempt to move.

He sighed, "I don't feel sorry for you. I envy you."

My head shot up, and I looked at him, shocked.

"What?"

"I envy you," he repeated. "I envy you, and I don't even know why. Since the first day I saw you, I have felt...." he stopped, closing his eyes and biting his lip.

"You don't know how lucky you are," he finally said, looking me in the eyes.

I was taken back. I didn't know what to say. I sat there, stunned by his words and his actions.

"How am I so lucky?" Little did I know that the answer was sitting right next to me.

He looked up, his eyes softening. He wasn't so angry anymore. He leaned forward and tucked a stray, damp hair behind my ear. His calloused fire like hand brushed my face. It wasn't an unpleasant feeling.

"You just are."

And with that, Cole opened his door, jumped out, and came around to open mine. He helped me out and led me to the front porch. I could barely take any notice of the house (because of the unfortunate, cold rain), but I did note its large size. The porch wrapped around the entire house. There was also a tire swing hanging from the large oak tree in the side yard.

He took his key out of his pocket and unlocked the door. The entry way was large with wooden floors, which led into the living room. I was instantly drawn toward the artwork in the spacious room. I walked in and stopped when I came to the first painting on the far side of the massive room. The first painting was of a Native chief sitting on a horse in the middle of a field. He looked straight ahead, an air of authority surrounding him. He was wearing nothing more than animal skin pants and feathers that were braided into his long, black hair. The sky was cloudless, only an ocean of blue contrasting with the dark copper skin of the warrior. I walked on until I came to the next picture. It was a black and white photo. There were three older Native women sitting in a circle, smiling widely into the camera. They looked like they were making baskets. They were all so beautiful, even though they were old in age.

I was so absorbed in the photo that I didn't even notice when someone came to stand beside me.

"Beautiful, aren't they?"

I jumped back, in momentary shock, and almost fell when someone caught my arm.

"I'm sorry," she said, her voice sweet and tender like a mother's. "I didn't mean to frighten you."

I straightened up and looked back to the beautiful girl. She was tall, taller than me by a few inches, with long, toned arms and legs. Her skin was a rich, deep copper, like Cole's, and her hair was long and black, curling at the ends. Her eyes were wide and deep chocolate, and she had such a beautiful face. She couldn't be any older than twenty, maybe nineteen. My stomach tightened just looking at her. She was so lovely, too lovely to be real.

"I'm Chenoa, Cole's sister," she greeted, her eyes twinkling.

It made sense now. It must be genetics that two people be so inhumanly gorgeous.

"It's nice to meet you," she continued when I remained quiet.

"It's nice to meet you too. I'm…"

"Adeline," she finished for me. "I know all about you."

"You do?"

"Of course. Cole has told me so much," she explained, her smile never leaving her face.

"Let's not exaggerate," Cole interrupted, while walking into the living room and standing beside Chenoa.

"Besides," he continued, trying to conceal his embarrassment, "Adeline needs to get home. I just needed to grab something."

"Well, you can wait," Chenoa snapped. "I'm not done talking."

Chenoa turned back to me, her smile even wider.

"Would you like something to eat, Adeline?"

"Um, no thank you."

I looked to Cole, then back to Chenoa. They were both staring at me, observing me. I blushed again and looked back to the black and white photo.

"Did you take this?" I asked, trying to avoid their gazes.

Chenoa looked to the photo fondly, "Yes. It was about three summers ago. We had a festival. This photo was my favorite. Paco didn't mind it either."

"Paco?" I questioned. It was another strange name.

"Our father," Cole explained. "Speaking of which, he and Elsu will be home soon."

Cole said this last part to Chenoa specifically. She rolled her eyes in response and looked back to me, smiling.

"Well, it was nice to meet you, Adeline. Please come visit us again," Chenoa said as she pulled me into an embrace. I awkwardly hugged her back, desperate to be back in the safety and security of my own home.

Cole led me toward the door. I looked back once more to the copper skinned beauty who was staring thoughtfully at the black and white photo.

Chapter Two

"I hope that wasn't as weird for you as it was for me," Cole grimaced as he zoomed past the other houses on the Little Shell Reservation.

"No," I lied. "Your sister is very nice."

"And nosey," he added.

I laughed while continuing to look out the window.

"So what did you need to get?"

"Well," he said, nervousness echoing in his deep voice. "Chenoa wanted to meet you."

Surprise raced through me. Was that all? No other reason beside the fact that Cole's beautiful sister, who was nothing more than a stranger to me, wanted to meet me.

"Really? That's why you took me to your house?"

He sighed, his eyes narrowing in frustration. He was hiding something.

"Cole?" I asked.

"She just really wanted to meet you."

It was silent the rest of the ride home.

Cole pulled into my driveway and then cut the engine off. We sat in silence for a few moments, watching the rain clouds float over my small house. The rain had finally slowed down. The only sounds were the music from the truck's stereo and the pitter-patter of small raindrops.

"Why did you leave school yesterday?" I queried carefully. It was a question that had been bothering me.

Cole closed his eyes and sat motionless.

"I had to warn my family and our tribe," He replied carefully, thinking through each word before speaking them.

"Warn them? Of what?"

He shook his head, embarrassed and ashamed, "I can't tell you. It's stupid really."

I nodded, "All right. I understand."

He looked completely taken aback. When he opened his eyes, they were filled with astonishment.

"You do?"

"Yeah. You don't even know me. If I were you, I wouldn't tell me either. At least not now. I would wait and see if I was trustworthy or not. Like I said, you need to get to know me," I explained.

He smiled and shook his head again.

"You are something else," he whispered.

"What do you mean?"

"You…you're so different from other people I know. I think you'll say one thing, and then you catch me off guard. Who are you?" he asked, looking me in the eyes. The truck began to spin.

I looked away, "I better get inside. Thanks for the ride."

Before I knew it, Cole was opening the door and helping me out. He walked me to my front door and said goodbye. He gracefully walked to his truck and drove out of the driveway. I waited until I could no longer see his taillights before I got my key out and opened the door.

I walked in, half expecting to find Emma already home. Of course, the house was empty and just the way I had left it. My cereal bowl was still on the table from this morning when I had left in such a rush, almost missing the bus.

I dropped my bag on the kitchen table and began to clean the kitchen. I checked the messages, but there were only old ones from a month ago wishing Emma a happy twenty-seventh birthday.

It took me a little while to get the dishwasher started. I took out some pasta and began to cook dinner. After dinner was started, I worked on some homework, but found it very difficult to concentrate. I was having a hard time keeping the Dyami family out of my mind. At least, the two members I had met.

I finally gave up on homework and started on the wash. The phone rang, causing me to spill laundry detergent all over the floor.

"Crap! Coming, coming!" I yelled to the phone.

"Hello?" I answered, a bit out of breath.

"Hello. Is Miss Emma Jasely available?" a deep voice asked.

"No, but may I take a message?" I took out a pen and paper from a drawer.

"Yes. This is Mr. Red Hakan. I am the chief of the Little Shell Reservation. Could you have Miss Jasely call me back as soon as possible?" The rough, aged voice requested.

"Sure...no problem..." The line went dead.

I hung up the phone and then wrote down Mr. Red Hakan's name, number, and a note for Emma to call him. I began cleaning up the mess in the laundry room, still curious about the reason behind Mr. Red Hakan's call. What exactly did he want to discuss with my sister? Did it have anything to do with Cole Dyami? The smell of burning pasta shook me out of my thoughts.

"Shoot," I mumbled, as I took the pot of boiling water and pasta off the oven top and poured it into a bowl. The pasta seemed to have formed a large, unappetizing clump.

"Smells good!" Emma said sarcastically as she walked into the small kitchen and placed her purse and jacket on the table.

"Sorry, I wasn't paying attention," I mumbled dryly.

"Obviously," Emma replied as she let her long, dark auburn hair out of its usual bun and let it flow around her face. Her hazel-violet eyes intensified.

I sighed as I began to de-clump our pasta dinner. I was more or less poking it and watching air bubbles form.

"Any messages?" Emma asked as she went through the stack of mail she got on the way in.

"Um, yeah."

"Who?" Emma inquired still not looking up.

"A guy from the Little Shell Reservation. He left a message. It's next to the phone," I replied staring at the clump of what was supposed to be our dinner.

I heard the sound of her heels walking toward the phone as she picked up the piece of paper and read it to herself.

"A Mr. Red Hakan?" Emma questioned to herself.

"You know him?" I asked casually.

"No, do you?" She began dialing the number.

"Nope," I whispered as I took the pasta and put it on three separate plates and poured some tomato basil sauce over it. It would have to do.

"Hello. This is Emma Jasely. Is this Mr. Red Hakan?" Emma asked, her sweet voice seeming confused.

A few moments of silence went by as I began setting the table and watching Emma's face carefully.

"All right. No, thank you Mr. Hakan. Good bye," Emma replied before she hung up the phone.

"What was that about?" I asked, genuinely interested.

"Nothing much. Just wanted to know if I could come down to the reservation tomorrow. They are having a meeting and wanted a reporter there to write a story for the paper," she explained, as she took out two bottles of tea for her and Henry.

"Oh," Relief washed over me. "You going?"

"Yeah. You wanna come? It's a Friday so you won't have school the next day. It could be fun," Emma nudged me, smiling persuasively.

Going to the reservation meant many different things. I could possibly see Cole, who I was still trying to avoid, wasn't I? I was still wary about Cole, about the secrets he was clearly trying to keep. But I could see that he didn't necessarily want to keep those secrets. That it was more of a burden, a heavy load he was tired of carrying.

"Maybe," I replied. "What's the story on?"

"He wouldn't say. Just said I would find out all I needed to know tomorrow," Emma sat down at the table and drank her tea.

I poured myself some water and began to take little sips until I heard the doorbell ring. Emma's face broke out into a smile. I rolled my eyes.

"Be nice," she hissed, as she jumped up and skipped to the door.

It wasn't like I didn't like Henry. He just tried way too hard to be nice to me. If he made Emma happy, then I was happy, but I just wished he didn't call me "sugar" every time he saw me.

"Hey, Emma! Hey, darlin'! How are ya?" he asked as he playfully punched my arm.

Or "darlin". I'm not fond of that name either.

"Good," I replied bleakly as I sat down at the table and began to pick at my food.

"I suppose you would be good after today!" Henry laughed as he and Emma sat down for dinner.

"What do you mean?"

"Don't play dumb! I saw you and that new kid getting all cozy at lunch. Say, what's his name?" Henry asked as he stuffed his face.

All the blood drained from my face, and my chest felt hollow. Emma gave me a questionable look.

"What?" she asked threateningly.

This was another reason why I disliked Henry. Having him work at my school as the ninth grade history teacher meant that he was watching me and reporting back to Emma. Emma may have been my best friend, but she was very strict when it came to boys.

Until quite recently, there had been nothing to report. I should have known Cole would not have gone unnoticed by Henry.

I wondered what would happen if I faked a heart attack. I really thought about falling out of my chair and dying. Anything would be better than this.

"His name is Cole," I said, answering Henry's question while still looking at Emma. "He's just a friend."

"Didn't seem that way to me," Henry shook his head as he took another swig of his tea. "Especially when you got in his truck after school."

"Maybe you should mind your own business and stay out of mine," I exclaimed angrily.

"Adeline!" Emma scolded.

I ran to my room, too embarrassed and frustrated to say anything else. Once I was safely inside, I slammed the door and fell onto my bed. I heard footsteps, and a knock soon followed.

"Go away," I grumbled.

Emma ignored me and opened the door. I could feel the weight of the bed shift as she sat down.

"What's gotten into you?" Emma tried to coax me out of my pillow.

"Nothing. I don't know what you're talking about."

"You're not telling me things. Leaving me in the dark. Now you're yelling at Henry for no apparent reason. What's wrong?" Emma asked, concern replacing the anger in her voice.

"I'm a teenager."

"Teenager or not, you still have to tell me things. Now, who is this Cole? And why were you in his truck?" Emma pulled me into a sitting up position.

"New guy from the Little Shell Reservation. He was just giving me a ride home because the bus forgot me."

"Again?"

I rolled my eyes, "Yeah, again. And it was raining. He was just being nice."

"Well, maybe next time you should get a ride with Henry," Emma sighed, still obviously not happy about the current boy situation.

I thought over that option. Riding home with Henry was out of the question. I would have rather walked the two miles through snow, hail, and rain to my home rather than sit in a small, enclosed space with Henry.

"Be careful, Adeline..." Emma whispered, shaking me out of my thoughts.

"What are you talking about?"

"You don't know this boy. Neither do I. Just be careful with whom you hang out with, okay?"

After a few more moments of silence, Emma left. I stood up and closed the door after Emma was gone and then fell back on my bed.

But she did have a point. I didn't know Cole. I didn't know anyone at my high school for that matter. I didn't hang out with anyone. Cole was the first person to actually try to get to know me. Sure, I was not totally buying his "I just want to get to know you" tactic, but then again, I've never had anyone really try to understand me. It had been so easy to be ignored and alone. I was content on simply surviving high school. I didn't want to climb the social ladder, or be homecoming queen, or anything like that. Sure, some may not call what I was doing "living", but I was satisfied with simply existing. It was easy, predictable. It was safe.

Suddenly, the sound of something crying outside my window caught my attention. I looked out my window and saw an eagle flying above my house. I stared at it curiously. It was just circling over the house, screeching every couple of minutes. I cringed away from the window.

I never liked birds. Not since the time when I was eight and Emma decided it would be a good idea to take me to the zoo. Everything was fine until we went to the hawk exhibit. The handler said they were safe to pet, but once my hand got within three inches of the hawk, it went berserk. It started screaming and took a bite out of my hand. I looked down to my pink scar and gently brushed it with my fingertips.

*

I was next to a river in the middle of a forest. I heard the loud cry of something above. When I looked up, I yelped in surprise. There was a bald eagle bigger than two combined. Its wings were massive, and its beak was sharp. The feathers were a shiny black and white with spots of brown. It landed gracefully in front of me on a log. The strangest part was its eyes. They were brown and so human like. Not only that, but there was a large scar beginning at the top of its head and stopping at the corner of its beak.

I felt as if it was glaring at me. My mind was telling me to run, but my legs were frozen stiff.

Suddenly, a familiar voice yelled from within the woods.

"Adeline! Where are you?"

I opened my mouth, but no words formed. The eagle seemed to have smiled at my weakness. He soon emerged from the woods and stopped when he saw the larger-than-life eagle and me. His eyes filled with tears as he whispered, "I'm sorry…"

I woke up screaming.

*

I ate breakfast slowly, trying to get rid of last night's dream. Emma quickly grabbed her coffee mug and ran out the door.

I was early for the bus, so I took out the homework that I didn't finish last night. Maybe that would get my mind off of the awful nightmare. I began to work on geometry, when someone rang the doorbell. Most likely Emma, who forgot her keys, again.

"Come on Emma! How many times do you have to forget before…."

I opened the door, and my jaw fell to the floor. Here, on my front porch with his large, black GMC truck in the driveway, was Cole Dyami, looking as handsome as ever.

"Hello Adeline," he greeted me. His voice was silkier than I remembered.

"What are you doing here?" I asked stunned.

"Picking you up for school."

"But, why?"

"Because I like you," he answered smoothly.

"But, why?" I repeated, trying to figure out if I was still in bed sleeping and he was just a dream.

"I have a feeling about you. Now, go and get your things or we'll be late," he pushed me back into the house.

I ran to the kitchen and grabbed my bag and books. I quickly checked myself in the mirror beside the front door, something I rarely did and what Emma did every day. My hair was decent, and my complexion was average. I took a deep breath, walked out the door, locking it behind me. I turned around and found Cole with his hand stretched out to me.

"Your bag?" he prompted.

"Oh, right," I handed him my bag.

He walked me to his truck and held the door open. I was more careful than I was yesterday and was able to get inside of the truck without assistance. He was in the driver's seat in no time, with my bag next to his in the back seat.

We rode in silence except for the CD player. He was playing the same CD from yesterday. A small smile tugged at my lips. Our conversation varied once again, but instead of music, we were now discussing literature.

"Best book you have ever read?" he asked seriously, a smile etched across his face.

"That's easy. *Hamlet*." Although it wasn't a book, it was my favorite play. I always found myself rereading it every year.

"Wrong!"

"How is that wrong?" I fumed. "It's an opinion. Opinions can't be wrong!"

"I said best book, not best play. Besides, Shakespeare is overrated…" he continued as he pulled into the parking lot.

"Oh really?" I asked, beginning to sound annoyed. "Then who's your favorite writer, oh wise one?"

He laughed, "Definitely Chaucer!"

I rolled my eyes as we made our way toward the locker hall. We continued to banter on about who was a better writer, Shakespeare or Chaucer. By the time we had gotten to my locker, we had agreed that Chaucer was the best at epic poems, while Shakespeare was the best tragic playwright. We were still discussing different authors when the bell rang, signaling the start of first period, homeroom.

"I'll see you in geometry," Cole said quietly.

"Okay," I whispered a moment late as he walked gracefully off to his class.

I walked into the classroom and quickly sat down in the last available seat in the back row. Students began to file in late. They sat down and began talking among themselves.

"Did you see the new guy?"

"Yeah. I even talked to him!"

I recognized the voices of Joanne and Sasha, the social climbers of the school.

"No way! What did he say?" Joanne questioned, seeping with jealousy.

"Oh, not much. Just small talk," Sasha lied as she flipped her fire red hair behind her shoulders.

"What's his name?" Joanne asked, still jealous, but too curious to let that stop her questions.

"Cole. I talked to him at lunch the other day," interrupted Brittany with Matt at her side.

"Big deal," Sasha puffed.

"Just letting you know his name," Brittany replied smoothly, as she sat down with Matt in the seat in front of her. He seemed quite anxious. Maybe being nice to Cole was Brittany's idea.

"Well, Adeline was the one that had his attention all day," Matt muttered bitterly while glaring at Brittany.

All three girls turned around and stared at me. I blushed, out of habit, and looked down to my geometry book. They finally turned back around and began to whisper to themselves, but I was still able to catch a little bit.

"What does she have that I don't have?" Joanne whispered bitterly.

"Don't worry, Jo. He probably felt bad for the girl…"

Although I knew I should blow off what Sasha said, it still stung. Cole and I had a lot in common, but doubts were always in the back of my mind, reminding me that I was in strange territory. I was riding the waves of something unknown. Something that could end up breaking me.

The next two periods, English and French passed slowly, but finally came to an end. I had never been so excited about geometry before in my entire life. I walked into the class half expecting Cole to be there waiting and the other half thinking he was just a dream that I was about to wake up from.

When I walked in, I was pleasantly surprised. There he was, sitting in the back row with a suspicious smirk on his face. I walked over, and he smiled as I sat down. Geometry went by quickly. Soon, the bell rang and I began packing up, getting ready to go to history. Cole was by my side as we walked into history.

"I have something to ask you," Cole finally said as we sat down.

"What is it?"

Cole seemed suddenly nervous; he couldn't stop tapping the floor with his foot.

"I was wondering if maybe, you know, if you would like to come to a campfire ceremony this Saturday with me?"

I was astonished. Was he asking me out on a date? Cole read my expression quickly, backtracking his prior statement.

"You know, as friends. The elders of my tribe tell stories of our past and stuff. I know you said you'd like to learn more, so I thought you might want to come…" he continued, seeming more relaxed. "There's a market too, earlier, during the day."

I nodded, "Yeah, that would be really cool. Thanks for inviting me."

Cole smiled triumphantly while taking out his notes. I followed suit, but I couldn't shake the feeling that maybe there was more to this campfire ceremony than what Cole was telling me.

Mr. Jackson brought the class to order and told us about a test that we would have Monday. The whole class groaned, but Mr. Jackson ignored it and continued with notes. Class was dragging by when someone dropped a crumbled piece of paper on the floor next to my feet. I picked it up and found my name written on the outside. I looked up to Cole and found him glaring at Tommy Fuller, best friend to Chandler Phalcon. Tommy basically worshiped Chandler; he would do anything for him.

I looked back down to the note and opened it:

Adeline Jasely,

I know we have not talked in the past, but I was wondering if you would like to go with me to the movies this weekend? I'd love to get to know you better.

Chandler Phalcon

I was in utter shock. Why in the world would Chandler want to go out with me on a date?

I suddenly heard a low growl from beside me. I was surprised to find Cole glaring at the note in my hands. He closed his eyes, trying to calm himself.

The rest of class was very tense. I glanced at him every now and again, but he would either be glaring at the folded-up note or burning a hole in the back of Tommy Fuller's head. The bell rang, and I grabbed my books as I carefully watched Cole's expression. He sat motionless, like a statue that belonged in a European museum and not in some high school classroom.

"Cole?" I asked vigilantly.

"So, Adeline," I heard Tommy Fuller come up behind me. "What do you say?"

"Excuse me?" I turned my attention to Tommy. We never talked, except for the times he needed a pencil or paper.

"About the note. I mean, Chandler must really want to get to know you if he is willing to give up a Saturday..." Tommy continued. I winced at his comment, not sure if he meant to insult me or not. I was about to respond when someone else beat me to it.

"She is not interested in Chandler," Cole answered through gritted teeth. "She never will be."

Both Tommy and I stood shocked, our mouths hanging open. Did he seriously just say that?

"Okay," Tommy replied as he left the room, eyeing Cole fearfully.

I stared at Cole for a minute before I grabbed my bag and stormed out of the room toward the cafeteria.

"Adeline! Wait!"

The nerve of him! I could make up my own mind. Like I would ever say yes to a guy who had a sophomore do his bidding. And what was with his extreme change in attitude? He seemed so upset and angry. Could it be he was jealous? I dismissed the silly notion. No, it had to be something else, anything else.

I ran past the line for food, too angry to eat. I was almost out the door to the school's parking lot when a fire-like hand grabbed my shoulder and pulled me back into the cafeteria.

"Adeline, wait. I'm sorry," He began.

"No! I don't want to hear it!" I interrupted angrily.

I started walking back out to the parking lot, and Cole didn't stop me. I kept walking angrily, not completely sure on where I was going.

"Where are you going?" a silky voice asked me.

I ignored him and kept walking until I felt him grab my arm and stop me.

"What?" I hissed irritated.

"I'm sorry, but you have to trust me on this. Chandler is no good. I'm just trying to help you," Cole apologized, looking me in the eyes.

My breathing became irregular again, and my heart began to pound from his powerful gaze.

"Why? Why is he so bad?"

"Let's just say he isn't the nicest guy around," Cole explained quietly.

"Well, it wasn't like I was going to say yes or anything," I whispered looking down to my feet.

"Really?" Cole seemed surprised.

"No! Why would I say yes to guy who can't ask me out himself?" I replied, feeling a little bit insulted.

Cole sighed with relief, "That's good. Now can you do me a favor?"

"Maybe."

"Stay away from Chandler. Don't ask me why, just please do it. I would really appreciate it," Cole requested earnestly.

I was about to tell him that I didn't need babysitting and that I could take care of myself, but when I looked into his eyes, I saw nothing but sincerity. He actually seemed to care.

I sighed, "Yeah. If it makes you feel better."

He smiled, and everything became a bit hazy.

"Thank you, Adeline. I really appreciate it," Cole smiled as he led me back into the cafeteria for lunch.

Chapter Three

The rest of the day went by quickly. Cole drove me home again and said he would pick me up the next day around noon for the campfire. The actual campfire wouldn't start until sunset, but Cole had mentioned the street market and that he would show me around his family's ranch. I was honestly looking forward to it. I walked into the house and was surprised to find Emma already home.

"Hey, Addie! Could you come here for a second?" Emma yelled from her room. It sounded like she was in her closet.

"Coming, Emma," I replied as I placed my bag on the kitchen table.

I walked into her room and wasn't that surprised to see all of the contents of Emma's closet sprawled across the bed.

"I see you have a date with Henry tonight," I said as I moved some clothes and sat on the bed.

She stuck her head out of the closet, "No. I have that story to do at the Little Shell Reservation, remember? You're coming with me."

I had completely forgotten. What would Cole say? Would he even be there?

"Maybe I should stay home. I have a history test Monday, and I really need to study if I have any hope of passing," I said, hoping she would let me off the hook.

"Adeline Connor Jasely, it is a Friday night, and the last thing you are going to do is study for some test," Emma replied firmly as she came out of the closet in jeans and the blue top Henry gave her for Christmas.

"I thought you didn't like that top," I replied, looking for a change in subject.

Emma was looking at herself in the mirror, trying to figure out what shoes would go with the outfit.

"No, I like it," she lied.

I walked into her closet and found the shoes she had probably been looking for.

"Here. These will go well," I said as I handed her the dark, blue flats that I gave her for her birthday last month.

She smiled, "You are the best. What would I do without you?"

I smirked, "Probably starve to death."

"Real funny, now go and get changed. We are leaving in twenty minutes."

"Why do I need to change? I'm staying here."

"No, you are coming with me. Now, will you change yourself or will I have to do it for you?"

I rolled my eyes and walked to my room. I opened my closet and found nothing suitable.

"Hey, Em! Can't I just wear what I have on now?"

"No! Wear that cute sundress I bought you!" she yelled back.

"A dress?" I asked as Emma walked into my room with her laptop at her side.

"Yeah, why not?" she asked, oblivious to the fact that we were only going to a tribal council meeting. Nothing to dress up for.

"I'll look stupid. Just let me wear jeans," I begged.

"Adeline, you will wear this dress, and you will like it," Emma commanded as she took the light green dress out of my closet and laid it on the bed.

She left and gave me privacy to change. I changed unwillingly and looked at myself in the mirror. I had let my hair down out of its ponytail, but I still wasn't satisfied with the person looking back at me. I never usually was. I wasn't ugly, just plain. I was nothing compared to my sister. She was every man's dream. Golden skin, beautiful, wide eyes, full lips, and curly auburn hair. I was pale with muted brown hair, and small hazel eyes. And in a dress I just looked pathetic.

"You ready, Addie?" Emma called from the kitchen.

"Yeah, coming!" I yelled back as I grabbed my brown boots and jacket and ran out my door. I walked up to Emma while putting my shoes on. She turned to look at me and frowned when she saw my feet.

"Adeline, really. Boots?" Emma asked, disappointed.

"I'm wearing the dress, Emma. Don't push it," I replied as I walked out to Emma's red jeep.

We drove off toward the reservation. We rode in silence except for the music in the background and Emma's humming.

"So why didn't you want to come with me? You usually like to come and help when a story is involved," Emma asked, breaking the silence.

"Oh, um, I don't know."

"Is this about Cole?"

My heart sped up at the sound of his name.

"What? No. Nothing to do with him," I lied.

"Really? So you don't like him?"

"Not like that. He's just a friend," I reminded her.

"Oh come on, Adeline, you can tell me! Do you like him?" The young, girlish voice was coming back. Emma could change her persona from concerned parental guardian to fun-loving older sister in a heartbeat.

I rolled my eyes, "No. He's just my friend."

Silence descended as she took that in.

"It's been awhile, hasn't it?" Emma commented.

She was referring to the fact that until recently my social life had been pretty much non-existent. Ever since my fallout with Lily, I never tried to make any friends.

"Just be careful, Addie," Emma whispered.

"Why?"

"Well, even if you say you don't like this boy, who's to say that he doesn't like you? You know, like you like you," Emma winked.

"Whatever Emma..." I rolled my eyes.

"Oh come on! Does he have a girlfriend?" she asked, pulling into the parking lot of the conference center.

Her question wiped away any hint of a smile left on my face. I had never thought of that.

He lived on the reservation. Of course he could have a girlfriend.

"You okay, Addie?" Emma asked, concerned at my silence.

"Yeah, I'm just going to go for a walk. You go ahead. I'll meet you inside," I replied as I jumped out of the jeep and began walking aimlessly.

"Okay! I'll see you later!" Emma called back.

I couldn't seem to get away fast enough. I suddenly realized that I had allowed myself the hope that maybe, possibly Cole was interested in being more than just friends. But even the prospect of friendship was dangerous, terrifying. Just because he wasn't interested in the girls at my school didn't mean that he didn't already have someone he was interested in here, on this very reservation.

I finally slowed down to my natural pace, just watching everything that was happening around me. There were many houses on each side of the dirt road. They were small, but quaint. Women and children were outside, either playing or taking laundry off the line.

I kept walking, watching all of the life around me. The sound of the children and their laughter was contagious. A smile tugged at my lips.

They were all amazingly beautiful. Their copper skin glowed from the setting sun. Their long, black hair blew in the wind and their eyes were wide and playful.

Suddenly, I heard the cry of an eagle, and time seemed to stand still. As if on cue, all of the women and children stopped moving, stopped talking, stopped laughing. They all looked to the sky, fear and confusion clouding their deep brown orbs.

I looked up and found an eagle, larger than life, circling the area above me. I looked back around to the people and found them staring at me, their expressions unreadable.

The mothers and other women yelled to their children telling them to go inside their homes. Soon, the area was deserted.

Why did they all leave?

I heard the familiar cry of the eagle as it circled above me. I looked up and became hypnotized by its flight pattern. It felt like hours had passed before a familiar voice broke through my thoughts.

"Adeline!" Cole yelled.

I heard the crunch of his footsteps as he ran toward me. I felt his warm, rough hands take and hold my face as he made me look into his eyes.

"Adeline? Can you hear me?" he asked. His voice was distant and fading quickly.

"What is she doing here, Cole?" someone asked, sounding infuriated.

"Cole?" I whispered. My vision was getting blurry. I looked over Cole's shoulder and found a taller copper-skinned man. Even with my blurry vision, I was able to make out that this man must be Cole's brother, Elsu. I was shocked. His eyes were a vivid, familiar brown and his long black hair was tied in a ponytail at the base of his neck. He was beautiful, but there was a long, ragged scar that began at the corner of his eye and met jaggedly to the corner of his mouth. He looked distorted and angry. I was afraid.

"Jacy probably spellbinded her," I heard Elsu say.

"Adeline, stay with me," Cole said, ignoring Elsu as I felt him lift me into his arms. I felt incredibly weak.

"And why would he do that?" Cole asked indignantly, almost mocking Elsu, as I felt him begin to walk. The voices were becoming more and more vague.

"He's doing his job. Protecting the tribe," Elsu whispered.

Then everything went black.

The gentle hum of velvet-like voices woke me out of my dreamless slumber. I kept my eyes closed because my body was still too weak to move. My eyelids felt like lead glued together. My senses came back to me slowly as the voices around me became more and more clear.

"She's the one. I know it," a soft, feminine voice murmured confidently.

"How do you know, Chenoa? We hardly know her," A low, rough, voice replied exasperated. He sounded so tired.

"Remember what you told me yesterday. Those feelings mean something, Cole. She's not some girl. Maybe she's the one we've been waiting for," Chenoa said self-assuredly.

"You don't know what you are talking about," Cole replied coldly.

"Cole's right, for once. He is not the Delsin or one of the Chosen. He's just some teenage boy with a crush," Elsu said, finally joining the conversation. He sounded disgusted and dismayed.

"Elsu, one more word and I swear..." Cole growled under his breath.

"You'll what?"

I heard Cole sigh and Elsu laughed, "Yeah. That's what I thought..."

They all became quiet, but even with my eyes closed, I could feel the tension that was building. What were they talking about? What's a Delsin? My head was beginning to hurt from all the perplexity. Suddenly, my body began to feel lighter and I could feel my eyelids beginning to move.

"She's waking," Elsu said bleakly, as I heard him leave the room. The tension from before melted away. I became aware of people watching me. I felt their intense gazes even with my eyes closed. When I opened my eyes, I thought I was in heaven. Here, right in front of me, were two copper-skinned seraphs. I heard Chenoa giggle as she whispered something to Cole I couldn't catch.

"Chenoa. Be quiet," Cole reprimanded. "Adeline, can you hear me?"

I stared up at him dazed, but nodded at his question.

He smiled, "Do you know where you are?"

I shook my head no.

"You're at my house. Do you know what happened to you?"

I looked over to Chenoa and then back to Cole. I nodded.

He sighed, "So you know that after you left your sister, you were walking through the streets when a couple of kids started playing baseball..."

Wait, baseball? No, they were looking at the eagle like I was.

Cole continued, "And that a fly ball hit you in the head. Then Elsu and I carried you back to our house, right?"

Wrong. Something was off.

I started to sit up, "No. That's not right. There was no baseball. There was an eagle. He 'spellbinded' me or whatever that means. That's what Elsu said."

Cole looked shaken while Chenoa seemed thrilled.

"I told you she's the one," Chenoa muttered.

"The 'one' what?" I felt so lost and confused.

"Nothing," Cole replied while glaring at Chenoa. "It's time to get you back to your sister. She's probably really worried."

"No," I replied angrily. "Tell me what's going on!"

Cole and Chenoa were stunned by my outburst.

Cole closed his eyes, "Adeline, please. Let me take you back to your sister."

"Only if you tell me what's going on," I demanded.

Cole shook his head.

"Cole, she has the right to know," Chenoa whispered quietly.

Before Cole could reply, the phone rang. Neither Cole nor Chenoa moved.

"It must be Paco," Chenoa sighed as she walked to the phone.

She answered it, and Cole continued to stare at me. I blushed under his gaze and looked down to my feet. My head was still a bit dizzy.

"You really shouldn't get involved with all this craziness…" I almost didn't hear him.

I looked up and saw sadness in his eyes.

"Involved in what?"

He didn't reply, but walked over to me and helped me stand.

"No. I won't do that to you," he whispered to himself as he led me to the front door. I almost didn't hear him.

"Paco is on his way home. The meeting is over," Chenoa said as Cole led me out the door.

"Tell him I'll be home soon," Cole replied as he led me to his truck and helped me in.

I looked to the house and found Chenoa standing on the porch looking to the sky. I followed her gaze and saw the same eagle sitting in the tree where the tire swing hung. The truck began to shake, like there was an earthquake. It took me a moment to realize that it was me who was quivering. Cole jumped into the truck and sped out of the driveway quickly.

"Hold on, Adeline. I'll get you back to your sister. Don't worry…" Cole's voice was trying to sound calm and collected, but I could hear the fear he was trying to mask.

Before I knew it, we were parked outside of the conference center. The clock in the truck read half past seven. Emma was going to kill me. Cole opened the door for me and helped me out.

"Adeline Connor Jasely!" I heard someone yell.

I looked over my shoulder and found Emma storming toward me.

"Hey, Emma," I murmured quietly.

"Don't you 'hey Emma' me. Do you know how worried sick I've been? You said you'd be right in, and here I am waiting for two hours…" Emma shouted, completely ignoring Cole who was standing by my side, surveying the sky above me.

"I'm sorry," I whispered, hoping she would wait until we were home for her to begin yelling at me.

"And who is this?" Emma demanded, pointing to Cole.

"Hello, Miss Jasely. I am Cole Dyami. It's a pleasure to meet you," Cole greeted eloquently, but still somewhat uncomfortably.

"So, you ditched me to go hang out with your friend," Emma accused, looking at me with betrayal and anger written across her face.

"Actually, Adeline was walking through the reservation when a couple of kids started playing baseball. A fly ball hit her in the head. My brother and I took her to our home to look after her before we brought her back to you," Cole explained causally. If I hadn't known any better, I would have believed him.

Emma's anger turned to concern as she took me into her arms and started searching my head for a bump from a baseball that didn't exist.

"Oh, Addie! Are you okay?" Worry and concern suddenly replaced the anger and frustration that once saturated her voice.

I looked over to Cole and saw the hinting in his eyes. He wanted me to go along with it and lie to my sister. I contemplated whether I should call out his lie or play along. The look on his stunning face seemed desperate.

"Yeah, I'm fine. You know me. Being at the wrong place at the wrong time and getting hit in the head," I lied. I actually sounded believable.

Cole sighed, relieved, while talking to Emma, "The bump has shrunk. Chenoa, my sister, is very good with injuries like this. You can hardly tell it's there now."

Cole and Emma were staring critically at my head. I knew that Emma would find no bump. She was more observant than Cole thought.

"Oh, yeah. I see it. It'll be gone by tomorrow," Emma said, agreeing with Cole while pointing to a spot on the top of my head.

I was shocked. Emma believed him.

"Speaking of tomorrow," Cole continued smoothly. "I was wondering if there was any chance Adeline could come over to the reservation and hang out. There's this market we have every month, and usually we have a campfire where stories of the tribe are told."

I had completely forgotten about that. Maybe it wouldn't be such a bad idea to get to know Cole after all. Maybe Emma was right. Maybe I do need to reach out to people too.

Emma looked to me with eyebrows raised. I nodded in approval.

She looked to Cole, "Maybe. What time should I bring her?"

"Oh, there is no need for you to drive down here. I would be more than happy to pick her up."

Emma looked to me again and said hesitantly to Cole, "I don't know."

"I promise I won't let her get into any trouble."

Emma smiled back, obviously charmed, "Well, okay. If you promise to have her back by ten."

"Of course," Cole replied.

He turned to me. "I'll pick you up around nine."

I nodded as he turned around to Emma and said goodnight.

It was a long ride home. After Cole had left, my sister suddenly remembered why she was so angry with me in the first place. She gave a long-winded speech on responsibility as I gazed out the window.

"Adeline, you can't ever do that to me again. The whole time during the meeting I was worried sick. What would have happened if Cole and his brother didn't help you out? You could still be on that street unconscious...." She went on and on.

I was barely catching a word. My mind was repeating the night's events over again in my head. Cole's conversation with his brother and sister was still very hazy. I was sure it was most likely a dream, a delusion my mind had made up.

When we arrived home, I listened to some more of Emma's lecturing and then took a shower, getting ready for bed. I laid my head on the pillow hoping for some rest, but my dreamless sleep from earlier had energized me. A million thoughts were swirling around my head. Why did Cole say I couldn't be involved? That he wouldn't do that to me? Was there some secret to this tribe that I was missing?

I crawled out of my bed and sat down at my desk with my computer. I turned it on, hoping its noise wouldn't catch Emma's attention. I pulled up my regular search engine and typed in "Little Shell Reservation, Chippewa Indians".

A lot of ads for hotels and restaurants popped up, but I closed those out quickly. I clicked on the link that spoke of the tribe's history. I skimmed the page and found that there were two different tribes from the same Indians. They were the two dominant ones, Little Shell and Turtle Mountain. Little Shell's reservation was in Montana and Turtle Mountain's was in North Dakota. What was strange was that in the late 1880s the Turtle Mountain Indians left the Little Shell tribe and became their own tribe. This information wasn't new. I learned it already from prior history classes. The real question was why was I so interested?

Why did this tribe, and Cole, for that matter, have anything to do with me? They didn't.

I heard the sound of Emma's footsteps, walking toward my room. I turned my computer off and then jumped into my bed, pretending to be asleep. I heard her crack the door open and stand there for a moment. Finally, the door gently closed, and I was left alone in the dark. I knew I should have fallen asleep immediately, but fear of the next day and what it would hold kept me awake. I was going to be walking into uncharted territory, into a life of a family, of a boy, I didn't even know. But even though I hardly knew him, there was this small tugging in my chest. A gentle yearning, like a small candle that wanted to know Cole, to understand him. To be his friend.

Chapter Four

I woke up the next day feeling anxious, almost forgetting that Cole was going to pick me up and take me to the campfire ceremony his tribe was having. My mind was still hazy from all that had happened the night before.

I was prepared for another speech from Emma as I walked into the kitchen, but found a note instead:

Addie,

I forgot to tell you that I would be spending the day with Henry. I'll see you soon. Love you.

Emma

I sighed as I took the note down and threw it away. Emma was never usually home on the weekends. Her life seemed to revolve around her job and Henry. I was usually toward the bottom of her priority list. Not that I minded too much. After all, I enjoyed the quiet, the time alone with myself. It was usually on weekends, when Emma was gone, that I would do most of my painting.

Art was the one medium, the one activity, I found the most joy in. It was a rarity that I could do it with schoolwork and helping Emma. She found my pieces charming, but I could see the worry, maybe even disapproval, in her eyes. No one can really live off being an artist. I needed a real job, not some hobby.

I poured myself some cereal and ate it gradually. I continually glanced at the clock and found time moving slowly. After I finished breakfast, I grabbed my history book out of my bag. Might as well study while I was waiting, but battle dates and presidents eventually became tedious. Subconsciously, my hand began making drawings on my notes. Not really paying much attention, the strokes of my pencil made designs and sketches. It wasn't until I decided to put away my history book did I realize I had been drawing a man. A familiar face that I had, apparently, been paying too much attention to. Ignoring the small tug in my chest, I grabbed the notebook paper, crumbling it before tossing it in the trash.

Suddenly, the doorbell rang. When I opened the door, I was greatly surprised to find not Cole, but a different, older man. He was clearly from the reservation, with his copper-toned skin. He looked aged, but the youth in his brown eyes was hard to miss.

"Uh…hello," I stuttered.

"Hello. Is Miss Emma Jasely home?" the man asked. His voice was silky, but rough at the same time. I had heard it from somewhere.

"No, she's gone for the day."

"Well, could you tell her that Red Hakan came by? I have the recording of the meeting for her," Mr. Hakan continued as he handed me an envelope with Emma's name on it.

"Sure, no problem," I replied as I stuck my hand out to take the envelope.

What shocked me the most was the reaction from Mr. Hakan when I grabbed the envelope and our hands brushed together. Mr. Hakan immediately tensed up and took a step back as if I had been a snake that tried to strike at him. His face paled, while his eyes lost their warmth, going cold.

"Thank you," he muttered as he turned quickly, jumping into his car and driving away.

Stunned, I stood on my front porch for a moment before I walked back in. I placed the envelope on the kitchen table and the doorbell rang again. I was more cautious this time as I looked through the peephole. I sighed, relieved, and opened the door.

"Hello, Adeline. How was your morning?" Cole greeted.

"Strange," I replied honestly as I closed the door behind me and locked it.

"What do you mean?" Cole walked me to his truck and opened the door for me.

"A guy from the reservation came by," I answered as Cole started the truck.

He instantly tensed up and sat very still.

"Really?" His voice was strained, on edge. "Who?"

"Red Hakan," I was careful in my response.

His fists tightened, the tendons becoming visible.

"Why?" he asked, still uneasy.

"He had to give something to Emma. A tape recording of last night's meeting. She was asked to write a story about it."

We sat in my driveway for a few minutes before Cole responded.

"Was that all?"

"Yeah."

"Did he do or say anything weird?"

I looked to Cole and found him with his eyes closed; a very apprehensive expression written across his beautiful features.

"Sort of," I replied truthfully. "Well, when he handed me the tape, our hands brushed and he jumped back like I shocked him or something…" I felt my cheeks heat up from embarrassment. This was so ridiculous. It couldn't mean anything. I looked over to him again but still found him looking anxious, embarrassed even.

"You okay?"

He finally relaxed, sighing, "Fine. No big deal."

He pulled out of the driveway and drove toward the reservation.

"Was that normal? That he came by?" I wondered while looking at the road.

He shrugged, "I guess so."

I let the conversation drop, my eyes glancing out the window again. We were quiet for a while until Cole began to chuckle.

"What?"

He looked over to me, "You know, I didn't pin you the dress wearing type." His laughter became a little louder. I felt my cheeks heat up in embarrassment.

"It wasn't my idea. Emma made me wear it. I know it's stupid…" I rambled on flustered.

It was quiet for a few moments.

"Well, you looked nice," Cole shifted uncomfortably in his seat. I looked at him with eyebrows raised.

"What?" he asked, exasperated. "Can't you take a compliment?"

I bit back a sarcastic remark, "Thanks."

"The only reason I brought it up was because I'm glad you're not wearing one now," Cole continued.

"I thought I looked nice?" I teased him.

He rolled his eyes, "Yeah, well looking nice won't help me around the ranch."

"Oh, so I'm working the ranch today?" I asked playfully, turning to him again.

He nodded, his eyes creasing in a smile, "Yes ma'am."

I laughed as we pulled into the reservation. We drove by many houses and I was happy to see people out and about. It looked like they were setting up for the market.

"What about the market?" I asked, pointing to the booths that were being set up.

"We'll get there," he answered. "It doesn't start for awhile anyway."

We pulled into his driveway and he shut the truck off. He jumped out of the truck and opened the door for me. Before we made it half way to the door, Chenoa rushed out and grabbed me into a tight hug.

Cole chuckled while Chenoa rambled on.

"Oh, Adeline! It's so good to see you! I missed you! How are you?" She prattled on as she pulled me into their beautiful home.

The house was just as magnificent as I remembered. The entry hall was large enough to fit a crowd of people quite comfortably. The beautiful, dark hardwood floors continued through the whole home. Beautiful black and white photos adorned the walls. The home was lovely, peaceful.

"Chenoa, breathe," Cole whispered as he followed Chenoa and me into the kitchen.

"Would you like anything to eat, Adeline?" Chenoa asked politely, ignoring Cole.

"Oh, I'm fine. Thank you," I answered as Cole opened the door leading from the kitchen to outside.

"We'll be at the barn," Cole called over his shoulder as he led me out the door.

"Are you gonna make her work?" Chenoa sounded exasperated, mortified even. "She's our guest."

Cole only shook his head and waved at his sister before closing the door. We walked along the fence line behind their house, which led to the barn and several acres of green pasture. I could see the horses in the distance grazing.

"It's beautiful," I murmured.

"Yeah, I know," Cole took a deep breath, his entire body relaxed. He was in his element, on the ranch with the horses.

We spent most of the morning feeding horses and fixing wire fence posts along their property. As we were walking the fence line, one beautiful palomino horse followed us. At one point, she nudged my shoulder, looking for a treat.

"Hey there," I laughed, turning around and stroking her beautiful neck. She pushed me again, but this time Cole came up to caress her.

"Hey there, Honey," He rubbed the spot in between her eyes. She leaned into him, almost as if she were trying to embrace him.

"Is that her name?"

Cole looked to me with pride, "Yep. This is my girl, Honey."

I patted her neck again, "She is so sweet."

"Yeah, it's kind of weird. She never usually walks up to strangers like that…" Cole mumbled, mostly to himself.

"Well, I just have a way with horses, I guess," I laughed, wrapping my arms around Honey's neck. She leaned into me, like she was agreeing with me.

"Yeah," Cole replied quietly, finally turning back toward the fence. "I guess you do."

Cole's horse, Honey, stayed with us while Cole continued to fix the fencing. I mainly watched and handed him tools whenever he asked. It was strange, being here with Cole on his ranch. I didn't know why, but I felt like I was really seeing who Cole was. The way he moved with the horses, carried fifty-pound bags of feed, tossing hay, all the hard work. He seemed to enjoy it, like this was his home, his comfort.

After fixing the last spot in the fence, Cole began leading us back to the house.

"Sorry for all this work," Cole apologized. "I needed to get it done before we went to the market."

"Don't be sorry," I said wiping the sweat from my forehead. "This was great!"

He laughed, startling Honey, who was walking right behind us.

"Great? Well that's a first. Most people can't understand why my dad still runs this place," Cole's calloused hands spread, pointing to the barn and the surrounding pastures.

"I think it's beautiful, really," I whispered, looking at the herd of horses Honey began calling to.

"Go on," Cole smacked Honey's side. "Go to your family."

Seeming to understand, Honey trotted toward the herd answering their calls.

Cole glanced down to his watch, "The market has just started. You ready to go?"

"Yeah," I said, my eyes still glued to Honey. "Yeah, let's go."

Chenoa was still in the kitchen, wiping the counters when we walked in.

"I hope my brother didn't make you work too hard," Chenoa glared at Cole.

"Of course not," I laughed. "I enjoyed seeing everything. It's beautiful here."

"Well, we were just passing through," Cole playfully pushed Chenoa. "We're heading to the market now."

"Have fun," Chenoa hugged me while simultaneously trying to push Cole.

"Chenoa, aren't you coming?" I asked. I felt rude to leave her when she had just welcomed me into her home.

Chenoa gave me another warm smile, "I'll catch up with you guys later! I'm going to wait for Elsu and the others."

And after leaving Chenoa, Cole led me back outside, making our way toward the market.

"It's a wonderful day, isn't it?" Cole began nervously, trying to make small talk.

"Who are the others?" I countered, completely ignoring his question. Suddenly, the thought of Cole having a girlfriend seemed more and more plausible. Maybe Chenoa was going to bring her to Cole later. My stomach dropped to my feet. The small tug in my chest pulled, the little candle was flickering again.

Cole sighed, "Just some of our friends. If you can call them that."

"What does that mean?"

Cole shrugged, running a hand through his onyx hair, "I mean, they are more Elsu and Chenoa's friends than mine."

"What? So you don't have friends?" I asked while playfully punching his arm.

He smirked, "Yeah pretty much."

I waited for him to say he was joking, but he didn't. He was looking straight ahead, but I knew his mind was somewhere else. Some place I couldn't see.

"You're serious. You don't have any friends," I was shocked. Cole was so likeable, kind, and a pretty good friend from what I had seen.

He laughed, glancing back down to me, "Now, I'm not a complete outcast, Adeline. I do have friends, but I mostly like to keep to myself and to the ranch. Is that so wrong?"

He purposely bumped into me, almost causing me to trip and fall.

I glared at him, "No, there's nothing wrong with that."

Suddenly, it made sense, how comfortable he was with the horses, with Honey. In the same way I found comfort with paints and paper, Cole found refuge in his family's ranch, in the hard work. It was his home. It was who he was.

"Now, what about you?" Cole asked after a few moments of silence. "Where are your friends? Or better yet, your boyfriend?"

He said the last few words very quickly. I almost stopped when he even mentioned the word "boyfriend". My love life had been very limited at best and basically non-existent at worst.

"I don't have a boyfriend," I replied quietly. "But what about you? Surely you have a girlfriend?" I turned the tables. This was my chance to once and for all convince myself that a future friendship with Cole would remain reserved. If there was a future to even have.

He laughed, "No. No girlfriend."

"Seriously?" I questioned, still not convinced.

He rolled his eyes, "Seriously! I swear you're starting to sound like my sister."

We continued walking until we finally saw the conference center. The road leading up to it was filled with people and venders. My eyes widened at all the activity. Cole seemed to enjoy my amusement. He was a very good tour guide, leading me from vender to vender; introducing me to people he had grown up with. Unlike the day before, no one seemed vigilant around me. Everyone was very welcoming.

"Adeline, this is Kai. She is the best basket weaver in the whole tribe," Cole introduced, a smile never leaving his face.

"Oh, Cole, stop it!" Kai laughed while playfully slapping his arm. "You know Chenoa would be very upset if she heard you right now."

Kai looked to me, her smile reaching her eyes, "It's very nice to meet you, Adeline." She took my hand and pulled me into a hug. I returned the hug awkwardly, smiling when she finally released me.

"Come, I want to show you something," Kai took my hand and led me farther inside her station. There were several ornate baskets, all so striking and wonderfully made. It was hard to believe that she made all of them by hand. Kai picked something off one of the tables and placed it in my hands.

"A gift," she explained. "To keep you safe in both spirit and body."

I opened my hands and found a dream catcher. There were small blue flowers braided in with the dark wood. It was beautiful.

"Forget-me-nots," Kai continued. "They hold in the good dreams, the ones you don't want to forget, while the dream catcher snatches the bad before they can get to you."

Moisture clouded my eyes. No one, especially someone I had just met, had ever given me something so beautiful, so meaningful.

"Thank you so much," I finally muttered, desperately trying to control my emotions. It was odd how something so small could have such an effect on me.

"Hey, Cole!"

We turned around and found a group of young people making their way toward Kai's station.

"Hey, guys," Cole greeted, meeting them halfway.

I immediately recognized Elsu and Chenoa, but the others were strangers to me. I stood there uncomfortably, waiting for someone to introduce me.

I glanced over to find another girl glaring at me. She was gorgeous, the definition of perfection and beauty. Her long, black hair flowed in the wind, framing her face. She was tall and lean, her copper skin glowing. And I suddenly felt unworthy. I couldn't compare.

And she knew it too. I knew by the way she was glaring at me, as if I were a bug that needed to be squashed immediately. I stumbled backwards under her intense gaze. I thought about running. Running until I was safe in my house, content with forever being average and ordinary.

Cole sensed my discomfort. He stood beside me, placing his hand on the small of my back and bringing me forward to meet his friends. He smiled widely while he presented me, as if he was proud. I couldn't meet anyone's eyes, especially that girl's. I was too much of coward.

"Adeline, this is Elan and Dylan," Cole said, a hint of a threat in his voice as he looked at his friends. Elan was tall and toned. His hair was long, a few inches below his shoulders. Dylan was a few inches shorter, but more muscular than Elan. His hair was longer, but tied in a ponytail at the base of his neck, like Elsu.

"Well, hello there, beautiful," Dylan stepped forward. Cole rolled his eyes. "It's so nice to meet you." I felt my face heat up.

"Cole, you've been holding out on us," Elan added, while still staring at me. "Are all the girls at that school this gorgeous?"

Now I was really self-conscious. Couldn't they see the other girl right beside them? Next to her, I was nothing.

"Are you idiots done embarrassing yourselves yet, or do you have more to add?" Cole asked, humor and a bit of irritation mingled in his voice.

"I'm just trying to make friends! Isn't that right, Ella?" Dylan turned toward the copper-skinned goddess.

She looked at me again. I was convinced that if looks could kill, I would have been six feet under.

She rolled her eyes, "Whatever." Ella walked away with Elsu by her side. Uncomfortable silence ensued.

"Don't worry about her, dear," Kai came up behind me, placing a hand on my shoulder. "She isn't very good with outsiders."

Dylan snorted, "She's not very good with people in general."

"Ella is Dylan's sister," Chenoa explained. "She likes to keep to herself."

"And to Elsu," Elan winked.

"Yeah, Cole. I'd say in a few months we'll be brothers-in-law!" Both Dylan and Elan howled with laugher.

"Yeah, yeah," Cole tried to repress his smile.

Soon, Elan, Dylan, and Chenoa left, but promised to come find us when the campfire started. Cole and I continued through the market, stopping every now and then when someone recognized Cole.

"Can I ask you something?"

"Sure," Cole replied after he handed me a cup of lemonade from one of the venders.

"Thanks," I looked down to the ground, watching my feet.

Cole waited for me to continue. I sighed, not completely sure on how to start. Cole waited patiently.

"Yes?"

"About last night…what happened exactly?" I began carefully, finally finding my train of thought.

"It's a long story."

"I have time."

"Well, what exactly about last night do you want to know?" Cole asked nervously.

"Well, why did I have to lie to my sister? And why did those people run? Were they afraid of that eagle?" The memory, even though it was still foggy, gave me chills.

Cole sighed, "It's better for you and Emma to know as little as possible. You know, be on a need-to-know basis."

I didn't like that answer very much.

"Well, considering I'm the one that got hit in the head by a baseball," I glared at him. "I think I deserve to know."

Cole smiled, but soon it faded, "It's nothing to worry about. I promise."

For some reason, I didn't believe him.

"Well, anyway, what about that eagle?" I continued. "Is that what everyone was afraid of?"

"No, not exactly," Cole stammered.

"Then what?"

"It's really stupid. You'll think I'm crazy."

I shrugged my shoulders. "Try me."

He hesitated before finally whispering, "They were afraid of you."

"Come again?"

He sighed, "You remind them of someone from a legend."

"A bad legend?"

"Sort of."

"Tell me," I urged.

"It'll be told tonight," he countered. "At the campfire."

"Oh." I let the conversation drop.

He led me to where the campfire ceremony would take place. Our conversation stayed very safe. Music, books, and movies were the main topics to discuss. If I ever tried to bring the conversation back around to the tribe and this mysterious legend, he would change the subject. I finally gave up and decided I would find out everything I wanted to know later.

Soon, it was time for the ceremony and nervousness set in. I couldn't exactly explain it, but I was worried. Worried about what I might hear, what I might learn. Suddenly, learning the truth about Cole's life, his heritage, frightened me. But I couldn't walk away either. Whether it was good or bad, I had to know.

We walked into the open field beside the conference center just as the sun began to set. A bonfire was ablaze when we sat down on the benches around the fire pit. There were many teenagers there, playing football and laughing. I think I saw Dylan and Elan tackling each other at one point. There were other older men there as well, the tribe's elders from what Cole told me. Paco, his father, was one of them.

The older men sat down around the fire and everything became very serious. The teenage boys that had been playing suddenly stopped and came over to sit on the ground, or where ever they could find a spot, so that they could hear the elders.

"Tonight," one of the elders began, "we will tell the tale of a legend from long ago. The legend of the split between two tribes that had once lived together in harmony."

I saw Red Hakan clear his throat before he began.

"Long ago, when our ancestors lived in peace, there came a need to feed the people. Famine had struck and much of the food was gone. The chief at the time, Heluka, was very worried for his people. So, in an effort to restore the food supply, Heluka went off to find new game that had not moved on or died out. He was away for many days and many nights. He soon grew weak from the lack of food and water. He had not seen any game for quite awhile and he was about to lose hope.

"Suddenly, while Heluka was climbing a mountain, he heard the cry of something behind him. He turned and there he saw the most beautiful creature his eyes had ever seen. She was an eagle, but not like one he had ever seen before. Her feathers glistened in the sun, like stars in the night sky. Her body, though it looked strong and invincible, was small. The color of her feathers was strange to Heluka. They were jet black with lines of light brown and white swirling from the head to the tail. Her eyes were a vibrant green and so much like a human.

"He stood stunned as he watched the beautiful creature before him fly and soar through the mountain valley effortlessly. She cried again and landed on a rock beside Heluka. He continued to observe the eagle carefully while she gazed at him.

"Then there was a rattle in the bushes next to where Heluka stood. All of a sudden, the eagle dove into the bushes, and the sound of a rattle and the tearing of flesh was all Heluka could hear. The eagle flew out of the bushes next to Heluka's feet and landed on the same rock as before. She was in the same position, but in her beak was the body of a lifeless rattlesnake.

"Heluka knew that this eagle had saved his life. If not for her, he would have been bitten, and he would have surely died. He took a step closer to the eagle. After she had finished her meal, she looked up to Heluka with intellect in her green, human-like eyes.

"He had said to her, 'I shall call you Onida, for you are what I have searched for and what I have found.'

"Onida never left Heluka's side the entire time he trained her. He had successfully trained her to hunt all kinds of animals for him. He had also taught her to fight in case of battle. She was good to him and he to her. They had grown close. They were no longer man and eagle, but were one when they fought and hunted. It was as if she knew his every thought and he hers.

"The time came for Heluka to return to his people. He had enough deer and elk meat to last his tribe for weeks. When he and Onida returned to the village, the people yelled in shock at an eagle so close to their chief. One man had a bow and arrow ready to be used.

"'Stop!' Heluka ordered. 'I have brought you food like I promised, and it seems that we have been blessed with the help of nature.'

"The people stood stunned when they heard this. Heluka called Onida to his side, and she came obediently. He explained what had happened while he was away, and the people were relieved. He taught many of the young men how to train eagles and hawks, like he had trained Onida. Soon, many of the young men were able to catch their own flying creatures and train them. The Chosen men, though few, were the men that hunted alongside Heluka and Onida.

"Soon, the village was overflowing with meat and skins. Everyone was well fed and happy, for the most part. The village was still at peace, but it seemed that there had been trouble brewing from within the tribe. Tama, Heluka's wife, had become very jealous of Onida. Many of the other men in the tribe were unhappy with Heluka as well. They had been taught to train the birds, but none had chosen them. They had been rejected by nature, and they blamed Heluka.

"Secretly, for many months, Tama and a few men from the village found their own hawks and falcons and trained them to hunt and fight. Heluka soon became aware when he heard news of rebels within the tribe.

"Heluka gathered his Chosen and together they went out to stop the rebels. When he and the Chosen found Tama and her men, he felt utter betrayal and sadness. Heluka tried to settle the matter through words instead of having to fight. Tama wouldn't hear of it, so fought they did.

"Civil war lasted a long time. Finally, knowing she and her men were outnumbered, Tama and her men fled the village, taking their hawks with them. But before Tama and her men had left the tribe completely, Tama and her hawk followed Heluka and Onida while they were hunting. When they weren't paying attention, Tama tried to attack and kill Onida. She failed miserably and was finally chased back to her rebel men.

"Heluka did not know what to do to keep Onida safe. So, in an effort to keep Onida by his side, Heluka and Onida joined together in body and became one. They had grown into a much larger eagle with a wingspan of two adult eagles combined. Heluka trained his men, the Chosen, to transform with their eagle partners. This was very powerful magic. Only those who were Chosen could accomplish it.

"Heluka and his men were able to shift back into their human form, and their eagles were able to transform to their normal forms as well. Word of this power became known to Tama and her army of rebels. Tama soon figured out how to take over the body of her hawk and taught her men. The difference was that this did not make the hawk more powerful. Since Tama and her men were not Chosen, the souls of the creatures were lost, and they needed to find new hawks each time they transformed. This was very dark, evil magic. Once the soul was lost, it could not find its way back to the light. Those who used this magic, those who used these innocent souls, were cursed.

"The two tribes fought bitterly for a long time with no end in sight. But one day, Onida and Heluka were hunting when they came upon a woman near a waterfall. She was beautiful and powerful. She was pale-skinned with clear, gray eyes. She mesmerized Heluka. He knew that there was something more to this woman than what he originally thought. She was a heavenly being sent from the Great Spirit to help Heluka and his tribe and to stop Tama's tribe from stealing more hawks and losing their souls.

"While the heavenly being was helping Heluka and his Chosen, they both fell hopelessly in love. They both knew that this was unheard of, but they could not stay away from one another. They were inseparable and soon were married. Tama soon heard of Heluka's new marriage, and her thirst for revenge became even more passionate.

"She devised a plan to destroy the heavenly being and to finish off Heluka once and for all. While the heavenly being was in the forest picking berries for the tribe, Tama, in the form of another hawk, swooped down and tried to destroy her. Heluka knew something was wrong when he could not find his new wife. He and Onida went searching. They were horrified when they found Tama killing the heavenly being in a mad rage. Heluka caught Tama by surprise and destroyed her, sending her soul into the depths of the earth.

"When Heluka transformed back to his human form, it was too late for his wife. She was slowly slipping away.

"She whispered, her divine voice sounding strained, 'I give you the last of my power and strength so that you may defeat them, my husband. Do not be deceived that, because you have killed her, that there will be no more war. There will be war for many years to come, for many generations. So take what's left of me and fight, my love.'

"She died in Heluka's arms. His grief was so strong and his heart so broken that not even Onida could heal him. He became tired of war, and he soon became tired of living. He took the power that the heavenly being had given him and made it into a wind-like element. He then banished it from the realm of the living, hoping no one would come after it and fight again.

"He transformed one last time, he and Onida becoming one. He then stayed that way for the remainder of his life. He and Onida died in battle while they were fighting Tama's tribe once more. His ashes were thrown into the river, near the waterfall where he had met the heavenly being…"

When Red Hakan finished the legend, it took me a moment to realize that tears were streaming down my face. My heart was still pounding. A man stood and cleared his throat. We all turned to him. He was very tall, with long, black hair in two braids. His dark, blue eyes were captivating and very familiar.

"There are dinner and drinks in the conference center for those who have not eaten. Thank you for coming. This concludes the campfire ceremony," he finished. He walked away, toward the conference center, I imagined. Everyone began standing and gathering their things. It took me another moment to realize that I was still sitting when people started to put out the fire.

"Adeline?"

I looked up and found Cole waiting beside me.

"Yes?" I croaked.

"Would you like some dinner or would you rather return home?" he asked cautiously.

"I wanna stay," I exclaimed eagerly.

He smiled, and held his hand out to me. I looked at it dumbly.

"Would you like some help?" he queried patiently.

I nodded, and placed my hand in his warm, calloused palm. My hand looked so small in comparison. He gripped my hand and gave a gentle squeeze. I realized he meant to try to help me stand up. I stood and then, hand in hand, we walked toward the conference center. My heart was pounding in my ears when he asked me something. I completely missed it.

"What?"

He chuckled, "What did you think of the legend?"

"Oh, I loved it, but…"

"But?"

"But it was just so sad," I replied, looking toward the ground watching the moonlight catch our shadows.

"Yes, the past seems to be that way," he whispered, looking straight ahead.

We walked into the conference center and found the large room packed. It looked like the whole tribe was here. And unfortunately, the whole tribe saw Cole and I walk into the room hand in hand. I blushed as everyone continued to gaze at us. I thought that Cole would drop my hand once we made it into the building, but if anything, he held it tighter.

"What's she doing here?" asked one of the older women.

"What's he thinking? He could have any girl in the tribe and he picks an outsider," another commented.

"Like father, like son," I heard another whisper.

They were right. I didn't belong here. What was I thinking? I tried to turn to run away, but Cole tightened his grip on my hand.

"Don't listen to them, Adeline," he whispered. "They're just jealous old women with nothing better to do."

I nodded, still not convinced, but willing to stay. He led me to a table where Chenoa was seated. I saw Dylan and Elan heading toward the table as well.

"How did you like the legend, Adeline?" Chenoa asked me as I sat down.

"It was beautiful, but so tragic."

Dylan and Elan, with plates full of food, pulled out chairs and sat with us.

"What's up?" Dylan asked, his mouth full of food.

"Nice," Chenoa commented, obviously disgusted.

"What?" he asked innocently. Everyone started to laugh.

Cole sat down next to me and nodded to Chenoa.

She looked to me. "Would you like something to eat? You haven't eaten anything in ages. Let me get you something."

"Oh, it's all right. I can get something," I responded, but Chenoa wouldn't hear of it.

"No, I don't mind," Chenoa said as she stood and skipped over to the food. Suddenly, the smell of hamburgers and hot dogs hit my nose, and my stomach growled in response.

"Hungry?" Cole smiled.

"Not really."

He chuckled, "Whatever you say."

Cole began talking to Elan and Dylan while stealing some of their food. I almost thought they would start fighting, but Cole calmed them down. I looked around the room and found a million brown eyes gazing back at me. I immediately looked down to the table, staring at the wood indentions.

"Don't be embarrassed. It's none of their business," he murmured.

"They're right though. I don't belong," I whispered in response.

"If you don't belong, then neither do I. You're my friend, and they will have to deal with that," he replied a bit louder, maybe to catch the attention of some of the older ladies who were still eyeing me.

"Yeah, Adeline," Elan added, "don't worry about what the old hags think."

"They have nothing to do besides gossip," Dylan continued, before taking another huge bite out of his burger.

"Here you go, Adeline," Chenoa said as she placed a plate with a hamburger and some chips on the table in front of me, along with a cup of lemonade.

"Thanks, Chenoa," I replied, still looking down as I took a bite of my burger. I hadn't realized how hungry I really was.

"No problem," she smiled cheerfully, "and don't worry about those ladies. They're just busy-bodies."

I nodded as I continued to eat. Cole continued to steal Dylan and Elan's food, while Chenoa and I watched in amusement. When I had finished, Chenoa bounced over to me, taking my plate.

"Oh, no. I'll get it," I tried to stand but Chenoa pushed me back down.

"I insist," Chenoa giggled as she took my trash and walked away.

Elan and Dylan stood up, "We'll see you later, Cole."

"Later, guys," Cole smiled.

Dylan walked over and shook my hand, "It has been an absolute pleasure."

Cole rolled his eyes while punching him in the arm, "Okay, she gets it. Now get out of here."

Dylan saluted, "Yes, sir!"

Elan laughed, following his friend.

"See you later."

"Bye," I giggled while watching Elan and Dylan head toward the door.

Cole and I talked for a while, but he continued to avoid discussing the legend. He was clearly uncomfortable. We suddenly became aware of someone else's presence as a man cleared his throat from behind us. We turned around in our chairs, and I looked up to find the same man from before at the campfire.

"Cole," he greeted.

"Paco," Cole replied, his voice completely void of his prior warmth.

Tension continued to build as the two stared each other down.

"And you are?" Paco titled his head toward me, slightly irritated.

I opened my mouth to respond when Cole introduced me, "This is Adeline. My friend from school."

"Oh, I see. Pleasure to meet you, Adeline." He didn't sound like it was a pleasure at all.

"Pleasure to meet you," I replied softly. I looked back down to the floor as he continued to gaze at me, judging me.

"I'll see you at home," Cole hinted warningly.

"Be home by eleven," Paco replied, just as threateningly, as he walked away.

"Sorry about that," Cole relaxed as soon as Paco was out of hearing range.

I looked up to Cole, "Who was that?"

"He's my father."

"Oh."

"You couldn't tell?" he laughed sarcastically.

"I don't know. I just didn't think there would be so much tension."

"He's just angry with me," Cole shrugged as he made little shapes on the table with his fingers.

"Why?"

He glanced at me regretfully and then looked back down to the table. Oh. His dad was angry with him because of me. Figures.

"Maybe I should leave. I don't like making your family feel uncomfortable. I'd hate to make them angry at you because of me," I tried to stand up, but Cole pushed me back down in my seat. Again.

"This has nothing to do with you. My family is just extremely superstitious. I promise," he replied earnestly.

That reminded me.

"You know how you said I reminded your tribe of someone in the legend?"

"Yes," he answered warily.

"Who is it? Who do I remind them of?"

"It's stupid. My tribe is just really superstitious," Cole replied, trying to buy himself some time.

"Quit making excuses," I countered. "So what if it's all not true? I'm still curious."

Cole sighed, seeming uncomfortable.

"What's wrong with telling me?" I asked, making him look me in the eyes.

"It's just really embarrassing," he finally admitted. "Some people have certain family members they are self-conscious of. Well, I have a whole tribe. I just don't want to freak you out."

I laughed, "Trust me, if I was freaked out by now, I would have left long ago."

He joined in with my laughter, "Well, thanks."

"But seriously," I continued, "tell me."

Cole hesitated.

"Come on," I encouraged. "Humor me."

"Okay," he agreed, "but not in here."

Cole led me out of the conference center. The market had already been cleared away. All that was left was the dirt road and the moon shining down, lighting our way.

"Is this better?" I asked, spreading my arms around me.

"Much," he agreed. "I feel like I can breathe now."

For some reason, I felt there was a double meaning to his words.

"So..."

"So what?" Cole asked.

I punched his arm, "Are you going to tell me or not?"

He laughed, "Hey! No need to get violent!"

When our laughter finally died down, Cole cleared his throat.

"Some people in the tribe," he hesitated again, "think you are the heavenly being."

Well, that was definitely not what I was expecting.

"Sorry?"

He rolled his eyes, "Well, they think you are her reincarnation. Stupid, I know. Most of them are the really old folks who still believe the legends and myths completely."

I was at a loss for words. Wasn't the heavenly being supposed to be beautiful and powerful? I was the complete opposite.

"Why do they think that?" I questioned quietly.

Cole sensed my change in attitude, "Don't take it personally. I told you, those people are crazy."

"But why do they think that?" I persisted.

Cole stopped walking and turned to me. We stared at each other for a long time. I suddenly noticed how cold the air had become; chill bumps were covering my skin. Cole slipped his jacket off and wrapped it around me.

"Thanks," I muttered, staring down at my feet. Silence followed.

"If I tell you, you're going to think I'm, or at least the tribe, is crazy."

"Why don't you let me be the judge of that?" I looked up into his deep, blue eyes.

He licked his lips nervously and sighed, "It's a dumb reason honestly."

"What?" I smiled. "Because I'm a pale face. There are plenty of pale women in Great Falls. Any one of them could be her."

Cole laughed, "No, it's not because you're white. If that were their reason, I wouldn't be worried at all."

"Why are you worried?"

He glanced to me again, "I'm just worried I'm really gonna freak you out."

I looped my arm in between his as we continued walking, "I won't freak out. Promise."

He smiled, "They think, or rather suspect, you are her reincarnation because of me."

"Why you?"

"No one ever really brings outsiders into the tribe. You know, like the campfire ceremonies. We are a small tribe, and we like to keep to ourselves," he explained. "So, when I brought you around they kind of got some crazy ideas from some crazy legends and boom, they have convinced themselves of some silly beliefs."

I felt his eyes on me. I looked up smiling.

"See? I'm not freaking out or running and screaming," I stated proudly.

He laughed, "Well, that's good. Otherwise, you would have a long run home."

"Speaking of which, I need to head back," I realized. "I need to get home before Emma."

"Where is she? I thought she would be at home waiting," Cole asked as his home finally came into view.

"Henry took her out for the day," I explained, shrugging closer into Cole's jacket.

"Who's Henry?"

"Emma's boyfriend."

"Oh."

"What?"

"I don't know. Just curious." He was staring at the stars, captivated by their beauty.

"Are you cold? You didn't have to give me your jacket…" I trailed off.

He smirked, "No, I'm fine, Adeline. Don't worry."

We drove back to my house silently and somehow, along the way, I had fallen asleep.

"Adeline?" someone asked. It sounded like I was dreaming.

"Huh?"

I heard the same voice chuckle as I was being lifted. It felt like someone was carrying me. I heard my front door being unlocked and opened.

"Where's your room?" he asked quietly.

"Take a left down the hall. First door on the right…" I muttered groggily.

I heard the door to my room open and then felt myself being laid onto my bed. The bed made the same creaking sound it did when I was awake. I felt my boots being taken off and heard them fall to the floor with a thud. Someone lifted my comforter over me and laid it down. I felt so warm.

"Good night, Adeline," the voice murmured.

"Don't…leave…" I said dazedly.

The voice chuckled, "All right. Just go to sleep."

"Okay. Promise you won't leave?" I asked, still sure I was dreaming.

"I promise," the voice assured me.

I fell into a dreamless slumber, faintly aware of someone's gentle humming.

ALLISON BLANCHARD

Chapter Five

The sound of birds chirping outside my window woke me around ten. I rubbed my eyes and looked around my room. My boots were lying on the floor carelessly next to my bed. I noticed that I was still wearing my jeans, green sweater, and someone's jacket. It couldn't be mine because the sleeves were way too long...

Suddenly, I realized that it was Cole's. It even smelled like him.

How had I gotten to my room? The last thing I remembered was driving home with Cole and then having such a strange dream. I smacked myself in the face. That wasn't a dream; it was real. Cole had to carry me into my own home and then tuck me into bed like a child. I groaned out loud at the memory.

I pushed the covers off, going to take a shower. After I had changed, I grabbed Cole's jacket and placed it under my pillow. I didn't need to explain that one to Emma. I would give Cole his jacket tomorrow at school.

I walked into the kitchen and found Emma sitting at the kitchen table, reading the paper while sipping her coffee.

"Morning, sleepy head," she greeted, not looking up from her paper.

"Morning," I replied as I retrieved cereal and milk from the cabinet. I poured the contents into a bowl, then sat down at the table and began to eat.

"How was your night?" I asked in between bites.

"Good," Emma sighed, finally folding her paper and setting it on the table next to her mug.

"What?" I questioned hesitantly.

"You sure were tired last night. So tired that someone had to carry you to bed," Emma took another sip of her coffee.

I awkwardly swallowed what was in my mouth. "Oh…you know about that."

"Yeah, he was here when I came home," Emma replied evenly. It was the calm before the storm.

"He was so nice, saying that you were safe in bed and that he wanted to wait until I came home before he left."

"I can explain," I started.

"Can you?"

I looked back down to my cereal, suddenly losing my appetite.

"I don't know what happened. I was tired and on the way home I fell asleep. He was just trying to be nice by not waking me up. Is that so wrong?" I asked quietly.

"No, it's not, Adeline. I just don't like the fact that you couldn't put yourself to bed. I thought I taught you to take care of yourself. You don't need a man -"

"To save me like a damsel in distress," I finished for her. I had heard this speech about a million times.

"Exactly," she continued. "Now, I'm not mad. Just frustrated. You're such a smart girl. I've never seen you so infatuated with a boy before." She said "infatuated" like it was a sin.

"I'm not infatuated with anyone," I contradicted. "We're just friends."

"I hope so," Emma whispered as she stood up and placed her mug in the dishwasher.

Emma walked toward her office, probably to finish her story for the paper.

I sat at the table just staring at my cereal that was now becoming soggy. I placed my bowl and spoon into the sink, planning on washing it later. I walked into my room and grabbed my school bag. After about an hour of studying, the phone rang. It rang twice before Emma answered it.

"Adeline! It's for you!" Emma called from down the hall.

I was shocked. Who would want to talk to me? I grabbed the phone next to my computer.

"Hello?" I answered timidly.

"Hello, Adeline?" the deep voice asked.

"Yeah, who's this?"

"Hey, this is Chandler from school. How are you?" His voice was smooth, confident, and arrogant. I was happy that he had called to talk to me. The look on my face may have insulted him.

"Um, good. How are you?" I responded uneasily. Since when did Chandler Phalcon call to see how I was doing? I didn't even think he knew I existed.

"Fine. I heard that you received my note Friday," Chandler said, oozing with self-assurance.

"Um, yep, sure did," I replied, not completely sure how to handle the situation.

"So I know this weekend didn't work out, but how about the next?" he asked persuasively. "I would have asked in person, but my schedule is pretty hectic."

I rolled my eyes at his self-righteousness.

"Yeah, well mine is too. I won't be able to hang out with you," I replied steadily, surprised at my composure.

He must have been surprised too, because there was silence on the other end.

"Oh really? Is it someone else?" Sarcasm seeped through the phone.

"No," I muttered, "I just have plans."

"With Cole Dyami?" Chandler asked, disgusted.

It was my turn to be speechless.

I heard Chandler smirk, "That's okay. I don't mind a little competition."

"No, I think you have the wrong idea," I tried to reply. The line had already gone dead.

I hung up the phone when Emma yelled from her computer, "Who was it?"

I walked into her office, "Someone from school."

"A boy?" she asked with an eyebrow raised. She was sitting in her chair, legs crossed, with a pencil in her hair holding her bun together.

"Aren't we Miss Popular?" she teased while she typed.

I rolled my eyes, "Oh be quiet."

"What did he want?" she asked curiously.

"He wanted to take me out on a date," I replied calmly. "How's that story coming along?"

She stopped typing, looking at me with wide eyes.

"A date?" She was clearly shocked.

"Yeah, no big deal. I said no," I replied, not appreciating my sister's stare. Was it really that hard to imagine that someone might want to ask me out? I guess so, because she kept staring at me like I had grown two heads.

"Is it really that hard to believe?" I asked quietly.

Her face relaxed, falling into a frown.

"That's not what I meant, Addie," she stood and pulled me into a hug.

"Quit calling me that," I cringed, looking for a change in subject while trying to shrug out of the hug.

"You know I didn't mean it like that, right?" she asked, ignoring my struggle.

"Yeah, yeah, now let me go," I whined.

Emma finally released me after she ruffled my hair.

I started to leave when she said, "And to answer your question, I'm almost finished with my story. I'll let you proof it when I'm done."

"Kay." I walked back into my room to study.

About an hour later, Emma called me into her office with her story ready.

"Coming, Emma!" I called back, running into her office.

The printer was on its last page.

"Can I read it now?" I asked curiously while leaning against the doorframe.

She skipped toward me with her papers at hand.

"Be absolutely truthful! I can take it," she instructed dramatically as she placed the papers in my hands.

"No problem," I rolled my eyes while I walked to her desk and began to read.

Great Falls Tribune

"Local Teens Trespassing on Native Land"

By: Emma Jasely

The Chippewa elders began to discuss the problem of unwanted visitors on their land while at the Little Shell Reservation's weekly meeting. It seems that teenagers from the Great Falls area have been seen on the property without permission, hunting and holding unauthorized bonfires.

"It's not that we do not appreciate their enthusiasm of our culture," Chief Hakan said to the tribunal. "It's just we would like some sort of respect. This land belonged to our ancestors and it's [the tribe's] job to protect it."

Chief Red Hakan went on to say that the tribe "enjoyed the visitors that were respectful" but would rather have the others obey the simple jurisdictions of the council of elders. The council held a vote on whether to tighten the laws of the tribe, considering the amount of laws that the unwanted visitors have broken, or whether to do away with visitors all together. The vote was nine to one. The council had voted to boot out visitors completely.

"I hate that it has come to this," Paco Dyami, a prominent council member, explained when he read the vote. "But these people, my tribe, our ancestors, they deserve better treatment than this and if it means that no newcomers may come, then very well."

The council meeting went on to discuss the new law that would state no visitors would be allowed onto the Chippewa tribe's land. Many of the elders ordered with much enthusiasm that no one without papers saying they belonged to the Little Shell Tribe would be allowed to "set one foot onto the Chippewa soil".

Many others simply wanted certain hours that visitors would have to obey. Those elders were overruled when Chief Hakan explained, "I feel that our tribe can no longer let outsiders come into our reservation. We have been taken advantage of, and it's time we, as a tribe, set our foot down. I cannot permit any visitors of any sort to be allowed onto the Little Shell Reservation."

Finally, the rule was made. No visitors, at any time, are allowed onto the Little Shell Reservation, effective immediately.

I was personally asked by Chief Red Hakan to write a story on the decision of the council meeting. I was also personally asked to give Chief Hakan's individual side of the story, no newspaper editing allowed.

"I just want to say that this is nothing personal or hostile toward the good people of Great Falls," Hakan explained to me after the meeting. "I'm just trying to do what's best for my tribe and what's best is no visitors. Period."

Chief Hakan went on to say that it was mostly the teenagers of Great Falls that have caused the disturbance among the tribe.

"We, as a tribe, hold nothing against the elders of the city. It's the kids that don't seem to hold our land and tribe with any respect. And to be quite honest, I do not want the tribe's youth to be influenced by the youth of Great Falls. We are doing our best to preserve our culture in every way possible. Therefore, it would be best if our youth would remain separate. Separate in every way possible," Hakan explained.

The Little Shell Reservation has made it extremely clear that no one outside of the tribe is to enter unless specifically asked by one of the elders.

I stared at the article in front of me, completely shocked and taken aback. No one was allowed to visit? Ever? It seemed so strange, especially considering the fact that most of the tribe was very welcoming to me, an outsider, only yesterday. Did Cole know about the new rule? Is that why his dad was so cold to me? Because he knew I was breaking a rule I didn't even know existed?

"Hey, Adeline! I've got lunch on the way. I ordered pizza," Emma called from the kitchen.

"Okay," I yelled back.

I placed Emma's article back onto the desk, slowly making my way toward the kitchen.

"What'd ya think?" Emma asked as she grabbed paper plates from the cupboard.

"Oh, it was really good," I replied quietly as I retrieved two sodas from the fridge.

I sat down and opened my can, taking small sips.

"You okay?"

I answered a moment late, "Yeah. Fine."

"Was it the story? About no visitors?" Emma asked, concerned. "I thought Cole told you."

"No," I replied quickly, "he didn't."

Emma opened her mouth to say something when the doorbell rang. She walked toward the door mumbling something about "fast service". I was surprised, no, more like dumbfounded, when Emma said, "Oh, hey, Cole."

"Hello, Miss Jasely. Is Adeline home?"

What was he doing here? Did he just hear about the new rule too? Maybe Cole was right. Maybe his tribe was a little bit crazy.

"Yeah," Emma replied reluctantly, "she's in the kitchen."

I heard him walk down the hall into the kitchen. I didn't look up, but stared at the bad yellow paint job on the walls. Emma and I did it two summers ago when she thought the kitchen needed to be brightened.

"Hey, Adeline."

"Hi."

"May I have a seat?" he asked politely.

"Sure," I replied, still staring at the wall.

He was silent for a moment after he took the seat next to me. I glanced down at the table and saw his dark, rusty-colored hands neatly folded together on top of the table. I immediately looked back to the wall in front of me and waited for him to start.

"What are we looking at?" Cole whispered into my ear.

I jumped back in surprise. How did he get that close? He chuckled when I landed on the linoleum floor.

"Ouch," I muttered.

"Here," Cole said as he offered me his hand, "let me help."

I slowly placed my hand in his as he helped me back into my seat.

"I'm sorry I scared you," he said as we sat down again in our seats.

"It's okay," I mumbled.

"So…" he began.

"So?"

"So, what are we looking at again?" he smiled, amused.

"What?" I finally turned to look at him.

He took my breath away like the first day I met him. His messy black hair was wet from the morning rain. Stray strands stuck to his face and almost covered his eyes. Almost, but they were still captivating. His deep blue orbs suddenly made me feel very self-conscience. He was smiling from ear to ear, white teeth showing. I looked down to his brown boots, trying to regain some control of my emotions.

"I was wondering why we were staring at the wall? It looked very interesting to you," he explained.

"I don't know."

I looked back up to his beautiful face and saw his smile gone, replaced by a frown.

"What's wrong?"

"Why didn't you tell me?"

"Tell you what?" Cole asked, his voice confused.

"About the law that the elders ordered, that no visitors were to come to the Little Shell Reservation."

He sat for a moment, his blue eyes thoughtful.

"I didn't tell you because it's not important," he replied with a clenched jaw.

"What do you mean it's not important? If I wasn't supposed to be there, then I should have left." It all made sense now. Why Cole's dad was not very friendly. Why Ella seemed to hate me so much even though she didn't even know me. I was breaking a rule. A very important one at that.

Cole shook his head, "Unless you have been holding bonfires and hunting on our property without permission, then you are allowed to come whenever you wish."

"But Emma's story said no visitors. At all."

Cole sighed, "The rule said no one can come unless an elder says they can."

"Since when are you an elder?" I asked, still critical.

"I'm not, but my father is."

I stared back in disbelief, "Doesn't your dad want me away too?"

Cole didn't reply but looked out the window behind me. I took his silence as a "yes".

"I'm not going let you and your dad fight because of me," I whispered.

"Please, Adeline. Don't start," Cole spoke softly as the doorbell rang. The real pizza boy was here.

"Hey, guys," Emma greeted happily as she walked in with two pizza boxes in her hands.

"Hungry, Cole?"

Cole looked to the pizza boxes, now on the table in front of him, "Oh, no thank you, Miss Jasely. I ate before I came."

"Are you sure? You are more than welcome to it."

"Thank you, but really I just ate," Cole declined politely.

"Okay, well make yourself at home, Cole." Emma grabbed two pieces and placed them onto her plate. She took her soda and whispered to me as she walked away, "I'm gonna eat in my office."

I looked back to Cole, surprised to find him walking out of the room. I quickly followed him, "Where are you going?"

"To get the books out of my car," he replied steadily.

"What books?" I was still confused.

"The books for our history project, remember? I told you my dad had plenty of resources we could use." He smiled while unlocking his truck's door. He began carrying several books into the house.

"Here, let me take some," I offered. He carefully handed me two thick volumes. My arms almost caved in at the weight. He made them look so light. We spread the books across the table and immediately set to work. Every now and then Emma would come in to check on us. She seemed mildly pleased that we were only doing schoolwork instead of whatever else her imagination had come up with.

After three hours of hard work and research, we had actually finished the project and the presentation. I even felt prepared for the test the next day. Strangely enough, the project and the studying were fun. At least, working on it with Cole was fun. I suddenly forgot about the tribal ruling and even about the legend that was supposedly about me. It was just Cole and I, two friends working together.

"Well, now that that's done, I guess I better be heading home." Cole began to close up his laptop and clean up the books.

"Oh, I guess so," I tried not to sound too disappointed as I helped him take his things back to his truck.

"I had a great time," he smiled as we stood outside his truck. "Even if all we did was work on the history project."

"Yeah, me too."

Silence descended as the sun began to set. Cole looked like he was about to say goodbye, when I finally worked the courage up to ask him something I had been wanting to know since he came today. Since the moment he walked in, somewhere in the back of my mind, I knew something was wrong.

"Why did you come over?" I finally asked, looking down at my feet. "I mean, what was the real reason?"

I knew that Cole didn't come over just for the project. No, there was another, much deeper reason.

"Can't a guy come over to visit his friend without there being a reason?" Cole asked, eyes fixed on the setting sun. There was a hidden meaning behind his words.

"What happened, Cole?" I asked sternly, knowing something must have happened on the reservation.

He sighed, looking down to his feet.

"Nothing happened."

He was like an open book. I knew something happened.

"Tell me," I urged.

Cole looked into my eyes.

"What happened?" I demanded.

He sighed before he began, "Elsu and I got into a fight."

"Because of me," I whispered, "because I broke the rule."

"No, Adeline," Cole surprised me, "because of me. Elsu has always had ill feelings toward me. Did I tell you that we are only half-brothers?"

"Yeah, I think so."

"Well, Elsu never really accepted me as his brother. He has always hated me, ever since I was a baby," he continued, "You see, our father, Paco, really loved my mother, more than their mother. Their mother, Dena, left our father after Chenoa was born. Couldn't handle motherhood I suppose."

"Then Paco met your mom," I assumed.

"Yeah, and then I was born," he stated carelessly, as if his life had no value. I was almost angered by his thoughtless tone. Obviously, he didn't know how important and vital his life was, at least to me. The tug in my chest pulled tightly.

"Well, anyway," he continued, "Elsu never really considered me his brother. Just a pest. Chenoa is the opposite. She's the best big sister."

The thought of little Chenoa being older and bigger than Cole made me smile.

"And so, Elsu and I fought again," Cole concluded. But I knew that there was more.

"Just because he doesn't like you? That seems odd."

"He is sort of odd," Cole laughed, "but don't worry. It was nothing, really."

We stood in silence for a minute before I asked, "What kind of fight? Like verbal or…."

"It was physical. But some words were exchanged," Cole smirked.

"Cole!" I scolded as I began checking his arms for injuries. "Are you all right?"

He began chuckling, and I glared at his humor.

"I'm not the one that lost. Elsu got the bad end of the fight," he replied calmly, taking his hands out of mine.

I couldn't believe that Cole's huge, muscled brother lost a physical fight to such a kind, non-violent person.

"Is he hurt?" My care and concern now transferred to Elsu.

"Just his ego."

I was suddenly unsure of the person standing in front of me.

"So you beat Elsu in a physical fight?" I asked, looking for clarity.

"Yes," Cole answered dismally, "does that bother you?"

"No. Just you don't seem like the kind of person who would use actions instead of words," I explained.

"I tried talking. He threw the first punch."

The thought of Elsu trying to hurt Cole made me feel uneasy. I looked over Cole again, making sure he was still okay.

"I'm fine," Cole assured me.

"I know," I replied sharply.

He laughed, "Well, if that's all, I really should head home."

But neither of us moved. We stood there, not wanting the other to leave. I was surprised when Cole reached over and tucked a strand of my hair behind my ear. He was about to say something when someone interrupted.

"Hey, Addie?" Emma called, sticking her head out the front door.

Sensing my tension, Cole let his hand down and stood further away from me. I immediately cursed Emma in my head.

"Yeah?" I asked, breathless.

She looked at me with eyebrows raised, "You okay?"

I nodded, "Yeah, what do you need?"

I glanced toward Cole and found him fighting back a smile. I wanted to smack him.

"Just making sure that you know that dinner is almost ready," she said, leaning against the doorframe.

I bit back a sarcastic remark.

"Don't worry, Miss Jasely, I was just about to leave," Cole replied as took his keys out of his pocket.

Emma seemed satisfied and walked back into the house. I knew she would still be watching us through the window though.

"Thanks again for helping me study."

"No problem," he replied as he opened the truck door.

"I guess I'll see you at school," I whispered, beginning to turn back to the house as the night sky began to drizzle.

"Wait," Cole grabbed my hand.

"Yes?" I asked eagerly.

"I'll pick you up. Seven thirty, okay?"

I nodded, succumbed to his gaze.

"Great. See you then," he said as he climbed into his truck. "Goodbye, Adeline."

He drove away, and I watched until his headlights were out of sight.

Chapter Six

He picked me up around seven thirty, like he had said. He stood there waiting on my front porch, looking more like a Greek god, than a high school student. I tried to give him back his jacket when I got in his truck.

"No, Adeline, you keep it for now," he smiled, "I don't want you to catch a cold."

"Ha ha," I muttered dryly, "I'm not that fragile."

But I still hung onto the jacket, gently placing it in my school bag.

The car ride was peaceful and quiet. We didn't talk much, mostly listened to music. It was a different CD this time, but the same band. When he parked, he immediately helped me out of the truck. He took my school bag and pulled his jacket out. He wrapped the jacket around me, ignoring my protests.

"Seriously, Adeline. I am not getting in trouble with Emma. I refuse to let you get yourself sick," he smiled, amused. "Besides, friends don't let friends catch colds."

I rolled my eyes at his lame joke. But no matter how hard I tried, he would not take the jacket back. He walked me to my first period class again, but instead of leaving he walked me into the room and to my seat.

Everybody watched as he handed me my books, "I'll see you in geometry."

Joanne and Sasha's mouths fell open. He left and I was alone with everyone's eyes on me. I could only imagine what they were thinking.

"So, you and Cole are pretty close, huh?"

I was surprised when I found Brittany Ryan sitting next to me, looking at me like I actually existed.

"Excuse me?"

"You and Cole. Are you, like, a thing?" she asked as she flipped her blonde hair behind her shoulder.

I bit my lip, "No, just friends."

"Really? Are you sure?" she asked. There was something else she was hinting at. I could tell by the way she eyed my, no, his jacket.

"Yeah, why?"

"Well, I was just making sure. I want to ask Cole to the sweetheart dance this Friday," Brittany explained while seeming very interested in her nails.

"Oh, what about Matt?"

Her eyes widened when I said his name. I instantly regretted it.

"You didn't hear?" she asked, surprised. "We broke up Friday night. No big deal."

No big deal? Matt Robinson and Brittany Ryan had been going out for as long as I could remember.

"No, I didn't. Sorry to hear about that," I replied, not sure of what else to say.

"No big deal," she repeated, "but, just to be sure, you wouldn't care if I asked Cole out?"

Envy and suspicion hit me hard, and I tried not to sound bitter.

"No, it's fine. I don't care," I lied.

"Sweet. Thanks, Madeline. I appreciate it," Brittany said as she stood and then sat next to Joanne.

"It's Adeline," I corrected, a moment late.

She didn't hear, or pretended not to, and continued talking to Joanne and Sasha. Most likely about the dance and who she was going to ask. For some reason, I was definitely not okay with Cole going anywhere with Brittany Ryan. She was so fake. Cole deserved better. Someone…not blonde. But now I was just being selfish. If Cole was into the plastic, fake tan, bleached blonde Barbie type, then I should support him, right? As his friend, I should not really care whom he chose to date. After all, how did I even know if he would say yes?

But what if he did? What if Cole turned out to be just like Lily? Then I would be invisible again. I could do that. I could live with that. I did it once. But the tug in my chest continued to pull, the small candle was burning even brighter. Would I honestly be able to let Cole go like I let Lily go?

Lily Shelton had been my best friend as long as I could remember. It was hard to believe, but we had slumber parties, went to movies, and even did homework together. She knew all my secrets, and I knew hers. But one day, she changed. One day we were sitting at lunch laughing and talking about how shallow some of the girls were. Then the next day, I woke up and found my best friend gone, and one of those shallow girls had taken her place.

Friendship never had worked out for me before. I thought I loved Lily. She was like a sister. But apparently I was wrong. And I was wrong about Cole. I had known it all along. The bell rang and I walked to my locker slowly, too engaged in my thoughts to notice someone beside me.

"Adeline?"

"Huh?"

"Are you all right?" His voice filled with concern.

"Yeah, Cole," I lied, "I'm fine."

We walked to my locker, and he leaned against the wall while I grabbed my books.

He continued to watch me as he walked me to English. I turned to him right before I walked into the room. I didn't want more students gossiping about me and Cole today.

"I'll see you later," I said softly.

He didn't reply, but reached his hand toward my face. My heart skipped a few necessary beats. He gently tucked a stray strand of my hair behind my ear, his hand skimming my cheek, "You will tell me what's wrong, Adeline Jasely."

He could read me like a book.

"I don't doubt I will."

He chuckled to himself while walking off to his class. I stumbled into English just before the bell rang. Ms. Cook seemed annoyed but said nothing as I took my seat.

"Hey, Adeline?" someone whispered from behind me.

I turned slightly in my seat to find Lily Shelton.

"Do you know what the geometry homework was? I didn't have time this weekend..." Lily asked, obviously stressed.

Even though Lily no longer spoke to me besides moments like these, I still helped her out when she needed it. Maybe I was letting her use me. Maybe I was hoping we could restore our friendship. Maybe this was how Cole and I would be one day. He would only ask what the homework assignment was, then return to his life as if he never touched mine.

"Yeah. It's page 302, problems seven through fifteen," I replied quietly.

"Thanks," she breathed as Ms. Cook glared our way.

The next two periods breezed by, and it was time for geometry. I walked in and was not too surprised to find Cole sitting in the back waiting for me. I smiled as I sat down next to him.

"You will never believe what happened in Spanish," he whispered as the class came to order.

"What?" I asked curiously.

"Brittany asked me to the dance this Friday," he replied quietly as he took out his homework.

My chest felt hollow, "Really?"

"Yes. She seemed very confident," he chuckled, "Of course I said no."

A smile had spread across my face.

"Really?" I asked with a bit more enthusiasm.

"Of course. I plan on going with someone else," he replied as if it was obvious.

My heart fell into my stomach.

"Oh," I whispered.

Mr. Holman continued checking the homework aloud, but I wasn't paying attention. I was trying to figure out who had asked Cole to the dance. Kelly? Or maybe Natalie? I went through every girl in my class that could have asked him.

"Adeline? It's time for history," Cole reminded me as I saw that the classroom was suddenly empty.

"Okay."

We walked to history in silence. I was still deep in thought when Cole and I sat down at our table.

"Okay, enough with the silence. Tell me what's wrong," Cole demanded.

I looked up to him dumbly.

"What?"

"You are upset about something, and I want to know what it is."

I looked down to my hands and suddenly wished I were anywhere but next to Cole.

"Who asked you to the dance?" I whispered.

He looked dumbfounded. "Brittany. I thought I told you this."

"I mean, who asked you that you said yes to?" I questioned, feeling a bit braver.

I looked to his face and found him smiling. Oh no. He really liked her.

"She hasn't asked me yet," he replied as the bell rang, signaling the beginning of class.

"Who is she?" I asked, now impatient.

He chuckled, "You."

My mouth fell open, and I almost forgot where I was when Mr. Jackson passed out the test. I closed my mouth and began my test. Even with all the studying, I was having trouble keeping my attention on history. Did I hear Cole correctly? He did say that he wanted me to ask him to the dance, right? I soon realized that I was doodling instead of writing my essay on the Louisiana Purchase. I quickly finished my work.

The bell rang, and Mr. Jackson reminded the class about the project that was due that next day as we all handed in our tests. Cole followed behind me as we walked to the cafeteria. We bought our food and sat down at our table in the corner of the room.

"So, what did you think of the test?" I asked, trying to buy some time.

"Easy. You?"

I nodded while I peeled my orange, "It was all right. Just a little long."

"Yes. It must have taken awhile considering the amount of drawing you did," Cole smirked.

"You should keep your eyes on your own test."

He laughed blissfully.

"Yes, ma'am," he mock saluted.

I laughed at his expression.

"Now about the dance," he began.

I looked back down to my tray, "Yeah?"

"Are you going to ask me, or will I have to go with Brittany?"

I immediately tensed at the mention of Brittany's name. His amused expression angered me a little bit.

"You're enjoying this, aren't' you?" I accused him.

He shrugged as he leaned back in his chair, a lovely smile across his already beautiful face.

I shook my head, "Cole, will you go with me to the dance this Friday?"

I was shocked that I had actually said it without stuttering. My heart raced as I looked to him for his answer.

"I don't know," he teased, "I'll have to think about it."

I threw my orange peel at him. He caught it before it hit him.

"Violence is not the answer," he smirked.

He leaned in closer to me and whispered, "I would love to go with you to the dance this Friday."

I gulped, "Okay, but just as friends."

"Oh?"

"I don't need any rumors about us floating around school. Plus, Emma will only let me go if we go as friends," I explained.

"I see. All right, just as friends," he agreed as he shook my hand.

I laughed at the gesture, but my voice sounded a few octaves higher than normal.

The rest day went by smoothly with no conflict from Brittany like I had expected. I guess no one knew whom Cole was taking to the dance yet. Cole drove me home and walked me to my door.

"I'll pick you up same time tomorrow," he said as I unlocked my door.

"Kay. Um, you know that you don't have to drive me to school and back? I can take the bus," I said while fiddling with my keys.

"I know, but I want to take you to school. You make the ride more enjoyable," he smiled, shoving his hands into his pockets.

"I'll see you tomorrow," he said quietly as he backed up, walking back to his truck.

"Bye," I whispered as he drove out of sight.

I walked into the house and immediately began dinner. Emma's favorite, chicken teriyaki. If I had any chance of being allowed to go to this dance with Cole, I needed to be extra sweet. I was still working on dinner when I heard Emma walk in.

"Hello?" she called as she walked into the kitchen.

"Hey, Emma," I greeted.

"What smells so good?" she asked as she went through the mail.

"Teriyaki chicken," I replied while placing the food onto plates.

"Really? What for?"

"Does there need to be a reason?" I asked as I set the table and grabbed our drinks.

"Will Henry be joining us?" I asked while I began setting a third place.

"Nope. He has papers to grade," Emma said suspiciously as she sat down and began to eat.

"Oh, then I guess we'll have extra."

We ate in silence for a few minutes before Emma questioned, "Okay, what's this all about?"

"What?" I asked innocently.

"I wasn't born yesterday, Adeline. What do you want?" She stated plainly as she took a sip of her lemonade.

I gulped the rest of my food and drank the rest of my lemonade before answering.

"I was wondering if there was any way I could be allowed to go to the sweetheart dance this Friday?"

I never thought I would ever utter those words. Neither did Emma because she looked as shocked as I felt.

"A dance? You want to go to a dance?" she gaped at me.

"Yeah," I muttered.

"By yourself? That hardly seems fun," she continued to eat her food. She was missing the point or didn't want to come to terms with it.

"I'm not going alone," I mumbled.

She dropped her fork, and it made a clanging sound when it hit the plate.

"What?"

I began chewing on the inside of my lip, out of habit.

"Who?"

"Cole," I whispered, "but we are only going as friends."

She closed her eyes and took a deep breath.

"Who asked who?" she asked while squeezing the bridge of her nose.

That was a good question. I wasn't even sure who asked exactly. I had asked officially but only after I knew Cole wanted to go with me.

"Um, it was sort of a mutual agreement."

"Who asked, Adeline?" she persisted.

"I did," I sighed. "It's a sweetheart dance. The girls ask the boys."

She sat unmoving, and I was afraid I had given her a heart attack.

"All right," she said, surprising me and finally relaxing.

"Really?" I asked ecstatic.

"Yes. Henry will be chaperoning, I think. Parents are allowed to too, right?"

"You're not a parent."

"A legal guardian. Same thing."

We sat glaring at each other before I sighed, "Okay, fair enough."

"Good."

We were silent as I picked up the dishes and began to load them into the dishwasher.

"What are you going to wear?" she asked as I continued to clean the kitchen.

I stopped where I was. What was I going to wear? I heard Emma chuckle, "That's what I thought. How about I take you shopping after school tomorrow? I'll get off work early and pick you up."

"You would do that?"

She walked over to me, and pulled me into a hug. I didn't protest this time.

"Of course. My little sister is going to her first dance with her first date. This is a historical moment," she teased.

"It's not a date."

"Whatever," she rolled her eyes.

*

That night I dreamed about the dance.

Cole and I were in the school gym talking when the music suddenly stopped. I looked toward the DJ and found him replaced by Chandler Phalcon. Suddenly, everyone that was in the gym was gone. They disappeared into thin air. It was just the three of us: Chandler, Cole, and I.

The tension could have been sliced with a knife as the two stood glaring at each other. Unexpectedly, Chandler jumped from where he was, near the DJ's equipment, and began charging toward Cole. Cole pushed me out of the way, and I landed on the floor in a heap.

The battle began. They circled each other, continual hisses and growls escaping from their throats. They were bent in a prowling position, ready to attack if needed. Chandler looked over Cole's shoulder to me and smiled pleasantly.

Cole growled, "Don't look at her!"

Chandler ignored him and continued to smile at me.

"Adeline…" he whispered seductively.

Suddenly, he was behind me, and I was standing again. His mouth was next to my ear, whispering, "I can show you the truth Adeline. Come with me."

I fearfully looked around for Cole, but found him nowhere. It was like he disappeared with everyone else that was in the gym.

"He's gone," Chandler whispered as he lightly brushed his hand on my bare shoulder.

"I can show you the truth," he repeated.

I was about to scream when an ear-piercing shriek interrupted me. I looked up and found an eagle flying toward us. I closed my eyes in fear of what was to come. When nothing happened I opened my eyes and found myself in a field in the middle of nowhere. It was a field of some sort of blue flower. I think they were forget-me-nots.

"What?"

The air was full of mist and fog. The sky was overcast, and the wind was lightly nipping at me. I looked around for something, anything, but found nothing. Only fog and flowers.

"Adeline!"

I turned quickly and found Cole running toward me. He embraced me, and I clutched him for dear life. My heart was pounding as he continually whispered into my hair, "I'm sorry, Adeline, I'm so sorry."

"For what? What's going on?"

He cupped my face in his hand and leaned down toward me. He was going to kiss me. My breathing became inconsistent as he leaned closer to me. Right before our lips were to touch, he began to fade away. He was no longer in my arms. I tried to bring him closer to me, but he was already gone. I was alone. I looked around, panicked.

"Cole!"

I woke up screaming.

Chapter Seven

The dream woke me around four, and I couldn't fall back asleep. I lay awake until around six thirty. I finally crawled out of bed, going to take a shower. After I had gotten dressed, I walked into the kitchen and began to pour myself some cereal. Emma came in a minute later.

"You're up early," she mused as she poured her coffee.

"Couldn't sleep."

"You sure you wanna go shopping? If you're too tired, we can wait," Emma said as she mixed her sugar and cream in her coffee.

"No, I want to go. Don't worry about it. What time will you pick me up?" I asked eagerly.

"What time does school let out? Two thirty?" She gathered her keys and purse.

"Yeah. Meet me in the parking lot," I replied as she ran out to her jeep.

"Kay! See you then!" she called back just before the door slammed shut.

I checked the time after I had finished my breakfast. I still had twenty minutes before my personal bus would pick me up. I entered my room, grabbed my school bag, and walked to my closet. I opened it and searched for the purse that I rarely used. I found it and then opened my chest at the foot of my bed. I opened the plastic bag with all of my babysitting and birthday money I had received over the years. I stuffed some of it into my wallet and placed my purse in my school bag. There was no way I was going to let Emma buy me a dress. We needed her paycheck to make ends meet.

I walked into the kitchen and cleaned up my bowl while I waited for the time to tick by. I mused over last night's dream and what could have triggered it. I could understand the dance part, but why did Chandler show up? Why were Cole and Chandler about to kill each other? And what did Cole mean when he said he was sorry? That was the last time I would eat teriyaki chicken before going to sleep.

The doorbell rang, followed by a light knock. I ran to the door keenly.

"Hey, Cole," I greeted, breathless as I took him in. Black hair in a mess, eyes shining brightly, and wearing my favorite smile.

"Hey, Adeline. Ready to go?" he asked politely.

"Yep," I replied as I locked the door behind me and walked with him to his truck.

"What are you thinking about?" he asked after we were on the road for a few minutes.

"What? Why do you want to know?"

He stared out the windshield and smiled.

"I don't know. Just wondering. You make interesting expressions when you're thinking about certain things. For example," he continued, "when you are worried about something, most likely Emma, your forehead wrinkles up and you bite your bottom lip. When you are angry, you glare at inanimate objects as if your looks could kill." He laughed. "When you are confused, or trying to figure something out, you stare at your hands and bite your upper lip. And when you are flustered, this is my favorite, your cheeks blush and your nose wrinkles. It's very amusing."

"Glad you find me so hilarious." I replied sarcastically.

He chuckled, "See, you're flustered. Though you're biting the inside of your lip, which is new."

"I am not flustered!"

I must have seemed even funnier, because he found it harder to contain himself.

"Done yet?" I asked dryly as we pulled into the parking lot.

"I'm sorry, Adeline. I'm not laughing at you, I promise."

"Uh huh," I muttered as I jumped out of the truck.

Cole was beside me in no time, walking me toward my locker.

"What did Emma say when you told her about Friday?" Cole asked as he held the door open for me. His expression was very serious.

"She was okay with it," I said. "She's taking me dress shopping after school today, so you don't have to take me home."

"Oh. All right." He seemed disappointed.

"What did your family say?" I asked while doing the combination to my locker.

"They were fine with it."

"No they weren't," I contradicted.

"How do you know?"

"Because that's your lying face," I replied plainly as he walked me to class.

"I have a lying face?" he asked, amused.

"Yep. I see it every time you try to hide something from me."

He walked me into the classroom again and, like yesterday, everyone watched us with eager anticipation.

"I swear, I learn something new every day with you," he said, shaking his head.

I blushed as people continued to stare at us and whisper amongst themselves. I looked back up to Cole and found him inches from me.

"I'll see you later," he smiled.

"Oh, okay," I muttered.

He turned and walked away, leaving everyone in the room watching as he gracefully left. I fell into my seat and began to get more and more annoyed and flustered as people turned to stare at me. Brittany, suddenly, stood and stalked toward me, anger and frustration written clearly across her face. Oh no.

"Hey, Madeline," she greeted me bitterly as she towered over me, hands on her hips.

"It's Adeline," I corrected.

"Whatever," she dismissed. "So, yesterday when I asked Cole to the dance, he told me he was going with someone else. Know anything about that?"

I gulped. The last person I should be afraid of is Brittany Ryan, but considering how many more torturous years of high school I had left, I was terrified.

"Um…no," I lied. Bad move. Brittany saw right through it.

"Don't lie to me," she threatened.

I sighed, "Yeah, I'm going to the dance with Cole, as friends."

The whole room became silent. Apparently, everyone had been listening.

"And why didn't you tell me this yesterday, Madeline?" she asked, seeming betrayed.

"It's Adeline," I corrected again, "and I didn't know we would be going together until after I talked to you. Besides, we're only going as friends…"

"So you waited until I wanted to ask him and then made your move?" she asked louder than one would consider polite. She wanted to make sure everyone heard.

"No. It's not like that," I opposed.

"Whatever, Madeline. I don't want to hear it," she dismissed dramatically as she went to sit down.

"It's Adeline," I growled under my breath.

The next two periods went by the same. Everyone stared at me, whispering about Cole and I going to the dance. Predictable. Every high school was the same. When something new and unheard of happened, everyone had to know. By third period, it seemed that the entire school population had heard that Cole Dyami was going to take Adeline Jasely to the sweetheart dance.

"Hey, Adeline!" someone yelled from behind me.

I turned around in the middle of a swarm of students shuffling to class, finding Lily Shelton running toward me smiling.

"Hi, Lily," I spoke shyly as she came up beside me.

"I heard that you are going to the dance Friday. I'm so excited!" she said breathlessly. I was shocked. Why did Lily Shelton suddenly care about what happened in my life?

"You are?" We walked into the geometry room.

"Yeah! I never get to hang out with you anymore. Maybe we could all go out to eat after the dance. You know, you, me, Eric, and Cole!"

I really wanted to say something like, "We don't hang out, because I couldn't fit into your superficial, shallow box."

But I didn't. Maybe she did feel bad about letting our friendship crumble. Maybe Emma had been right all along. I looked at Lily and saw the sincerity and guilt in her brown eyes. I was probably going to regret this.

"Yeah, Lily," I agreed, "that would be a lot of fun."

Her freckled face broke out into a grin, her brown eyes sparkling.

"Awesome," she said as she sat down in the seat in front of me.

I turned to my left and found Cole, in the seat next to me, smiling.

"Hello, Adeline, Lily," he said charmingly.

"Hey."

"Hi, Cole," Lily greeted him happily, "I was just talking to Adeline about the dance. Maybe you, Eric, Adeline, and I could go out to eat before or after the dance. What do you think?"

Cole looked to me for approval.

"I told her that it would be fun, if you don't mind." Cole could see how uncomfortable I was, but he could also see how happy this was going to make Lily.

He looked over to Lily, smiling warmly, "That sounds lovely, Lily. Thank you."

"It'll be amazing," she winked.

*

My mind was so filled with thoughts of the dance and Lily's newfound interest in our shattered friendship that I had completely forgotten about our history project. It wasn't till we were walking to history class did I suddenly remember. Luckily for me, Cole hadn't forgotten. He turned in the paper, set up his laptop, and began presenting in no time. Of course, all of my attention was on Cole, but I wasn't the only one. All of the girls in the room seemed to be completely in love with him already. Soon enough, our presentation was over, and the next pair was already talking about their subject.

"Good job," I whispered as we took our seats.

"Thanks. You too," he smirked.

I rolled my eyes and continued to watch the rest of the presentations. Before I knew it, I was in the lunch line with Cole on my right and Lily on my left. She couldn't stop talking about the dance.

"And I can't wait until the sweetheart king and queen will be crowned. I bet you guys win," she gushed.

I shook my head, and Cole chuckled.

"And about the dresses," she continued, suddenly serious, "maybe we should go dress shopping together. It could be a lot of fun."

"Emma and I are going after school. You could come with us if you want," I offered. I instantly regretted the words as they came out of my mouth. I was just setting myself up for disappointment. But her eyes lit up like a Christmas tree.

"Really, Adeline? You mean it? Yeah, that would be cool. I just have to call my mom, but that would be awesome," she smiled appreciatively.

We all paid for our food, and Cole and I headed for our usual table.

"Why don't you eat with us?" Lily asked innocently.

Cole interceded smoothly, "We like to eat alone if you don't mind."

Lily's mouth formed an "O" and then she winked at me, again. I glared at Cole as we found our seats.

"Did you have to say that?"

"Say what?"

"You know what I mean. Now she thinks we're more than friends," I mumbled the last three words.

"Let her think what she wants. It doesn't matter what other people think anyway," he said sincerely.

I stuffed my sandwich in my mouth and swallowed before asking, "Hungry?"

He laughed, "Not really. I had a big breakfast."

"Whatever," I muttered as I continued to eat. "So," I began after swallowing my lemonade, "I researched your tribe this weekend…" I had been meaning to tell Cole ever since hearing the legend.

I waited for anger, betrayal, anything, but he sat with a pleasant smile.

"And what did you find?" he asked curiously.

"Well, I read about the split, between the tribe, but it wasn't like the legend. They split for land and stuff," I explained.

"I see," he mused to himself.

I looked down to my cup and watched the ice slowly melt.

"Adeline?"

"I was wondering…um…" I stuttered.

"Yes?" he asked patiently.

"I was wondering," I began again, "which is true? The legend or the split for land and government recognition?" I looked up and found him gazing out the window.

"I told you. It's all myth. None of it is true," he replied, still in his own world outside the window, "The whole tribe is crazy."

He turned his head to face me, "Let's not get into this. I hear enough about the tribe when I'm at home."

I nodded, feeling guilty I even brought it up.

"So, what did you think when Brittany asked me to the dance?" he asked, scooting closer to me over the table. I rolled my eyes. What was I supposed to tell him? That I wasn't too thrilled at the idea of him becoming Ken and running off to Malibu with Barbie?

"Well, I didn't like it," I replied truthfully.

"And?" he prompted.

I leaned in closer, "I didn't like it. End of story."

"Okay," he whispered as he tucked a stray strand of my hair behind my ear. But instead of pulling his hand away, he gently caressed my cheek. I flickered my eyes down to the table. I looked up into his eyes again and saw confusion. He caressed my cheek one last time and then leaned back in his chair. I leaned back as well, missing his touch.

We continued conversation on other safe topics, steering clear from anything to do with the tribe.

"How's the ranch?" I asked before taking bite from my apple.

Cole's face instantly lit up, his eyes creasing, "Good. I'm training this new stallion my dad just brought in. His name is Sky. Adeline, he is huge…" And on and on he went. I could barely catch most of what he was saying, but I smiled and laughed along. Cole loved the ranch, loved being there. It was who he was. I was beginning to see that.

"We'd better go. I'd hate for you to be late for class," Cole said as he stood, throwing our trays away. I looked around and found the cafeteria nearly empty.

"Okay," I mumbled as I grabbed my bag and followed Cole as he walked me to class, still talking about the new stallion and the ranch.

School finally ended. I waited in the parking lot while watching Cole leave. I felt strangely empty as he walked toward his truck without me. I was walking toward Emma's red Wrangler when Lily pounced on me. Literally.

"Boo!" she yelped playfully.

"Hey," I greeted. "So, I assume you can come?"

She nodded eagerly. We walked up to Emma's Jeep. I walked around to the driver's side, and Emma rolled down her window.

"Lily Shelton is going dress shopping with us. Is that okay?"

Emma seemed confused, guarded even. "Are you sure?"

"Yeah," I hesitated, "I'm sure."

"Okay," Emma smiled again.

I smiled as Lily jumped into the back seat and I sat upfront with Emma.

"Thanks so much Miss Jasely. I really appreciate you letting me tag along," Lily spoke politely as we pulled out of the school and drove toward Main Street.

"No problem, Lily, and you can call me Emma," Emma said as she looked at Lily through the rearview mirror.

Sooner than I would have liked, I was thrown into a dressing room with at least twenty different dresses that Lily and Emma were making me try on. I knew to expect this kind of behavior from Emma, but I didn't remember Lily being so demanding. When we had walked into the boutique, both Emma and Lily's eyes had widened in excitement. They looked like children in a candy shop. I had been suddenly thrown from one section to another, having dress upon dress piled in my arms to the point that I could no longer see over my head.

"I don't think that will work," I had said to Lily as she placed a neon pink, floor length gown with a plunging neckline in my ever-growing pile of dresses. The thought of that on my body made me self-conscience.

"Adeline, the point of dress shopping is to have fun and try stuff on. You will try this on, and you will have fun doing it," Lily had huffed.

"Good luck with that one," Emma had whispered as she continued to look at shoes and accessories.

And now, here I was, the pure image of humiliation. The bright color did nothing to my skin, but made me look paler and my hair darker. My eyes looked browner and the circles under them became more apparent. The lack of sleep was getting to me. The revealing neckline did nothing but expose the little bit of chest that I had. Overall, I looked pathetic.

"Come on, Addie! Show us!" Emma whined.

"Yeah, Addie! Show us," Lily repeated.

I sighed, "It really isn't pretty, like you think. Can't you just trust me and let me try something else on?"

"No ma'am," Lily said sternly, "We'll be the judges."

I sighed, but pulled back the curtain and revealed myself in all my neon pink glory.

Both of their faces looked dissatisfied and a little bit overwhelmed.

"I told you," I grunted as I tried to fix the strap on my shoulder.

"Pink is not your color," Lily mused to herself as she ushered me back into the dressing room.

"You could say that again," Emma muttered.

This time, I looked to my modest pile of dresses that I had picked out. I took off the pink gown and picked out the light green dress I found when I first walked in. I thought it was perfect, but Lily thought it was too plain. I had hid it in the bottom of the pile, out of sight. I slipped it on and it felt right. Before I looked in the mirror, I took a deep breath. The last dress was a disaster, so I mentally prepared myself for the worst. When I turned around, it was anything but a tragedy.

I actually looked pretty. The light green color showed off my features in a very flattering way. My dark hair actually looked more auburn and my eyes looked more honey than hazel. My skin suited nicely with the color. I twirled inside my dressing room a few times, letting the hem of my dress dance around me. Although it was strapless, it felt comfortable and perfect.

"Ready?" Emma called from outside.

I took a deep breath and then flung back the curtain. This time, they both looked pleased. Shocked, but pleased.

"Oh my. Adeline, you look hot!" Lily gushed.

"I told you that green is your color," Emma said proudly.

I nodded and then twirled for them to get the full view.

"I think this is the one," I said as I finished my twirling.

"How much is it?" Emma asked as she came toward me, looking for the price tag.

"What's it matter to you? You're not buying it," I said as I grabbed my bag and took out my purse as proof.

"Adeline Connor, I am going to buy this dress. You should save that money for college," Emma replied as she continued to look for the tag.

When she found it she looked a bit taken aback. I looked at the tag myself. I had enough saved up, but I knew there was no way Emma could buy this. Her paycheck for this week wouldn't even cover it.

"I've got the money, Emma. Don't worry," I whispered.

She sighed and pulled me into a hug. Lily pretended to be interested in one of the dresses in the back of the store and left Emma and I to our sisterly moment.

"I'm so sorry about this," she whispered regretfully, "One day, we'll be able to buy whatever we want and not have to worry about the prices."

I knew all about Emma's plan. It was what we have both been working toward. Emma was working her way up in the ranks at the Great Falls Tribune for the past five years. Just a couple of more promotions and we would move and she could work for any newspaper she wanted, for the pay we wanted. Her dream was the *New York Times*. It was our dream. At least, it was then.

"I know, Em," I said, embracing her back, "but for now, I've got this, okay?"

"Kay," she replied, letting me go to change.

The shopping trip had been a success. Lily and I found dresses for the dance and Emma bought some shoes. After we had dropped Lily at her house, we went home and found Henry in the kitchen with Chinese takeout.

"Hey, babe," Emma said as she hugged him from behind.

"Hey, sugar," he said as he turned around and kissed her deeply.

I sighed, retreating to my room to put away my dress. This was another dream Emma had. She wanted to be married by the time she was thirty, then have two kids by the time she was thirty-five. Jack and Sara were their names. I would be in college by then and on my own. Her plan was picture perfect.

Mine, on the other hand, was still in the works. Up until about a week ago, I had my whole life planned out. I would graduate high school in two and a half years, go to some college out of state, get a degree in journalism, take some art classes, find a good job, buy a house, and travel all over the world to every place I had dreamed of. I wanted out of this small town.

A lot changed in one week. In one week, I rethought my plan on college out of state. I rethought my plans of traveling the world. In one week, my only dream was somehow getting the small Native American reservation up the road to accept me. In one week, I wanted something more than anything I had ever wanted before. Something I never even thought I would want. I wanted Emma's dream. I wanted to get married and have kids. I wanted everything Emma already had, but differently.

I wanted Cole's friendship. I wanted the feeling I had with him all the time. I would never admit this to Emma, but I liked the feeling of being small around him. I had been raised to stand up for myself and be independent. I was taught that I didn't need a man to live. I was capable on my own. In one week, that idea repulsed me. I liked the feeling of being dependent on someone else. I liked not having to stand up on my own all the time. I liked knowing that he would protect me if need be. Although, he more than likely did not feel the same way, I liked to imagine. I liked to imagine him protecting me like in my dreams.

I fell onto my bed with a thump. The bed made its usual creaking sound. I rolled onto my side, looked out my window, and saw the sky slowly turn from blue to pink as the sun began to set. I sighed at my wishful thinking. I was going out of my mind. Cole's face entered my thoughts, and I smiled contently. His hair was messy and his blue eyes shining. I closed my eyes as I tried to remember every part of him that I had stored in my mind. I tried to remember the way my skin crawled when he stroked my cheek and played with my hair.

"Adeline?" Emma yelled from the kitchen, tossing me out of my daydream.

"Yeah?" I asked sitting up.

"Dinner! You hungry?"

"No, you guys eat without me," I yelled back while lying back down.

The last thing I needed was Henry and Emma's affection choking me. But instead of lying back down, I went to my closet and retrieved the art supplies I hadn't touched in a while. I began painting, not sure where my mind was. I let my hands move and create images. It usually wasn't until I was done that I knew what I had been painting. I was so consumed in painting. In the same way Cole felt free on the ranch, I felt free, felt more like the real me, as I lost myself in my paints. It wasn't until I heard Henry leave that I noticed it was ten thirty.

"Dang," I muttered. I forgot about my English assignment. I slowly walked to the kitchen and didn't see Emma. Guess she went to bed. I walked back to my room and changed into my pajamas. I crawled into bed with a yawn. I would work on the homework tomorrow. But before I fell asleep, I took one last glance at my latest project. It was Sky, the stallion Cole had told me about at lunch, his long black mane blowing in the wind. The Dyamis' pasture seemed to go on for miles. I smiled while slowly drifting to sleep.

Chapter Eight

I had trouble sleeping again, with dreams that turned into nightmares. Even Kai's dream catcher wasn't helping. I knew it was silly to think it would. Maybe my subconscious had believed it was powerful.

I washed my cereal bowl and walked into the living room. I grabbed my bag and began working on the forgotten homework while I waited for Cole to arrive. I was almost done with my last sentence when the doorbell rang.

"Good morning, Adeline," he greeted me, his voice like silk.

"Hi, Cole," I murmured.

"Ready to go?"

"Yeah, hold on one second," I said as I walked back into the living room and grabbed my stuff. After I retrieved my bag, I locked the door behind me. He walked me to his truck and opened the door for me. I jumped in, and he was in the driver's seat a moment later.

"How was shopping?" Cole asked as we drove down the road.

"It was good. Lily and I found our dresses," I replied while staring out the window. The sky was very beautiful, a clear blue with a few clouds.

"Really? What does yours look like?"

"Nice try, but you'll just have to wait for the dance," I glanced at him.

He was smiling with one hand carelessly holding the wheel and the other up against the window. He ran his hand through his onyx hair and then shook his hair out.

"Fair enough," he mused.

I looked out my window again, trying to collect my thoughts. We finally pulled into the school parking lot. I was a bit confused when Cole didn't immediately turn the truck off and head toward the school.

"Tell me more about you," he gently demanded, blue eyes boring into mine.

"What?" I stuttered.

"I want you to tell me everything about you, not sparing anything."

"Why?"

"Because there's more to you than what you let people see," he spoke softly, surprising me. "I want to know what you think, why you think the way you do, what you do in your free time. I want to know everything."

The passion in his voice almost knocked the wind out of me.

"Um...okay..." I stammered, trying to find the words. How was I supposed to respond to that? Write a novel containing all of my inner thoughts and desires and hand it to him?

"Well," I began, "I don't really know where to start."

"Start with your name," he said simply.

"You know my name."

"Your full name and so on. It'll all come to you."

I coughed in my hand before I began.

"Well, my name is Adeline Connor Jasely. Emma calls me Addie, though I find it annoying. I, uh, go to this high school, and I live with my only sister, Emma..."

I continued my autobiography as Cole walked me to my classes. Every time I looked to him while I talked he seemed so interested, like he was watching his favorite movie at its climax. Each time we had to part, he made me promise to continue where I last left off.

I was confused about his sudden interest in my life. There was nothing special or unique about it. No mystery or twist in the end. It didn't seem a quarter as interesting as Cole's life. Although I knew very little, I felt like there was some hidden secret or mystery that I needed to solve. I continued with my life story as Cole walked me to lunch.

"And sometimes when Emma isn't home I paint or draw," I finished while I sat down with my food.

"What do you paint?" he asked eagerly.

"Nothing too interesting," I shrugged while opening my bag of chips, "I just let my hands do what they want and see what happens."

"I'd love to see them someday," he said sincerely.

The small tug in my chest pulled again but more insistent this time, like it was trying to finally gain my full attention.

"Now, what about you?" I asked, changing the subject, "Since I have to tell you everything about my boring life, you're gonna have to tell me about yours. An even trade."

He smiled sadly, "Your life isn't boring."

"Maybe not to you. So, are you going to tell me all about you too?"

He looked around the cafeteria suspiciously. I followed his gaze but found nothing of concern.

"What?"

"I promise I'll tell you, but not here. Can you come with me after school?"

I could tell by the tone in his voice and the look in his eyes that he really was going to tell me everything about himself, not sparing anything. The small tug in my chest pulled sharply. The candle was no longer flickering, but glowing brightly.

The rest of the school day flew by, and before I knew it, I was walking toward the parking lot, looking for Cole. Usually, he met me after class, but I was surprised and a little concerned when I didn't find him there. I began to really worry when he wasn't at my locker or his. I was half way to his truck when I saw him, but he wasn't alone. Right there, in the middle of the school parking lot, in front of everyone, were Cole and Chandler. And by the looks of it, they seemed angry. I could hear their voices as I moved closer.

"Just stay away," Cole threatened him, resentment in his usually silk-like voice.

"It's a free country," Chandler replied, eyes narrowed, "I can talk to whomever I want."

"Not to her," Cole growled.

By this time, everyone in the parking lot was watching with eager eyes, hoping a fight would start.

I walked up beside Cole, "What's going on?"

Neither of them looked my way. They just kept glaring at one another, trying to burn a hole in the other's skull.

"Nothing," Cole finally answered, still glaring at Chandler, "Chandler was just about to leave."

"Hello, Adeline," Chandler greeted me, finally tearing his eyes from Cole, "How are you?"

It sounded like a snarl rumbled from Cole's chest.

"I'm fine," I said, looking to my feet.

Chandler took a step toward me, but Cole pushed me behind him so that he was blocking Chandler from me. I looked across the parking lot and saw Lily and Eric standing beside Eric's green Expedition. Lily looked startled while Eric's enthusiastic expression proved he wanted to see a fight and I was afraid his wish would come true.

"Let's go, Cole," I whispered.

He ignored me and continued to stare Chandler down.

"Cole," I pleaded, "just ignore him, and let's go."

I wanted to be as far away from this place as possible. I hated being the center of attention and the topic of gossip. So having two guys fight over me wouldn't help my cause. Cole gave Chandler one last growl before he turned me around and walked me to my side of the truck. He opened the door and helped me in. He walked around to his side and jumped in. We hit the road before I could blink.

"What was that about?" I asked angrily.

"Not now, Adeline." The speedometer continued to steadily increase. "Put your seatbelt on."

His knuckles were white from holding onto the steering wheel so tightly. I obeyed him and quickly fastened myself in. I waited a few moments for him to calm down before I spoke again.

"What happened back there?"

He sighed and closed his eyes for a brief moment.

"You wouldn't understand," he breathed, jaw clenched.

"Then make me," I demanded, determined. Cole promised he would tell me everything. He could start with this.

He sighed again, "Wait until we stop. Then I'll talk."

I nodded in agreement and looked out my window. The world outside was flying by. All of the trees and houses were a blur. I thought we would be going to the reservation, but when we passed the turn, I realized we weren't.

"Where are we going?"

"You'll see."

I sighed and continued to watch the world outside the truck fly by. After about twenty minutes of driving, we finally slowed down. I looked out my window and noticed that we had arrived at the cemetery. I glanced over to Cole, but found him staring straight ahead, face void of all emotion. Cole finally slowed down and parked. I followed him through the many graves and tombstones. I almost ran into him when he stopped in front of a memorial. It was very serene and peaceful. A small angel statue stood above the grave.

Cole fell to his knees and began straightening up the flowers that adorned the headstone.

"Hey, Mom," he whispered.

I felt my heart fall. I slowly sat down next to Cole, unsure of what to do. Cole never talked about his mother. All I knew was that she died right after Cole had been born. He never made it a big deal about it, never talked about her. But right now, as I saw his face crumble, saw his emotional pain become physical, my heart cried out to help, to do anything to ease his heartache. Silence descended as we sat with Cole's mother. I gently took Cole's hand in mine, desperate to comfort him.

"I come here a lot," he finally spoke, his usually strong voice broken. "I ask for her help whenever I can't work something out. Lately, I've been coming a lot more."

I stayed silent, letting him talk about whatever he needed.

"I brought you here because this is who I am," Cole looked up to me, "You wanted to know."

I nodded, resting my head on his shoulder. He took a deep, shagged breath.

He spoke with his eyes closed, "Are you sure you want to know? The truth, I mean…"

I almost forgot why he brought me here in the first place. Somehow, all of the chaos seemed to have disappeared. We were in his bubble, his personal refuge and safety.

"Yes," I answered firmly.

But Cole remained silent, his eyes glazed, looking off into the distance.

"What happened back there with Chandler?" I asked softly, trying to gain his attention again.

He sighed, "I sort of started it. The reason, I don't really know. I don't trust him."

"So? That's not a very good reason to try to start a fight."

He shook his head, "It's hard to explain. It's a long story."

"I have time."

"You know how I told you some people in my tribe believe in the legends, as if they were reality?"

I nodded.

"Well, I think Chandler might be one of them."

I laughed, "So? Chandler is a bit crazy. What else is new?"

Cole didn't laugh.

"No, Adeline, it's a bit more serious than that." The smile disappeared from my face.

"What do you mean?"

"I mean, I think that he thinks you might be the reincarnation." Cole placed his head in his hands.

"Okay," I continued, "I don't see the problem. So he's really crazy. Big deal."

"It's a big deal, because he's from the other tribe!" Cole shouted.

I sat in silence. I had never seen Cole so angry or upset.

"I'm sorry," he calmed down, "I'm just stressed."

"Yeah, I can tell."

"You see it doesn't really matter what my tribe believes, because they won't do anything. But Chandler's tribe..."

"The Turtle Mountain?" I questioned.

"Yeah," he nodded, "if they really believe in the legends, then there is some danger...for you."

"What do you mean?" I asked, suddenly wary.

Cole was quiet for a time. For a moment I thought he wasn't going to even bother answering. His eyes remained focused on his mother's grave. He lightly brushed the engraved words with his fingertips.

Algoma Dyami
Mother, Wife, Friend
"Love never fails."
~ 1 Corinthians 13:8

His voice startled me when he spoke again.

"These stupid legends are what killed my mother," he whispered, anger flickering in his blue eyes, "and I refuse to let them control my life any longer."

I was shocked, unable to form a coherent statement. These legends, that Cole put off as ridiculous, just stories his tribe had made up, were the reason he didn't have a mother.

"You see," he began again, "people from both tribes mistook my mother for the reincarnation. For reasons I still don't know."

He was quiet again, head hanging in defeat. I cleared my throat and fought the tears stinging the back of my eyes, "But I thought you said your mother died in childbirth."

Silence was my answer. I instantly regretted saying anything.

"Yeah," he finally said, "that's what I've been told. What I've been trained to say whenever someone asks."

Silence fell as the wind blew around us. I wasn't even cold, just numb. I didn't expect Cole's story to be so tragic, and I had a feeling it was only going to get worse.

"If they think you could possibly be the reincarnation," he began again, "then they might want to hurt you," his face seemed strained, broken.

"Like your mother?"

He nodded solemnly. My heart began to pound.

"But why would they even think I could be her?"

Cole sighed, "I told you."

I stared at him dumbfounded.

"Because of me. Because of our friendship," he explained. "My father still blames himself for my mother's death."

"Why?" I breathed, "I still don't understand."

"According to the legends, to the prophecy," he murmured, "my family is in the direct line of Heluka, the Delsin of the Chosen. And according to this so-called prophecy, the descendent of Heluka will rekindle the magic of the Chosen, but only when the reincarnation is near, to protect her."

He glanced at me, "It's stupid, I know. Makes no sense considering my mother wasn't even Chippewa. The next in line should be Elsu. Even if this wasn't all make believe."

I nodded, still trying to understand, "So, it's possible Chandler and his tribe might think I am this reincarnation, just because you and I are friends?"

"It's more than that," he murmured.

"What else is there?" I was baffled.

"Things…strange things have been happening to me ever since I was little," Cole looked at me, and I saw fear, doubt, and worry clouding his eyes. "Stuff I can't explain. I don't think I'm normal."

"Like what?" I asked, holding his hand tighter. I felt like he was going to disappear, slip away, like in my dreams. He took a deep breath before he began.

"I was eight and Elsu was sixteen. Chenoa and I had been playing on the tire swing in front of our house when Elsu and some of his friends pulled up after school. He ran inside and then came out with his jacket.

" 'You're not supposed to go out tonight. It's a school night. Father won't be happy,' Chenoa had said. Elsu turned around before getting into the car, 'Why don't you try to make me stay?' I didn't like the way he was talking to her. Elsu never gave Chenoa the respect she deserved. Even though they were full blood siblings, he still treated her like dirt, only a smidge better than me. I finally spoke up, 'She won't, but I will.' His friends boomed with laughter, and he became flustered. He regained composure and I immediately knew what he wanted without him even speaking. He wanted me to fight him and he wanted to win."

"I had never fought anyone before or ever tried, so I was hesitant, of course, but with Elsu's friends there, I knew he wouldn't back down. Not even if he was fighting his little brother. He stalked toward me, shoulders back, eyes narrowed on his prey - me. I stood quickly and brought my fists up to my face. His friends boomed with laughter again. Elsu gave a little smile. He was sure he was going to win and his only concern was what Paco was going to think when he came home. Chenoa tried to stop Elsu by grabbing and hanging on to his arm. She begged, 'Please Elsu, he's only eight. Don't hurt him!' He pushed her to the ground and continued to walk toward me. My blood boiled at the way he had just treated Chenoa."

"As he continued to stalk toward me, my whole body began to shake violently. My anger and rage at my older brother was slowly beginning to devour me. Suddenly, I could no longer hear the teenage boys in the car in my driveway or even Chenoa's muffled sobs. All that mattered at that moment was me and Elsu, me killing Elsu. I wanted to rip him to shreds and, with my lack of self-control, I think I would have done it. He was completely unaware of my sudden disposition, simply curious. When he was about two feet away, I lost complete control and attacked. The only thing I remember is the sound of Elsu's struggle, Chenoa's cries in horror, and the sound of a car screeching away, down the street."

"When I had finished and gained some sort of myself back I carefully began to look over the damage that I had caused. The playhouse that Paco had built for Chenoa was nothing but boards and dust. Chenoa was huddled up against the tree, sobbing and clutching her doll. I dreadfully began searching for Elsu, or what was left of him anyway. I finally found his beat up and battered body half way across the lawn, face down. I instantly rushed toward him, but stopped when I heard Chenoa cry, 'No, Cole! Please stop!' "

"I looked back to her and saw the fear in her big, brown eyes. Guilt and remorse swept over me like a tidal wave. Tears hit the back of my eyes when I heard Paco pull up into the driveway with Red Hakan at his side. They immediately rushed to Elsu, and I watched from the shadows, ashamed of what I had done. 'I think he'll be all right,' Chief Hakan had said, 'but his face is torn up pretty bad. He'll need stitches and there'll probably be a scar.'

Paco only nodded and then turned to look at me. The disappointment in his eyes was too much to handle."

"I broke out in a sprint, unsure of where I was going. All I knew was that I wanted to get as far away from the reservation as my legs would carry me. I ran and ran and ran, letting the sweat roll down my face along with my tears. I wanted to run for forever, away from home, away from the tribe, away from myself and the monster I had become."

"I finally stopped when my body gave out. I fell and lay in the grass hoping and praying I would die soon. It started to rain, and I hoped I would drown. I stood, sweaty and weak, and began walking aimlessly through the forest. My mouth was dry. I continued to walk when I heard the sound of rushing water. I walked a bit faster and stopped when I came to the most magnificent waterfall I have ever seen. I jogged feebly to the river's edge and crammed as much water down my throat as humanly possible."

"After I had my fill of the water, I looked around my surroundings with more attentiveness. The rain continued to pour, but the trees and flowers seemed to have made the thunderstorm above me fade away. I sat down at the trunk of a tree and decided that I was going to live there and never return home."

I stared at Cole, numbed by his story. He continued to look at me, with what seemed like wariness in his eyes.

"Wow," I breathed, "what happened next?"

"I fell asleep, and then I woke up to Paco carrying me through the forest whispering, 'It's okay, Cole. Don't worry. Elsu will be fine.' "

Cole became silent, hanging his head in shame. My heart was breaking. Not for Elsu, or even for Chenoa, but for Cole. It was in that moment that I realized that my heart would only ever break for Cole.

"I'm...I'm so sorry," I whispered as I embraced him with all the strength I could muster. He embraced me with equal force, holding me close.

"You must have felt so lonely," I sobbed into his chest. His heart was beating unsteadily, like mine.

"I'm not the one you should feel sorry for," he sighed into my hair regretfully.

I looked up into his eyes and saw the guilt and sorrow that he must have been dealing with for the past nine years every time he looked to Elsu and saw his scar. It must have hurt a lot.

"But you are the one I feel for Cole," I whispered, "You'll always be. You're my friend."

"I don't deserve your kindness," he smiled sadly.

"Yes, you do," I contraindicated as I pulled away from him to stare into his face. He shook his head.

"But I appreciate it. More than you will ever know," he said, wiping a stray tear from my cheek. I sat staring at his broad chest and his red long-sleeved shirt stained with my tears.

He sighed, "There's something happening to me...to my tribe and I'm scared."

He surprised me. He suddenly seemed so small, like a frightened child.

"Scared of what, Cole? You can tell me anything," I urged him while taking his large hand in mine.

"I can't say. I don't even know what is happening. I just...I feel like I'm falling into something I want no part of. Like any day, I'll wake up and not be me. I'm afraid that I'll wake up as that monster and never be able to be myself again," he whispered painfully. My heart ached for him. I looked up into his eyes, "You aren't a monster, Cole. You will never be a monster. You weren't then and you aren't now."

He shook his head, "Things are changing. I don't know what to do anymore. I'm tired of all the secrecy. I just want a normal life."

"Well," I whispered, "you have a completely average, ordinary friend who is here to help." A smile graced his face for a moment, but faded quickly.

"But I'm afraid for you too."

He smiled while taking my hand and bringing it to his lips. He lightly brushed his lips against my hand, causing goose bumps everywhere he touched.

"Now, I believe I should take you home," Cole said as he stood up and led me away from his mother's grave toward his truck. I turned my head and gave a silent farewell to the cemetery and all the secrets it held.

ALLISON BLANCHARD

Chapter Nine

I was blindly moving around the kitchen, fixing dinner without even thinking about it. My mind was trying to comprehend everything that had just happened. The small tug in my chest throbbed; the candle was beginning to burn.

After we had left the cemetery, Cole drove me back to my house. This time, he had walked me to my door. I waited for him to say goodbye and that I'd see him tomorrow. Instead, completely shocking me, he roughly pulled me to him, embracing me. His body was trembling. He was scared. He needed a friend.

Before I could say or do anything, he kissed me roughly on the cheek then swiftly ran back to his truck. He was gone before I could make sense of anything that had happened.

When Emma arrived, with Henry not too far behind, I was able to function normally. But once I was excused to my room, I locked the door and fell onto my bed, exhausted.

A million and more thoughts were swirling around in my mind as I thought about that afternoon and what Cole had said. I wanted to know why Cole was scared and what he was afraid of. If he gave me some clue, maybe I could help him.

Cole's story about Elsu was intriguing as well. I didn't completely understand how an eight-year-old boy was able to give a full-grown sixteen-year-old the scar that Elsu had. Cole said he didn't remember much, but maybe he was leaving something out, some minor details he thought wouldn't matter. Or maybe they did matter and he didn't want to risk telling me. I needed to figure out his mystery, and the result of this afternoon only left me with more questions and very few answers.

What would have Cole done that made him sound like a monster? Would Chandler have come to school the next day with a scar like Elsu's? I winced at the thought. No. Cole would never hurt anyone since Elsu. I still found it hard to believe that Cole caused that distortion on Elsu's face. I shuddered again.

I rolled over onto my side and sighed. What if Cole was a monster? Would I still be his friend? I didn't need to think twice. Of course I would be his friend. No matter what he thought he was or who he was, I would always be there for him.

Cole's face when he told me his story was still fresh in my mind. He seemed so pained and guilt ridden. He seemed afraid of my reaction, like I was going to walk away and never look back. The thought of never seeing Cole again sent a sudden chill through my body. The tug in my chest reacted painfully to the thought. I didn't think I could see myself without Cole now. We were both too involved in what was still a mystery, at least to me.

*

"What happened yesterday? Everybody's been talking!" Lily asked eagerly as she and I sat down in our seats for English. It was still bizarre that Lily was continuing to show such interest in me.

"Nothing, Lily. Don't worry about it," I muttered as I pulled my binder out of my bag, hoping she would drop the subject.

"Don't 'nothing' me. What were Chandler and Cole talking about?" Lily continued, unshaken by my tone.

"Nothing," I repeated.

"I heard that it was because Chandler wanted you to ask him to the dance instead of Cole," Lily added, "My, my, Adeline Jasely, who's popular now?" There was a hint of jealousy in her voice, an edge.

English dragged on and I found it harder and harder to concentrate on the topic.

"Miss Jasely? Off in dream land, are we?" Ms. Cook asked, pulling me out of my thoughts. I blushed as the class snickered.

"No ma'am'," I mumbled while looking down to the floor.

The bell rang, and I hurried out of the classroom before Ms. Cook or Lily could stop me.

I wasn't paying attention and I suddenly hit something hard and fell onto the floor, my books and papers falling everywhere.

"Great," I muttered as I tried to quickly pick up my things.

"I'm so sorry, Adeline. Here, let me," I heard a deep, rough voice.

I looked up and found Chandler Phalcon with his hand stretched out to me. I grabbed my last book and stood up by myself, with no help from Chandler. Chandler put his hand back in his jacket pocket as he continued to stare at me, undisturbed by my lack of courtesy.

"It's okay," I said as I turned to walk away. Chandler always made me nervous and ever since hearing from Cole what he may believe, I was going to be extra cautious around him.

"Wait," Chandler stopped me, grabbing my elbow and forcing me to face him again, "Let me make it up to you."

I stared blankly at his dark hand on my elbow. My heart accelerated in all the wrong ways. I tried to shrug out of his grip, but he just held tighter.

"It's okay. No harm done," I stammered, my eyes scanning the hallway for Cole.

"I insist. How about I take you out for lunch? My treat," Chandler whispered as he pulled me closer to him. This time, when I tried to shrug out of his hold, someone helped me.

"Get your hands off of her," Cole growled as he pried Chandler's hand from my elbow. Cole then pulled me beside him, his arm firmly around my waist.

"I was just apologizing," Chandler defended.

"You're sorry. She gets it. Message received," Cole asserted bitterly.

His hold around my waist tightened as Chandler leaned in closer to me.

"That offer still stands," Chandler winked. Cole growled in response.

Cole turned us around and walked me to class in silence. He remained in the same, stoic like trance throughout geometry and history. Quiet, distant, and protective. He finally broke his silence while he was walking me to lunch.

"Do you want to get away? From the school, I mean?"

I was puzzled by his question. We stopped in front of the doors to the cafeteria as he waited for my response.

"You mean ditch class?" I questioned, amused.

He smiled, "Yeah, you wouldn't care?"

"Nope, just get me home before Emma," I responded as he walked me to the parking lot. I was a little less than thrilled when he pulled up into my driveway.

"What are we doing here?" I asked, puzzled.

"You wanted to be home before Emma, so here you are."

I rolled my eyes, "Not what I meant."

We sat in the truck a few moments, both unsure of what to say.

"So, why the sudden urge to skip?"

"I needed to get away…"

I nodded, "So, I am still a suspect?"

He looked at me questionably.

"You know, am I still considered this heavenly being?" I asked, still baffled by such a notion. Maybe things had changed since yesterday.

He laughed dryly, "I don't know. I'm not exactly on speaking terms with many in the tribe."

"What about Dylan and Elan? They seemed normal."

Cole smirked, "I don't know how normal you could think they are."

"Well, do they believe in all these legends and stuff?"

Cole's smile fell, "Yeah, they do actually."

"What?"

"That's actually the real reason I transferred to this school. Everyone at the reservation is starting to really believe this prophecy," he laughed again, "They're even preparing for war."

"War?" Now I was concerned.

"Yeah," Cole shifted uncomfortably in his seat. "According to this prophecy, there will be a war over the heavenly being and her power."

I looked at Cole hesitantly.

He smiled, "But it's all garbage. None of it's true. They'll realize it soon enough."

But for some reason, I wasn't completely convinced. And I don't think Cole was, either.

I looked out the window when, embarrassingly enough, my stomach growled.

Cole chuckled, "Hungry?"

"Yeah, I didn't eat a big breakfast," I cringed embarrassed while unbuckling myself and opening the door.

"That's a shame. Breakfast is the most important meal of the day," he stated, smiling as he helped me out of the truck.

I rolled my eyes and took my keys out as he walked me to my door. I unlocked the door and Cole followed me to the kitchen. I set my bag on the table and immediately went to the fridge. I pulled out leftovers from the other night and began heating them in the microwave. I took two water bottles from the fridge and placed them on the table. Cole sat down and began to take small sips from his bottle. The microwave beeped and I placed the food on two plates.

After I sat down at the table Cole declined the plate, "Oh, no thank you, Adeline. I'm fine."

I rolled my eyes again, "Cole Dyami, I don't know what your problem is, but you are going to eat my food and like it. I'm not that bad of a cook."

"It's not that, Adeline. It's just that I'm not very," He paused, looking for the right word. "polite when I eat."

"What do you mean? You can't be as bad as me," I dismissed as I took another bite.

"No, I think I can be pretty bad…"

"Cole, I don't care. Just eat. For me," I pleaded.

He seemed defeated as he took his fork and started to poke at the cheese and macaroni.

"I can't," he pushed the plate away, placing his fork back down on the plate.

"Why not?" I was confused and exasperated.

"You know when I told you that something strange is happening to me?" Cole reminded me, suddenly serious.

"Yeah."

"Well, this is one of the things. Eating. I don't know how to explain it, but one day I was at dinner eating and I…well, I couldn't stop." he finally explained, somewhat ashamed.

"So, you eat a lot? Is that it?" I asked, not so surprised. Many guys his age eat a lot.

"No, Adeline," he shook his head, pushing the plate away from him even further. "I eat more than what one would consider normal."

"I don't care. You can have all of the leftovers if you want," I countered, still not getting his point.

"What I'm saying, Adeline, is that I would clean your entire kitchen if I got started," he finally admitted, mortification clearly written across his features.

"Well, when do you eat?"

"At home."

"Why is that? Why do you eat a lot?" I questioned, suddenly losing my appetite and pushing the plate away.

"I don't know. Paco says it's because I'm growing, but that doesn't make any sense. No normal teenager can eat as much as I can," he replied, deep in thought.

I thought for a moment before stating simply, "Well, maybe you aren't normal."

He laughed, "Gee, that explains it!"

We both laughed for a while until Cole's laughter faded, looking down to his folded hands on the table.

"Are you worried?"

He sighed deeply, "Yeah, I just…I don't know what's happening to me. I don't like being in the dark."

"And Dylan and Elan don't help," Cole continued, frustrated, "They're still trying to convince me that I'm…" but he stopped abruptly.

"Convince you that you're what?"

"Convince me I'm the Delsin, the Chosen leader," he mumbled, shaking his head.

I leaned in closer to him and placed my hands on top of his. He titled his head to look at me, deep, blue eyes piercing through me.

"I'll always be here for you," I whispered. I didn't trust my voice.

He smiled slightly, "I appreciate it. More than anything."

"But can you promise me something?"

He leaned his head closer to me. His warm breath tickled my nose.

"Anything."

"When you figure out what is happening, anything at all, will you tell me?"

His faced seemed strained, and I knew the answer before he would say it. He wouldn't be able to keep that promise. My heart fell.

"I don't know, Adeline. If it's what's best for you, then maybe," he replied, his hands now holding mine.

"And something else," I added quickly, before I lost my nerve, "Promise you won't leave."

He seemed puzzled. "I'm not going anywhere. What are you talking about?"

I sighed and closed my eyes.

"I mean, don't leave me. Promise that you will stay my friend, no matter what happens."

He caught me off guard when he pulled me into a fierce hug, his large arms encircling me.

"I promise that I will always be your friend, Adeline. You have my word," he whispered into my hair. He took a deep breath while his hand made light circles my back. I nuzzled my head into his chest and listened to the gentle hum of his heartbeat and breathing.

Cole went home around two thirty, and I was left alone with my thoughts. I stumbled into my room and sat down at my computer.

It took a few minutes to boot up, but when it did I immediately pulled up my search engine. I typed in "Little Shell Chippewa Indian Legends". I clicked on a few different links, but found nothing of relevance. It was like the Little Shell Reservation was making sure no one would be able to figure out anything about them, besides some legends and myths that did not really relate to the tribe in the present. Nothing even mentioned the legend that was told Saturday.

I left my computer and walked into the kitchen to begin dinner. Emma would be home soon. I continued to prepare dinner, not really aware of what I was doing. I think I was making potatoes and fish. I couldn't be sure. My mind was about ten miles down the road, wherever Cole was. He seemed so scared and alone this afternoon. Something bad was happening on the reservation, and there was nothing that I could do about it.

But there had to be something that I could do to help. I didn't know why I felt this way, but I felt like Cole had to be protected and that it was my job to do it. I didn't want to see him fall into something he didn't want to do, or be forced to live a life he never chose.

Maybe if I talked to Paco, he would tell me something about what happened that afternoon Elsu received his scar.

I internally cringed at the thought. Paco Dyami didn't like me very much from what I could tell. I doubted he would tell me anything about his family. Maybe Chenoa would tell me something. I smiled at my plan and wondered why I hadn't thought of it before. Chenoa would definitely tell me.

I wiped my hands on a dishtowel as I retrieved the yellow book. It took me a few moments to find their number. My heart raced when I heard the first couple of rings. It rang for a long time, and I started to lose my nerve. I was about to hang up, when I heard a click and then a smooth, silky voice.

"Hello?"

I squealed when I heard the voice. I wasn't expecting Elsu to answer.

"Hello?" he asked again, this time irritated.

"Um, hi. Is Chenoa there?" I stuttered while wrapping my fingers around the telephone cord.

"May I ask who's calling?" Elsu asked again, now curious.

"Adeline Jasely," I gulped.

I heard a frustrated sigh before he said, "Sorry, she's not here."

The phone line went dead. I stared at the receiver dumbly before hanging it up. That was very strange. I knew that Elsu didn't like me, but why would he stop me from talking to Chenoa? I was still staring at the phone, frustrated, when Emma walked into the kitchen.

"Adeline Connor Jasely, you've got some nerve!" I heard her say firmly as she slammed her purse and keys onto the kitchen table.

"What?" I asked as I turned to face her.

Her eyes were narrowed, her forehead creased, and her hands were fixed on her hips. Uh, oh.

"Don't you dare play dumb! I received an interesting phone call from Henry today. What were you thinking? Ditching school?" she scolded, her voice rising with her temper. I swallowed the lump in my throat as my heart dropped to the floor. I was dead for sure.

"I...I can explain," I stuttered while Emma continued to tap her foot on the floor angrily.

"Well, I'm waiting," she fumed.

I sat down at the table, "Maybe you should sit down."

She looked like she was about to refuse, but she soon sighed and sat.

I stared at my hands nervously while I tried to figure out an excuse. Nothing came to mind.

"Adeline..." she began warningly.

"I'm sorry," I muttered. It was all I could think of.

"Why did you skip class with Cole?" she spoke softly, but with all of her anger behind it. I gulped again. I didn't know she knew about Cole too.

"Are you two in some kind of trouble or something?" Emma asked, disappointed.

It took me a moment to realize what she meant.

"Oh gosh, Emma, no! We're not in any trouble like that," I sighed, embarrassed. I covered my face with my hands, too flustered to look Emma in the eye.

"So, no drugs or anything. You know how those Native Americans can be," she sighed, relieved, but still irate.

I snapped my head up at her accusation of Cole and his tribe.

"No, Emma. How can Native Americans be?" I demanded, my blood boiling. She didn't even know Cole, let alone his tribe. She was taken aback by my sudden change in demeanor.

"I just meant that a lot of Native Americans are into drugs and stuff. I don't want you caught up in that," she defended her comment.

"Well, don't worry. Cole isn't like that," I glared at her, "Don't accuse him of things that aren't true."

Her eyes widened like she suddenly had an epiphany. She sighed heavily.

"Oh, Adeline. It has finally happened," she shook her head while smiling sadly.

"What are you talking about? What's happened?"

"You love Cole, or you at least think you do," she accused, eyes full of discontent, "I always knew that this would happen one day. I just thought it wouldn't happen so soon."

I gaped at her full of surprise. Me in love with Cole. The idea was absurd.

"That…that's not true," I whispered desperately, trying to make Emma believe me.

"You're lying, and you know it," she sighed, "Now, I don't feel like you should go to the dance, but I don't want your dress to go to waste. So you will go to the dance and be home by ten. After that, I'd rather you not see Cole anymore. Start taking the bus again."

I was shocked. I had no idea she knew about Cole taking me to school.

She read the astonishment on my face, "Yeah, Henry told me about that, too."

I suddenly wanted to kill Henry with my bare hands. This was his fault.

"You…you can't do this!" I yelled, slamming my fists on the table.

Emma jumped back, "Yes I can. I am your older sister, and you will do what I say!"

"No!" I yelled, tears stinging the back of my eyes, "You're not Mom!"

Emma gawked at me, sadness slowly etching its way onto her face. I made a cheap shot, but she was coming at me in full force.

Ever since Mom and Dad died, Emma forfeited all teenage experiences and became a parent to me at a young age. While I grew up, she did everything for me, and I did everything I could to help her. I had surrendered all of the experiences kids like me were to have. I needed to help Emma out as much as possible, but sometimes, I wished that I could have been normal and done normal things, like going to dances without an older sister to make the decisions.

She nodded sadly while walking to her room. I yearned to take back my words and hug her, but I stood my ground. I was tired of being the good one and doing everything to make her life easier. For once, I wanted her to do something for me. The tears that I had been fighting back poured down my cheeks as I stood, taking in shagged breaths. The dinner that I had made was sitting on the table getting colder with every passing minute, and I didn't care. I suddenly needed to get away from there, away from the house, and away from her. I sprinted down the hall and out the front door. I ran down the street and didn't know or care where I was going.

Tears were blurring my vision, and I thought I saw someone in a car drive by me, but I didn't take much notice. I slowed to a walk as my chest and lungs ached with pain. I tried to take deep breaths, but the cold air only made my throat sore. I continued to walk numbly, not completely aware of what was happening around me. I heard a dog bark in the distance, but besides that, there was no other noise.

How could Emma say those things about me and Cole? She didn't even know him, and I didn't think she even knew me anymore. It was strange what this boy had done to me. In such a short amount of time, he had changed me. I was no longer hesitant about depending on people. I was now able to trust people to take care of me. Or at least trust him. For almost my whole life, I only had me to talk to. Yes, Emma was there, but I was the shoulder she needed to cry on. Very rarely was it the other way around. Now, Cole was the person I could go to, and I didn't want Emma to take that away from me.

My eyelids became heavy as I continued to walk. My whole body felt heavier and I wanted to sleep. I tried to shake it off, but found it useless.

I continued to walk aimlessly for a long time. It could have been hours or days, I wasn't sure. I thought I had heard someone call my name, but I ignored it. I just kept walking. Suddenly, I saw lights come from behind me, and I turned to find a black truck with the lights on bright. I shielded my face with my hand. The light was hurting my eyes.

I heard the car door slam shut and someone walk toward me.

"Adeline," he said, his voice filled with relief, "are you all right?"

I stared dumbly at him and nodded my head. He walked closer to me, and I fell into him, exhausted.

"It's okay," he whispered, "I've got you."

Cole lifted me into his arms and carried me back to his truck.

"Chenoa, you drive back to her house."

Cole jumped into the passenger's side without me slipping from his grasp. He sat me in his lap, and I curled into his embrace.

"She says I can't see you," I sobbed into his shirt.

I felt him sigh, "I know."

"She says you can't drive me to school," I sobbed again.

I squeezed my eyes, trying to stop the tears. He held me tightly against his chest.

"I know."

"She says I love you," I whispered sleepily. I felt so warm. He breathed in sharply.

"I know. It's crazy," I whispered as I fell into slumber.

The last thing I remember was Chenoa whispering, "Cole, she needs to know."

"Not now, Chenoa. Not now," he breathed while continuing to rub my back and hold me close to him.

Chapter Ten

I woke up to voices in my living room. I was too tired to move, so I listened quietly.

"Thank you so much, Mr. Dyami. I'm sorry you had to stay out so late," Emma spoke softly. It sounded like she had been crying.

"It was no problem, Miss Jasely. We are just happy that Adeline is all right," Paco Dyami replied. He sounded nicer than I remembered.

"And thank you, Chenoa and Cole, for going to all of this trouble."

"You're welcome, Miss Jasely," Chenoa exclaimed happily, her voice honest.

"Anything for Adeline," Cole vowed sincerely. His words were full of fervor and honesty. How could Emma doubt him? I stirred and I heard Emma rush to my side to wipe the hair from my face.

"Addie?" she whispered. I could hear a fresh wave of tears about to come on.

I opened my eyes slowly and found Emma's red-rimmed eyes and tear stained face. I looked around the room and found Paco, Chenoa, and Cole watching me intently.

"Adeline?" she asked again.

I looked to Emma, "Sorry."

She sighed, relieved, "It's fine, just don't ever scare me like that again."

I nodded and closed my eyes as she pulled me into a hug. I opened my eyes after she had released me. I was shocked to find Chenoa and Paco already gone. But to my happiness, Cole was still standing where he was before. He smiled when our eyes met. My breathing became irregular, and Emma noticed. She turned her head to Cole and looked back to me.

"You have ten minutes, Adeline, then he has to leave," she whispered as she stood to leave.

When Emma left the room, Cole and I just sat there, staring at one another. I tried to get up, but Cole was at my side before I could blink.

"Don't move," he said gently. He pushed me back down and then sat on the floor next to the couch.

"Thanks," I finally whispered, not meeting his eyes. The small tug in my chest pulled again, but this time it tightened like a rope around my heart.

"You can't ever scare me like that again. Do you understand, Adeline?" His voice was desperate and tired. The way he said it was different from the way Emma had. She said it like a parent. He said it like he was dependent on me, like he needed me as much as I needed him.

"I didn't mean to scare you," I searched his face for the reasons behind his words.

"Well, you did," he stated simply, "When Emma called and said you were missing…I swear, Adeline, my whole world fell from underneath me. I was thinking the whole time I was looking for you, trying to figure out why you would run, where you would go. When Emma told me about the fight you two had and what was said, I felt so responsible. I'm so sorry."

Guilt washed over me as I listened to him.

"It's not your fault! I'm the one who ran," I pleaded.

He shook his head and looked toward the floor, "No, Adeline, it's my fault. Maybe Emma is right. Maybe we should no longer be friends. Maybe that's what is best."

I stared at him, my heart breaking. Fresh tears threatened to spill over, but I tried to push them back. I opened my mouth to speak, but no words formed. When he turned to look at me, his mouth fell into a frown and remorse covered his beautiful face.

"Oh no, Adeline. I didn't mean to…please forgive me," he whispered as he sat on the couch next to me and pulled me into him. I tried to muffle my cries in his shirt, but found myself only crying harder.

"You…you promised," I croaked, "You promised not to leave me."

"I'm not going anywhere. Forget what I said," he whispered passionately.

We sat that way for a few moments, before Cole said, "I should leave now. You need to sleep."

I nodded as he brushed the stray tears from my cheeks.

He stood and brought me with him. He turned to leave, but turned quickly around and placed a kiss on my forehead. My eyes widened and my heart raced. I felt myself blush as my breathing became shagged. His lips felt like fire against my skin.

He brought his head back and whispered, "Good night, Adeline."

"Night," I mumbled as he let me go and walked out the door.

I was faintly aware of Emma when she walked into the room.

"Adeline?"

I pretended that I didn't hear her.

"Adeline?" she asked, this time louder.

I turned my head toward her, "Yes?"

She sighed, "You need to sleep."

I nodded and walked to my room. I closed the door behind me and changed for bed.

I crawled into the bed and tried to fall asleep, but Cole's kiss had left me wide-awake.

It was strange how Cole affected me. Usually, I would agree with Emma about men and teenage relationships. We had a plan for my life.

Boyfriends were out of the question. Like Emma had said, women did not need men. We were capable without them. They would only be distractions. Sometimes I doubted Emma's affection for Henry. I supposed the only reason she had stayed with him for so long was because she didn't want to die alone.

I suddenly second guessed the plan Emma and I had made. I doubted my views about men and romance. Even though Cole and I were only friends, I didn't want Emma to tell me I couldn't see him. I needed Cole now. We were both too involved. I knew his secrets, and I felt like he knew mine. Although there were more mysteries I didn't know, I had the strange suspicion that they would soon be revealed.

*

I couldn't believe how fast the week had gone by. Before I even knew it, I was sitting in Emma's bathroom with Lily applying makeup and Emma doing my hair. Emma was still wary about me and Cole, but she didn't want to keep me from going to the dance. I needed some high school experiences, she reasoned. And the guilt from my running away helped too. So here I was, playing Barbie at Lily and Emma's will.

"What is that?" I asked, horrified as Lily pulled out a tool from her makeup bag. It didn't look friendly.

She rolled her eyes, "It's an eyelash curler, Adeline. Chill."

I held my breath as she curled my eyelashes.

"See, not bad," Lily smiled.

"Whatever," I mumbled.

When Emma and Lily had finished, they did not permit me to look into the mirror until I was in my dress. What I saw was startling. The girl I saw had a beautiful face with a creamy complexion. Her eyes were greener than their usual hazel. Her hair was hung loosely in curls around her face. Overall, she was beautiful. It took me another moment to realize that she was me.

"Whoa," I breathed.

"You look amazing, Addie," Lily gushed.

I looked to her and found her in her dress. She was wearing a light pink halter with her dirty blonde hair in a French twist.

"So do you, Lily. You look beautiful," I smiled as she spun around Emma's room. I then saw a flash and a multitude of different colors.

"Ha! Gotcha!" Emma bragged as she began taking more pictures.

"At least warn me," I muttered as I tried to get my eyes to refocus.

Lily stopped spinning, "Take a picture of me and Adeline!"

Emma had the camera ready as Lily and I posed. Another flash and another multitude of colors.

"I want a copy of that," Lily said as she walked over to Emma and looked at the different pictures. Suddenly, the doorbell rang and Lily squealed.

"That should be Eric. I told him to pick me up here," Lily spoke in a rush as she took one last glance in the mirror and then ran to the front door. I followed a few paces behind to give Eric and Lily some privacy. I walked into the kitchen and looked at the clock. Cole would be here in five minutes.

I walked into the living room when I thought enough time had passed for Lily and Eric. Eric was holding Lily in a romantic embrace while whispering something in her ear, making her giggle. Apparently I hadn't given them enough personal time. I turned to leave the room again when Lily stopped me.

"Eric! Stop! Adeline, come back," she giggled.

I walked back into the room and found Lily waving me over and Eric with a frown.

"Sorry for ruining the moment, Eric," I teased.

He rolled his eyes, "S'ok."

Lily slapped his torso.

"Be nice," she warned.

I supposed that he wasn't as happy about being seen in public with me as Lily was. After all, he had a reputation to uphold. He winced, and Lily rolled her eyes and smiled at me. The doorbell rang just as Emma walked into the room.

"Adeline. The door," Emma prompted.

I nodded and took a deep breath as I opened the door, unsure of what I would find.

He looked like he had just stepped off of the red carpet. Cole's hair was in its usual, handsome disarray. He was wearing a tuxedo similar to Eric's, but he looked better. Much better. His blue eyes widened in surprise when he saw me. He smiled widely.

"You look beautiful, Adeline," he whispered as he continued to look me over.

"Thanks," I blushed as I stepped to the side to let him in.

Lily winked at me, and Eric shook Cole's hand. Cole then turned back to me and brought out a corsage of blue forget-me-nots and tied it around my wrist.

"Thanks," I blushed again.

"Ok, pictures!" Emma said as she got the camera ready.

Several flashes later, we were ready to leave for the dance.

"I'll see you later," I called as Eric, Lily, Cole, and I walked toward the cars.

"I'll be there in an hour. Behave," Emma whispered to me as I made my way through the front door. I acted like I didn't hear her and continued to walk toward Cole's truck.

After Cole had helped me in and gotten in on his side, we were on the road following Eric.

"You really do look amazing," Cole said as he took my hand and held it to his lips. His warm breath caused chills to course through me.

I blushed, "You don't look so bad yourself."

He chuckled against my wrist.

"Why, thank you."

We drove in comfortable silence as we followed Eric and Lily to the school. Cole parked in his usual spot with Eric about two cars away.

"Now, promise me you will dance," Cole entreated as I took his arm and walked toward the gym.

I rolled my eyes, "I can't dance."

"Everyone can dance," he contradicted.

We continued to walk through the crowd of people as we came closer to the entrance to the gym. A huge sign hung above the gym door with the words "Sweetheart Dance" in bright pink and white letters. Balloons and streamers decorated the flagpole outside of the gym door.

"I can't," I replied, "You'll be embarrassed."

He stopped midstride and turned to look at me with accusation in his eyes.

"I would never be embarrassed of you," Cole whispered while pulling me closer to him. People began to stare.

"Cole," I blushed under everyone's gaze, "people are staring."

He leaned his head closer to my face and then whispered huskily in my ear, "Let them."

I shivered and he noticed. He chuckled as he kissed my forehead for the second time in two days. My cheeks heated up and my pulse sped. I suddenly forgot about anyone else that was near. It was just Cole and I. Nothing else mattered.

"Let's go," he finally said as he took my hand and led me through the gym doors.

The only lights in the room were the neon lights hanging from the ceiling. Music was pumping and I could feel the bass pulse through my body. People were swaying to the music. I looked away quickly when I caught sight of Matt and Brittany dancing. At least I knew they were back together now. Cole walked me over to the punch table and poured me a cup.

"Thanks," I shouted over the music as I gratefully took the cup. I hadn't realized how dry my mouth was. I gulped it down, and Cole watched thoughtfully.

"Sorry."

"Don't be. You're adorable," he said as he began to twirl one of my curls.

I blushed as I continued to gaze into Cole's eyes, unaware of anyone else around. I thought I heard Joanne and Sasha say something to Cole, but I couldn't be sure. Cole didn't act like he heard them.

The song that had been playing ended, and a slow number came on. I recognized it immediately. It was one of my favorites, and I was surprised anyone else would know it.

I looked toward the dance floor and found Lily and Eric slow dancing, completely absorbed in each other.

"Let's dance. I'll teach you," Cole took my hand and led me toward the middle of the dance floor. I followed willingly, knowing Cole wouldn't do anything unless he was sure I wouldn't fall on my face. Cole placed one hand on my waist and the other in my grasp. I placed my hand on his shoulder, and we began to waltz. It was very different from the other couples and their dancing, but for me and Cole, it was right. We continued to glide around the floor, and I was surprised that I hadn't fallen yet. I was very proud of myself.

"See, anyone can dance," Cole smiled as he dipped me.

I closed my eyes thinking I would hit the floor. When he brought me back up, I realized how close we had become. I began blushing after I opened my eyes and saw his blue orbs staring back at me.

"You can trust me. I won't let you fall," Cole whispered as he brought us closer and we continued to sway.

"Uh huh," I mumbled as I was hypnotized by his eyes.

We continued to dance through the next song and then the next until I lost count. We were in our own world. In that moment, I wasn't in some badly decorated, stuffy school gym. The music didn't even make sense. I wasn't listening to anything but Cole's steady breathing, trying to match mine with his.

"Excuse me. May I cut in?"

Cole stopped our swaying, and it took me a moment to realize that someone was talking to us. I turned around and found Chandler standing confidently with his eyes looking me up and down. It wasn't the same way Cole looked at me. Chandler was mostly looking at my bare skin rather than me.

A low growl erupted from Cole's chest.

"No," Cole hissed ominously.

"I don't believe I asked you," Chandler said, hungry eyes still fixed on me. I gulped, and looked to Cole.

"He's right. It's your choice," Cole whispered, still not taking his eyes off of Chandler.

I decided not to be rude and agree to Chandler's request. Maybe I could convince him that I wasn't interested in him. Maybe I could talk him into leaving Cole alone.

"Sure," I mumbled.

Cole bent down to my ear and whispered, "I won't be far."

He disappeared through the crowd, and I was alone with Chandler. Well, not really alone, but Cole wasn't near. Chandler pulled me close to him and placed his hands securely on my waist. I hesitantly placed my hands on his shoulders. We began to sway to the music, and I tried to look anywhere but directly at him. His gaze was starting to make me nervous.

"Have you reconsidered? Maybe we could go out tonight. After the dance," he asked, startling me.

"Uh, no. Sorry, but I'm gonna be busy," I lied, trying not to seem awkward.

"And why do I think you are lying?" Chandler asked, surprising me by pulling our bodies closer and leaning his forehead against mine. My palms began to sweat as panic swept in.

He was too close, and Cole wasn't around.

"I'm...I'm not lying," I stuttered.

Chandler began to rub my back with his right hand. The urge to run became persistent.

"Yes you are," he whispered, "but I know how to change your mind."

His left hand began to make circular motions down my back, and I prepared myself for his next move. He was leaning his head toward my lips and I was trapped. I couldn't squirm out of his grasp. I was ready to scream when I felt wind whip across my face and I noticed that Chandler was no longer rubbing my back. I couldn't even feel him near me.

When I opened my eyes, I found everyone looking to the north side of the gym where the food and punch table were turned over. Chandler was lying in the midst of the damage. I heard him curse under his breath.

I looked around the gym, scanning the crowd for Cole. What surprised me was that I found him standing over Chandler, shaking violently. I immediately remembered the story Cole had told me.

As he continued to stalk toward me, my whole body began to shake violently. My anger and rage at my older brother was slowly beginning to devour me. Suddenly, I could no longer hear the teenage boys in the car in my driveway or even Chenoa's muffled sobs. All that mattered at that moment was me and Elsu. Me killing Elsu.

My eyes widened in horror as Cole began to shake even more. His whole body became a blur. I ran toward him, pushing people out of my way.

"Is he having a brain hemorrhage?"

"Did you see what happened? Chandler flew, like, twenty feet!"

"What's wrong with Cole? Is he sick or something?"

I finally made it to Cole and grabbed his arm. My own body began to shake.

"Cole," I choked, "stop."

Cole seemed to have calmed down because his shaking became less apparent, and he was no longer a blur.

"Ad-Ad-Adeline," he stuttered, teeth clenched together, "we need to leave. Now."

I nodded, and led Cole through the crowd. I looked over my shoulder and found Tommy helping Chandler. He seemed fine, but he was glaring at Cole as we walked away.

We made it out of the gym without interference from any teachers or Emma, and I was thankful. When we made it to the truck, Cole opened the passenger's side and lifted me in. I didn't protest. His jaw was still clenched, and his eyes were narrowed in absolute rage. He slammed my door closed, glided over to his side, and jumped in. The truck came alive and screeched out of the parking lot. His hands clutched the steering wheel until his knuckles were white.

"Cole," I whispered, "it's okay."

He sighed heavily, "There's something wrong with me."

"No, there isn't. You're only human," I denied.

"That's the problem. I don't think I am anymore," he mumbled.

His words shocked me, and I stayed quiet. Not human? I always felt like there was something mystical about him, but I never thought it would be true. Besides, he said he didn't believe in the legends, that they were just myths. Nothing more. He continued to drive until we parked in his driveway. I didn't even notice the reservation sign. Everything was a blur. He cut the engine off and we sat in silence.

"I'm sorry. I'm so sorry," he whispered. He sounded so weak and alone. I turned to face him and scooted closer to him.

"You have nothing to be sorry for."

"I ruined your evening."

"Not even close. You made it better," I said as I took his face in my hands and made him look at me. His face was hot against my cold fingers.

"Better? You call me almost killing someone in front of you 'better'?" he cringed, disgust in his tone. I shook my head.

"That's not what I meant. You make every moment better. Every moment with you is thousands of times better than being anywhere else. You wouldn't have hurt Chandler. You couldn't."

He smirked, "You don't know what I am capable of." The edge in his voice was different.

"Maybe so, but I don't need to. I know you and I know you wouldn't have hurt him."

The porch light went on, and Cole sighed.

"Chenoa is probably wondering what we are doing home so early," Cole muttered.

But he made no effort to leave the truck and head inside. Instead he simply sighed, his eyes focused on something in the distance. I followed his gaze and saw he was looking at the herd off in the pasture.

"How are the horses doing?"

"Sky is amazing," Cole beamed, his mind focusing on something positive, "I've been working him at night, when no one else is around. He's still a bit skittish, but he trusts me."

I smiled and he smiled in return, but it didn't quite reach his eyes.

"What?"

"You don't care, do you?" he asked, suddenly changing the subject.

"About what?"

"About my family, my tribe, and our secrets. It doesn't bother you or scare you?"

My answer was simple.

"No."

He sat, staring at me with wonder in his blue eyes.

"I just have one question," I whispered.

"Yes?"

"What other things have changed? What's actually going on?"

Cole's eyes wavered from mine, "Well, I'm fast. Faster than I used to be."

"I know," I replied sarcastically, "You drive like a maniac."

He laughed, and it sounded heavenly.

"That's not what I meant," he finally responded, sounding serious.

"Is that what happened tonight?" I asked, remembering how quickly Chandler was in front of me and then on the other side of the gym, thrown into the food and punch tables.

Cole frowned, "Yeah, same thing."

"What made you do that?" I asked warily.

"I didn't like the way he was holding you," Cole growled under his breath, "It didn't look like you liked it either."

"Oh," I muttered, "you're right. I didn't."

"I'm sorry if that embarrassed you. I have a problem with self-control," Cole apologized, his eyes cast down.

"You didn't embarrass me, just worried me. I thought you may have gotten hurt," I replied, searching his body for any injuries.

"Me? You were worried about me? I'm the one who almost killed Chandler and you are concerned for me?" he asked, anger seeping through his usually calm demeanor.

I was taken aback by his tone. He sighed sadly, calmed somewhat.

"I'm sorry."

"It's okay," I whispered.

We sat in silence for a few moments before Cole opened his door. He walked silently over to my side and held the door open for me.

"I forgot about dinner. You need to eat," he explained as he helped me out.

I nodded and followed him into his home. The warmth and smell of yeast rolls hit me hard and invigorated me. I suddenly was starving. Cole led me into the kitchen where Chenoa was busily making chicken and dumplings. The rolls were sitting on the granite counter top beside the oven. Cole led me to the table and pulled the chair out for me. I sat down and watched as Cole sat down across from me. He looked stressed.

"It's fine, Cole," I whispered while I took his hand in mine over the table. "I'm not upset."

"That's the problem. You should be. Any sane person would," he murmured, seeming desperate to get his point across.

He wanted to warn me, but I didn't need it. I was warned long ago that I shouldn't be involved, but it was too late.

"Hungry, Adeline?" Chenoa asked as she brought me out of my thoughts.

"Yes. Thanks, Chenoa," I replied gratefully as I dove into the dinner.

I was half way through my chicken and dumplings when I noticed Cole's hand clenched and tapping against the table nervously.

"You okay?" I asked after taking a sip of my lemonade.

He nodded, but continued his tapping.

"He's afraid that Paco and Elsu will arrive home soon," Chenoa explained while taking a sip of her tea, "He's afraid of what they will do."

"Chenoa," Cole warned.

"Be reasonable, Cole," Chenoa replied just as threateningly, "Word about what happened at the dance will surely get to Paco and Elsu. I'm surprised that they haven't phoned yet."

"How do you know about the dance?" I asked, pushing the food around on my plate. I lost my appetite when I thought about the dance.

"This is Great Falls, Adeline. Who hasn't heard about what happened is the better question," Chenoa smiled while adding more food to my plate.

Cole shifted uncomfortably in his seat. The headlights of a car pulling into the driveway set everyone on edge.

"Chenoa, stay with Adeline. I'll handle this," Cole said while standing and walking out the front door.

"Handle what?" I asked after I heard the front door close.

Chenoa seemed uncomfortable now.

"Some people in the family look down upon Cole's friendship with you," she replied.

My heart sank. I knew whom she was talking about.

"Mr. Dyami and Elsu?"

"Yeah," Chenoa responded, "but I like you!"

I laughed, "Thanks, but I don't want to get Cole in trouble. Do I need to leave?"

"Not without Cole," she replied, suddenly serious. I was surprised at her sudden change in disposition.

"Sorry," she apologized, reading the shock on my face, "It's just important that you don't enter or leave the reservation without Cole."

"Why?"

"It's hard to explain."

"I have time," I replied determinedly.

She sighed as she ran her fingers through her beautiful black hair.

"You're stubborn, you know that?"

"I've been told. Now are you going to tell me?"

"Only if you promise not to tell Cole that I told you. He has a hard time believing it all himself."

"You have my word," I promised, not completely sure about what I was about to hear.

"There is a myth that most people in the tribe believe. It's more like a prophecy. There's said to be men and women with strange talents throughout the tribe. These people are direct descendants of Chief Heluka. In the legend, it speaks of transformers, men that have inherited Heluka's ability of shape shifting. Specifically, eagles of the mountain. These men and women are called the Chosen."

"The Chosen are a group of mystically talented men from the tribe that are selected to fight the rebels. You see, this prophecy corresponds with the legend you heard Saturday, the one about the split. Well, the tribe doesn't think it is a myth. They think it is historical fact and that the prophecy will occur soon."

I nodded, "Cole has explained most of this, but what does this have to do with me?"

"You remember the heavenly being?"

I nodded.

"In the prophecy, the heavenly being's soul is reincarnated. When she is revealed, the Chosen begin to show up in a sense. Their job is to protect her from the rebels, who want her power for revenge," Chenoa explained patiently.

"Okay," I sighed, "Why does that make the tribe hate me?"

Cole had explained the tribe's misconception, but it still didn't make too much sense.

"They don't hate you," she sighed, "They are afraid of what the rebels would do if they harnessed your power."

"My power?" I scoffed, full of disbelief. Now I understood why Cole found it so hard to believe the stories of his tribe.

"Yes," she replied as if it was truth, "The tribe believes you are the reincarnation. They are afraid of your power."

"I'm nothing to be afraid of. I'm nothing special," I shook my head, still not believing, "and why does this make me not able to go anywhere without Cole?"

"Because one of the rebels could attack at any time. Even with Jacy on duty, you are still in danger."

"Jacy? Who's Jacy?" The name sounded familiar.

Chenoa sighed, "I think I've said too much."

"Yes, you have," a deep voice from behind me boomed.

Chenoa's eyes widened in surprise, and I could see the guilt sweep over her flawless features. I slowly turned around in my chair and found Paco Dyami, Elsu, and Cole in the kitchen.

"Hey, Dad," Chenoa greeted sheepishly.

"Go to your room, Chenoa," he ordered, eyes fixed on me. He didn't seem angry, just serious.

"Yes, sir," she replied.

"You too, Cole. Elsu," Paco ordered, turning his head toward Cole and Elsu.

"But…" Elsu contradicted.

"Now," Paco replied forcefully.

Elsu turned to leave, but Cole still stood, eyes, filled with apology and sadness, fixed on me.

"Cole," Paco warned.

"I have to take her home," Cole replied, just as forceful.

"No, you don't. I will. Now leave."

Cole sighed, and turned to go to his room. My heart dropped when Paco walked toward me. He sat down in the seat Cole had once occupied. I noticed that they looked very similar. They had the same dark hair and dark blue eyes. Very strange for a Native American.

"Now Miss Jasely," he began formally. It reminded me of Cole. "I hear that you had an interesting night. I hope you are well."

I nodded dumbly, unable to find my voice.

"And I am sure that you have some questions. Anyone would," he chuckled. His face broke into a grin, but disappeared as quickly as it came. It made me think it didn't even happen.

"Um, yes, sir."

"Well, ask away," he replied.

"Who…who's Jacy?" I stammered, remembering my question. My voice cracked.

"Ah, well. He is a friend of the tribe," he replied, "You've seen him. He flies over the village about five times a day."

"Flies?" I asked, suddenly feeling afraid for the first time.

"Yes. Chenoa told you about the shape shifters. Well, he was one from about a hundred and forty years ago," he replied, leaning back in his chair, relaxed.

I gulped, "That's impossible."

"Oh, it's possible. It's just people like you that don't believe it. That's why Cole is having such a hard time grasping it. His mother was just like you."

"I don't understand," I whispered.

"I know, and that's all right. You shouldn't."

We sat in uncomfortable silence for a few minutes. My heart was pounding and my hands were sweating.

"Any more?"

"Um, well…yes," I croaked.

"Yes?"

"What's happening to Cole? He seems afraid," I whispered, unsure of Paco's reaction.

He sighed, and his lips became a tight line, "Now that is a question I cannot answer."

"Can't or won't?" I asked, feeling braver.

"I believe I should take you home now," he dismissed my question as he stood and walked toward the door. I quickly followed.

The car ride home was quiet and tense. I sat uncomfortably in the passenger's seat of Mr. Dyami's black Ford SUV. The radio was on a country station. Mr. Dyami quietly whistled to every song that came on. It was about ten songs. I'm not sure what made the ride seem longer, the country music or me being used to Cole's insanely fast driving. I would have been home twenty minutes earlier if Cole had been the driver.

When Mr. Dyami pulled into the driveway, I saw the porch lights come on immediately. I was late for curfew, and Emma was probably irate. Before I even made it to the porch, Emma burst the door open.

"Where have you been?" she yelled.

"I'm sorry, Miss Jasely. It was my fault. We had Adeline come to our home for dinner, and time escaped us. Please don't blame her," Paco explained.

I was shocked. Why would Paco Dyami cover for me? Wouldn't it be better if I were grounded so I wouldn't bother him or his family?

"Oh. Well, I guess that changes things," Emma stuttered, "Thank you for bringing Adeline home, Mr. Dyami. I feel bad that you had to come all this way."

"No problem at all. Goodnight, ladies," Paco smiled as he tipped his hat and walked back to his car.

I walked inside the house with Emma not far behind.

"What were you thinking? Leaving after what happened? Did you even see it? Chandler could have been hurt. What was Cole doing?" Emma rambled as she followed me to my room. I stopped in the middle of the doorframe, turning around sharply.

"I'm sorry, but I am tired. I don't feel like talking about it right now. I'll see you in the morning," I said abruptly as I closed my door.

Emma stopped the door with her foot, "We will talk in the morning, Adeline."

"Fine," I snapped as I shut the door.

I sighed heavily as I got ready for bed. After my shower, I changed into my pajama pants and t-shirt. I crawled into bed and turned off the light. This night had not turned out at all like I had expected. What Chenoa had told me was so hard to believe. It sounded like a fairytale. I never read fairytales as a little girl. Emma preferred to read the newspaper to me when I was young.

Nothing Chenoa said seemed logical either, not when I was supposed to believe that there were flying shape shifters around. That was impossible. I couldn't think of anyone who would want to hurt me, but the thought of the men Chenoa talked about sent chills up and down my spine. Maybe Cole's family was just trying to scare me away. I couldn't think of Chenoa doing that. She seemed so honest when she told me. She acted like she really wanted me to know, to warn me even.

I lay in bed for a few minutes, trying to fall asleep, when I heard a tap on my window. At first I ignored it, but after the third time, I got up and pulled back my curtains. What I saw surprised me. There was my personal angel, standing at my window with a goofy smile spread across his face. I opened my window, and the cold air caused my hair to stand on end.

"Cole?" I whispered, "What are you doing here?"

He walked closer to my window. Our house was only one story, but the window was several feet from the ground. He took my hands in his and stood on his tiptoes. He was still smiling.

"You are okay?" he whispered relieved as he brought my hands to his face. My whole body was warmed, especially my cheeks.

"Yeah. Why wouldn't I be?" I asked, confused. I didn't know why Cole was standing at my window at about midnight, but I didn't care. He was with me.

"Come with me. I promise Emma won't even know you're gone."

I knew that I should have said no, that it was too late. I should have said we couldn't see each other, but I didn't.

"Sure. Let me get my shoes."

He gave my hands one last squeeze before he let me go. I rushed to my closet and grabbed my sneakers. I put on my jacket, technically Cole's, and then walked back to the window. It wasn't that far of a drop, but it didn't look pleasant.

"I'll catch you," Cole whispered as he held his arms out to me.

I nodded as I climbed through and sat on the edge of the windowsill. I took a deep breath and jumped. My feet didn't even touch the ground. When I opened my eyes, I was staring at Cole's beautiful face.

We stood there for a few moments, with Cole holding me and my arms wrapped around his neck. My heart was pounding loudly in my ears. He finally set me down, took my hand, and led me through the woods in my back yard.

When I thought we were far away enough from the house, I asked, "What are you doing here?"

He stopped walking and we were both very still. He turned to face me, smile gone. I felt my own smile disappear.

"Cole?"

"I needed to make sure you were all right," he said simply as he pulled me into his arms. He nuzzled his head into my hair and took a deep breath.

"Does this have to do with what Chenoa told me?" I asked into his chest.

He tensed when I mentioned Chenoa.

"Yes," he replied grimly.

"Do you believe it?"

"Not all of it."

"How much?" I asked looking into his face.

The moonlight enlightened his features and made him even more breathtaking. I found it hard to concentrate on what he was saying.

He sighed, "The part about you being in danger. Even if I don't believe it, doesn't mean other people don't."

"But I thought you said this was all ridiculous."

He glanced down to the ground, not meeting my eyes. So things had changed.

"What would they do to me, Cole?" I asked, fear finally making its appearance.

"Nothing," he replied sternly, "because they won't touch you. I'll make sure of it."

He held me tighter and I laid my head on his shoulder.

"Do you believe that there are men that can turn into eagles?" I asked.

He sighed heavily, "No."

"What about Jacy?"

"Jacy is a myth. He's not real. Just something the elders tell the little kids so that they aren't afraid of the dark," Cole reasoned.

"Then why were you angry that he spellbinded me that time when I passed out?" I asked recalling the memory clearly.

He sighed again, "You remember that?"

"Yes," I said lifting my head to look him in the eye.

He closed his eyes and drew in a deep breath, "It's so hard to tell you."

"Why?"

"Because I'm afraid you will leave. You are the closest thing to a friend that I have," he whispered, eyes opened and staring intently at me.

I returned his gaze, "I'm not going anywhere. I can't leave you."

"You say that now."

"I'll never leave you Cole. I can't," I replied, desperately trying to make him believe me.

He caressed my cheek with his hand, and the blood rushed to my cheeks.

"I can't let you get involved," he finally whispered.

"It's too late for that Cole."

"I suppose you are right. Just promise me something."

"Anything," I agreed.

"Promise me that you will stay away from the reservation. For now at least, okay?"

"Okay, but why?"

He ran his hand through my hair and held me closer to him.

"Those men, called rebels, are looking for you. They have been looking for over a hundred years."

"Would they come to the reservation?" I asked, shivering at the thought of such men coming for me.

"They might," Cole replied honestly, "Paco says they come every generation to see if the heavenly being has been reincarnated."

"Do you think I'm her?"

He bent his head down and stared into my eyes. His eyes were their usual deep blue, but grayer than normal.

"No," he whispered. Somehow, I didn't believe him.

I nodded, "Is this all really happening?"

"I'm afraid so."

"When were you going to tell me?"

"I wasn't. You weren't supposed to find out," he replied, "I was going to keep you safe until we knew the rebels were gone. Like I said, they only come once a generation."

"From where?"

"North Dakota. They are a part of the Turtle Mountain Tribe," Cole whispered, eyes narrowing when he mentioned the tribe. "Chandler is one of them."

My eyes widened and my breathing became shallow. Of course I knew Chandler was part of that tribe, but Cole never seemed too concerned before. He was convinced everyone was crazy, not using common sense. But now, things were different. Now, I was starting to think that I really could be in danger.

"Adeline? Are you all right?"

Forget the fact that this all seemed illogical and was probably a myth, but the thought of someone from the other tribe being so close terrified me.

"Adeline?" Cole asked, panicked as he held me closer and brought my face to look to his.

"Is he one of them?" I croaked. Cole remained quiet. "But I thought these legends weren't true? Just superstitions?" I asked, praying he would say yes.

His face fell, and I knew the answer. Whether or not I believed in birdmen or any other mystical creature, I knew that there was danger.

"I don't know," he finally answered, eyes cast down to the ground.

My eyelids became heavy, but I wasn't ready to go back to bed.

"Cole, I don't know if I believe all of this, but answer one thing. Chenoa talked about men from the tribe being Chosen. Are you one of them?" I whispered, afraid of his reaction. When he didn't answer, I looked up and found him with his eyes closed and his lips in a tight line.

"No."

"Are you sure? You said Dylan and Elan believed you were!"

"You need to go back to sleep. You must be tired," Cole said as he took my hand and started to lead me back to my house.

"Wait. Why won't you answer me?"

He stopped and turned toward me.

"Paco and the others believe I am, but I don't believe in the myths," he finally replied, voice monotone.

"But you just said you believe in the rebels and me being in danger. Why wouldn't you believe in being Chosen?"

"Because, Adeline...I just don't," he sighed. "Now, you need to get home and get some sleep."

He led me back to my house quietly. Just before he lifted me back through my window, he kissed my forehead and then rested his head against mine, eyes closed.

"Goodnight," he whispered as he lifted me into my window.

My heart was still pounding, "Night."

I watched him run back through the woods, and I wondered how long it would take him to get home. He said he was fast, and for his sake, I hoped it was true. He didn't need to get into any more trouble with his family. I closed my window after I knew he was gone. I climbed back into bed after I had quietly taken my sneakers off and placed them in my closet.

I wrapped the covers around me, but I wasn't warm enough. These blankets were nothing compared to the warmth of Cole when he held me. I finally drifted off to sleep, hoping I would wake up in the morning and all of this nonsense of legends and prophecies would have been a dream.

Chapter Eleven

My dream had turned into a nightmare. I was with Cole at the waterfall he had told me about, skipping stones. Everything was perfect. There were no worries, or birdmen, or Emma, or anything. Just me and Cole.

Everything took a turn for the worse when I heard the cry of something above. I looked up to the sky and found the largest eagle with black feathers flying above me. It was the same one from all of my other nightmares.

I screamed to Cole, but he didn't hear me. He was still skipping stones as if nothing was happening. I screamed for him again, but he still wouldn't turn. Suddenly, Chandler ran into the clearing, panting heavily. I screamed for both of them to look out, but neither acted like they heard me.

The large eagle swooped down and landed on Chandler's arm. The eagle was twice Chandler's size, but he held him up with no trouble. Cole finally turned to face Chandler and the eagle. I screamed again, feeling danger approaching. Cole began to shake violently, like he had at the dance. His whole body began to blend and then I could no longer see him, just a blur.

I heard another cry, but it wasn't from Chandler's eagle. It was from where Cole was standing. Cole had suddenly disappeared and then there was an eagle where he once was.

The eagle was far larger than any eagle that I had ever seen. His wings were great and broad. His beak was jet black and his feathers were the same onyx with lines of lighter brown and white swirling from the head to the tail. The eagle's eyes were a mesmerizing deep, cold blue.

It took me a few moments to realize that the eagle was Cole. I watched in horror as Cole began to circle Chandler and his eagle. Chandler turned his head toward his eagle and nodded. The eagle was gone in a flash and the battle between Cole and the black eagle began. I was so preoccupied with the eagles that I didn't notice Chandler approach.

"Adeline," he whispered.

I turned around and found him a few inches from me. I stumbled backwards when I noticed the dagger in his right hand.

"Don't be afraid," he cooed, "I'm not going to hurt you."

I gulped as he came closer. I continued to walk backwards until I was at the river's edge. I looked across the river helplessly as I knew that I couldn't swim across. The current would be too strong. I looked back toward Chandler as he continued to stalk toward me. Tears fell down my cheeks as I realized that this was the end.

Unexpectedly, the sound of a cry broke me out of my thoughts. Chandler and I both looked up and saw Cole flying straight down toward Chandler. Cole hit him and they both flew across the clearing and hit a tree. I heard a sickening, bone breaking noise.

I woke up screaming.

My nightmare had left me in a haze the entire morning. I woke up with a jolt when my dream had finally ended. I sat up in bed, trying to steady my breathing. I proceeded through my morning routine in a daze, not completely aware of what I was doing. It took ten minutes for me to recognize that I had conditioned my hair three times.

I sighed as I dressed and headed to the kitchen. I heard the coffee maker beep, and I jumped back, landing on my backside. Every little noise or shadow seemed to make me jump. I was suddenly wishing that Chenoa hadn't told me all that she knew the night before.

I stood, turned the coffee maker off, and unplugged it from the outlet. I walked to the fridge and took out some orange juice. I poured it into a glass and sat down. Food was very unappetizing at the moment.

I was slowly drinking my juice when I realized that I was alone. Emma wasn't home.

I looked to the counter next to the sink after placing my glass in the dishwasher. There was a note from Emma saying that she had an emergency meeting at the paper and that I was not to leave the house. We would talk when she returned home. I sighed again, but jumped when the phone rang. The phone continued to ring, seeming impatient.

"Coming, coming," I sighed.

"Hello?"

"Adeline?" the voice on the other end squealed eagerly.

"Hey, Lily. What's up?" I asked, calmed somewhat. I was afraid of who it would have been, if not Lily.

"Why did you leave last night?" she practically yelled, "What happened? Did you see how Chandler flew across the gym? Food was everywhere!"

"Yeah, I saw it, and I'm not sure how it happened," I lied, "Cole and I left because we felt like it. No big deal."

"Adeline Jasely, you are going to tell me what happened. I'm dying here!" Lily whined.

"Lily, I'm telling you the truth. I only know as much as you do. I'll talk to you Monday. I've got stuff to do, okay?" I explained, hoping she would drop it and let me go.

"Fine," she huffed, "but I want all the details about you and Cole in English!"

The line clicked and went dead. I sighed as I hung up the phone and looked to the clock. It was only half past ten. I began pacing, not completely sure why I was so nervous, but I soon realized what it was. I hadn't heard from Cole since last night. I continued to pace in the small space in the kitchen, replaying what happened last night like a movie in my head.

I had never done anything like that before. I had never snuck out of my window to go meet a boy. Other girls did that, not me. It was very strange how willing I was to jump out of my window and into the arms of a boy I hardly knew. But that was it. I did know him. No matter what Emma or my sensible side said, I knew Cole better than I knew anyone.

I was sure that he knew me too. Inside and out, better than I even knew myself. It seemed that he was there for me more than anyone had ever been in my entire life. For so long, I had only me to lean on. Now someone was there for me, but I was still afraid that any day I would wake up and he would just be a dream. A fantasy my imagination had conjured up in the midst of my loneliness.

I thought I had everything before Cole. Life wasn't bad, just predictable. I went to school, cooked for Emma, went to bed, and repeated the process. I now woke up, not sure about what to expect when I walked out the door.

I continued to pace through the kitchen, then into the living room for about ten more minutes until I heard a knock on the door. My heart jumped as I quickly made my way to the door. I took a deep breath, opening the door.

"Hello," Chandler greeted as he smiled cockily.

My heart instantly fell, and my stomach became a multitude of tight knots.

"Hi," I croaked, suddenly lonely. Emma was downtown and Cole was at the reservation. I didn't think the neighbors would hear me scream.

"May I come in?" he asked, leaning toward me and trying to stick his foot in the doorway. I stopped him with my foot and angled my body to block his path into my house.

"No, sorry. I'm kind of busy. Do you need something?" I asked, hoping he would take the hint and leave.

"Yeah, but I think we should go in," he replied, untouched by my tone.

He either missed the hint or just ignored it.

"I don't think that is a good idea," I whispered. My nightmare was still fresh in my mind. I began to tremble when I thought about it.

"Why not? I promise I won't bite," he chuckled to himself. I heard the sound of tires screeching in the driveway. We both turned to see a massive, black GMC truck parked in my driveway. My spirits were lifted.

"Get in the truck, Adeline," Cole ordered as he jumped out of the truck and glided toward me and Chandler. I stood motionless, feeling the tension seeping from both Cole and Chandler.

"I said get in the truck," Cole demanded forcefully while continuing to glare at Chandler. I tried to slide past Chandler, but he saw my move and blocked it before I could step my foot around him.

"I just came over to tell her that I was fine. You know, after last night," Chandler spoke to Cole, angling his body to block me from leaving. Cole began to shake, and my eyes widened in hopelessness. I didn't think he would be able to control himself this time. But just as soon as Cole began shaking, he stopped and recovered. He looked past Chandler to me and smiled slightly. Blood rushed to my cheeks, and I ached to be near him.

I tried again to get past Chandler, but this time he grabbed my arm and whispered, "Where do you think you're going? I just want to talk."

I gulped, knowing that there was more to his words than he was letting on. Maybe he did know and believe in the legends, like the other rebels. It didn't matter what I thought about them. All that mattered was whether Chandler did and if his tribe was looking for me. Suddenly, Cole was behind Chandler in a flash and grabbed him by his arm, twisting it.

"Don't you touch her."

The amount of force and passion behind Cole's words left me breathless. Chandler slightly turned his head to glance at Cole and whispered, "And what are you going to do about it if I do? Shift?"

Cole's eyes widened in horror and confusion.

"How much do you know?" he whispered, his grip on Chandler's arm becoming tighter.

"More than you think," Chandler replied ominously.

Cole's expression and the tone of Chandler's voice caused goose bumps to rise on my skin and adrenaline to pump through my limbs. So I was in danger. They continued to stare each other down, and I was still in between Chandler and Cole. Cole let go of Chandler's arm and looked to me.

"Adeline," Cole whispered, eyes on me, "let's go."

I looked to Chandler, then immediately back to Cole and nodded. I reached my hand to his open palm and passed Chandler with no interference. Cole grabbed my hand and pulled me along to the truck. I looked over my shoulder and found Chandler staring at Cole and me.

Cole helped me in, but instead of getting in on his side, he shut my door and walked back over to Chandler. Both glared as Cole said something to Chandler. Cole turned to walk away, but Chandler must have said something that made Cole turn back around in surprise. Chandler nodded, smirking as he walked down the driveway and disappeared in his dark blue Jeep. Cole finally turned to face the truck when Chandler's taillights were out of sight. Cole walked to his side of the truck and got in.

"What happened?" my voice was shaking.

Cole sighed as he placed the key into the ignition and turned it lightly. The truck came to life, but neither of us moved.

"Cole," I whispered, "what happened?"

He put the truck in reverse and pulled out of my driveway, speeding down the highway.

"Adeline," he finally replied. His voice seemed distant.

"Yes?"

"I'm so sorry," he apologized, eyes still on the road.

I kept staring at him, guilt and sorrow swimming in his eyes.

"Do they know about me?" I asked, hoping he would say no. "Do they think that I am the reincarnation?"

His lips became a tight line.

"I think so…"

My heart fell to the floor as I turned my head to look out the windshield. The sky began to drizzle. Soon, the rain began to pour harder. My whole world seemed to be changing and I was unable to stop it. Ever since meeting Cole, my life had been shifting, going through a metamorphosis. For better or worse, I wasn't sure. But even if this all ended badly, I could not bring myself to regret meeting this beautiful boy in the seat beside me.

"Adeline," he whispered.

I turned to look to Cole and saw that we were already parked in his driveway.

"What are we going to do?" I asked. "What do they want?"

He looked me in the eyes, and as usual, my pulse sped to an unhealthy rate. My mouth dried as I watched him lean closer. He wrapped his arms around me, whispering in my hair, "You won't have to do anything. I'm going to protect you from them."

He pulled away and the tug in my chest pulled, stronger and more insistent this time.

He jumped out of the truck and came to my side to open my door. He helped me out and embraced me again, as if we didn't have much time left. We stood for a few moments, completely absorbed in each other.

"Cole! Adeline! It's raining. Get inside!" Chenoa yelled from the porch.

Cole took my hand and led me to the house. Chenoa held the door open and Cole led me to the kitchen where there was warm chicken soup waiting for us. Chenoa silently walked to the stove and poured me a bowl while Cole pulled a chair out for me. I sat down and watched as Cole took the seat beside me. He took his jacket off and placed it around me. I realized then that I had been shaking. From the cold rain or fear, I wasn't sure.

"Here you go," Chenoa said as she placed the hot bowl in front of me with a spoon and napkin.

"Thanks," I breathed.

"Chenoa," Cole said, "Chandler was there, waiting for her. How much do you think he knows?"

The atmosphere took a sudden turn and Chenoa's usual bubbly personality was silenced as she sat down. The chair scratched across the hardwood floor.

"I don't know what happened, Cole," she explained, not looking me in the eye. "Maybe we have been underestimating them, their knowledge. Paco thought they were suspicious before, but now I think they know for certain."

"When do you think it started?" Cole demanded, his hands becoming tight fists.

"At the dance. After your little display," she replied quietly. "I suppose that confirmed his suspicions."

"I thought he just believed I was strange."

"Well, not anymore," Chenoa sighed.

"What's happening?" I asked, after I took another sip from my soup.

"Chandler knows more than we thought. He believes in the legends just like the other rebels. I'm so sorry, Adeline," Chenoa apologized, brown eyes refusing to meet mine.

"Well, what do we do now?" I asked. "What about Emma? I wasn't supposed to leave home."

"If I had left you there, Adeline, Chandler may have taken you to his tribe."

Cole stopped when he saw the fear in my eyes.

"It would not have been good. You are safe here. I'll talk to Emma," Cole said, calming me somewhat. I looked to Chenoa for reassurance that everything would be all right, but she seemed just as anxious as me, or even more so.

"Cole," Chenoa finally said, "you need to tell the elders."

"I know. I'm going now. You stay with Adeline and don't leave the house," Cole ordered while walking toward the front door.

"What? Where are you going?" I asked while tripping out of my chair and almost falling to the floor. Cole grabbed my arm and helped me find my balance.

"I need to talk to the elders about something important. You need to stay here with Chenoa. I promise I will be back soon," he explained, tucking another strand of hair behind my ear. He embraced me one last time before he left.

After Cole left, Chenoa took me to her room to give me a makeover, but I had a feeling that she was just trying to get my mind on to something besides crazed Native Americans that wanted me for revenge.

Her room was a pale yellow with beautiful crown molding. There were two large windows that overlooked the side yard with the tire swing tree. The windows also led to a small balcony. The bed was a canopy with a light blue bedspread that looked like silk.

"When I'm done, you won't even recognize the person in the mirror," Chenoa giggled happily as she led me to her bathroom. She made me sit in the chair, looking into the mirror, as she got her makeup out and spread it across the marble counter.

"Chenoa, what's going to happen?" I whispered. "I'm having trouble believing it all." I fiddled with my hands as Chenoa continued to pull and twist my hair.

"Yeah. I can tell," she sighed while brushing through my hair.

"What does it matter if I do or don't believe it all?" I asked while flinching. The rain had made my hair even more tangled and Chenoa wasn't exactly being gentle. Chenoa huffed and slammed the brush down on the countertop. She then began to pull and twist my hair. Painfully. We were silent for a time. I began to think Chenoa wasn't even going to answer.

"That's just the point, Adeline. It does matter. If you and Cole don't believe then it will only make it that much harder to protect you. You don't want to know what the rebels would do if they found you. They have already gotten so close. They know where you live," She finally responded.

I looked down to the white tile and began to count them as she continued to pull my hair. It was all I could do to not scream in frustration.

"What about Emma? Would they hurt her?" I asked quietly.

"I don't think they would do anything to Emma. We already have Jacy watching over your house when Cole can't be there," Chenoa explained.

"Wait, Jacy?" I asked, finally looking up to the mirror to find my hair with about a million curlers tucked in it.

"You've met him, but of course, you wouldn't believe me."

"Try me." I glared.

She stared at me through the glass to see if I was serious.

"You know that day you passed out? You saw that eagle flying over the village. His name is Jacy. Father told you about him."

"Mr. Dyami said he was a hundred and forty years old. Is that true?"

"The Chosen are shape shifters, like I said before. When they are in their eagle form, they stop aging. But once they turn back to their human forms, they resume the process," Chenoa replied quietly while she continued to curl and then spray my hair.

"Why would he look after me? Didn't he spellbind me or whatever it's called?"

"You don't even know what that means."

"Then tell me," I pleaded. My scalp suddenly began to itch.

"I can't tell you about Jacy."

"Then what does it mean to spellbind?"

She stopped curling my hair and went to her drawer, taking out a different brush. She then began to take out the curlers without answering me.

"Chenoa, why won't you talk to me?" I asked wincing as she continued to pull my hair.

"Because I promised Cole."

"Promised him what?"

She sighed, "That I wouldn't say anything that could put you in danger. If you know too much that could put you in even more risk with the rebels."

"I need to know," I whispered as Chenoa took out the last of the curlers and began to brush through the curls.

"There. You're done. What do you think?" Chenoa asked as she brought my head up to look into the mirror. I wasn't really looking at myself in the mirror. My eyes were glued to Chenoa's creamy copper skin, her bouncy mocha hair, and her large caramel eyes. She smiled slightly when her eyes met mine through the glass.

"You like it?"

"Yeah," I nodded, "it's pretty."

I continued to look at her through the mirror trying to find the answers She smiled widely as she pulled me out of the chair to face her. Her smile was gone by the time I had turned to her.

"I want to tell you, Adeline, I do. But he's my brother. I have to do what he asks of me. And there's more to it than you know. I can't refuse to do what he asks."

"Why?"

Chenoa looked down to the floor. Taking my hand, she led me to her magnificent bed. The bedspread did feel like silk, or maybe satin.

"The Chosen are an elite group in the tribe. They are very important. The leader of the Chosen is called the Delsin meaning 'he is so.' Even though Cole doesn't believe it, he is the Delsin. That also means that what he orders cannot be overruled. I have to do what he asks of me."

"Then how are you able to tell me this?" I asked.

"Because I didn't answer *your* questions. That's what he forbade me to do. Your questions that are specific about the Delsin and the heavenly being," Chenoa smiled, feeling triumphant.

"But he only said that *you* couldn't. He didn't order other people to do the same, did he?" I asked, eyeing Chenoa carefully. "Maybe I could talk to Elsu..."

"Oh no, Adeline! There is no way Elsu would tell you a thing. He may not respect Cole, but he would never talk to someone like you."

"What do you mean 'someone like me'?" I felt embarrassed all of sudden.

Chenoa took a deep breath, "Cole's mom was a white woman from the city, and Elsu hates Cole, so you can see where I am going with this. It's nothing personal. He just has a thing against people who aren't from the reservation."

Silence descended, and my mind went back to Cole's mother's grave. So much grief had been caused by this legend. Could it honestly have had something to do with his mother's death?

"What exactly happened to Cole's mother?"

"That would be breaking one of the rules. Sorry, can't help you," Chenoa replied while wagging her finger at me.

I sighed, "Isn't there anyone who could help me? If I am this reincarnation then I have a right to know what's happening."

Chenoa stared at me, eyes widening.

"Do you think you are her?" she whispered.

"Uh, I don't know..." I stuttered. I didn't really mean I thought I was, but if it was going to help me get the answers I was looking for, then I might as well go along with it.

"This isn't something you pretend, Adeline. You either think you are her or you don't."

The tone of her voice shocked me. She was being serious.

"Okay."

"Okay to what? You think you may be her?" Chenoa asked, honey brown eyes staring through my soul.

"I think I may be starting to believe all of this," I replied quietly trying to avoid her gaze.

She smiled slightly, and her face relaxed.

"Well that changes things."

Chenoa became absolutely giddy after I told her that I was beginning to believe everything that was happening. After what happened this morning with Chandler and at the dance, I was starting to think that I really was in danger and that maybe the legends did exist. All of what Chenoa was saying made sense - if I was in a fairy tale. Maybe I was in some sort of fantasy world and didn't know it. I only hoped that it would have a happily ever after.

Chenoa led me to their garage and said that she was going to take me to someone who could answer my questions. Cole had never made a rule about that. Chenoa's truck was in the corner next to another Ford truck, which belonged to Elsu.

"I'm glad you're starting to believe all this now. Maybe if you do, Cole will come around," Chenoa interrupted my thoughts as she opened her door and slid in the driver's seat. I followed suit and fell into the smell of leather and tobacco, a very familiar, comforting scent. She pulled out of the driveway with ease and we were heading down the road to wherever we were going.

"Can you answer any questions?" I asked as soon as we hit the highway.

"Maybe..." she hesitated as she turned the radio on low volume.

"Why is Cole so resistant to believing?" I finally whispered after several minutes of silence. Chenoa mused to herself before answering, "Cole blames all of the tribe's superstitions and beliefs for never allowing him to know his mother. He'd rather just pretend none of it exists."

I nodded, glancing back out the window. "How did Cole know I was in trouble? I mean, how did he know Chandler was at my house?"

Chenoa smirked, "He didn't."

"What do you mean?"

"He was going over to your house to see if you were all right. And he'd kill me if I told you, but he missed you," Chenoa explained, smiling brightly.

I looked down to my hands, a blush slowly making its way onto my cheeks. He missed me.

"It just so happened that Chandler was at your house. You're lucky Cole came over when he did," she went on.

I nodded in agreement and continued to stare outside, watching the rain beat against the windows. The rain was making the outside world look like a distorted oil painting. The houses flew by and soon we were no longer driving past houses or the small shopping centers in the reservation. There were only trees and the road we were on.

Chenoa continued to drive until a dirt road appeared to the right. She made a sharp turn and drove down the dirt road for a few more minutes. Soon the road ended and there was one modest-looking wood cabin. The wind and rain made it look less welcoming than I would have liked.

Chenoa parked the truck to the side of the house and grabbed an umbrella from the back seat. She came around to my side in a flash and held the umbrella out for me. We ran to the porch through the soaking rain.

"Now, her name is Enola, and she can be quite strange. That's why she lives out here, away from the rest of the tribe. She means well, and she can answer your questions. She doesn't exactly care about what other people think," Chenoa explained as she knocked on the door, while closing the umbrella Thunder erupted, and I jumped when the door flew open.

"Calm down, Adeline," Chenoa whispered so that only I could hear.

The woman was old in age. Her long white hair and the wrinkles on her face could tell anyone that. Her eyes were wide and attentive, a dark brown that seemed to captivate. She was wearing a long, ivory gown, I supposed for sleeping, and her feet were bare. I was afraid we had woken her. She continued to look me over, taking me in. Her ancient, brown eyes looked me over, catching every detail and memorizing it.

"Algoma..." she whispered as she stretched her hand to caress my cheek. Her face broke out in a grin, like she had found a lost friend. Chenoa gently grabbed her hand before she could touch me, "No, Enola. This is Adeline. The one I told you about." Enola's face fell when she realized I wasn't the person she thought I was.

"Oh, why is she here?" Enola asked while still staring at me, disappointed.

"She has some questions to ask you. Will you help her?" Chenoa inquired quietly. It was like she was talking to a small child. Enola nodded and turned to walk back into the cabin. I followed as Chenoa closed the door behind us.

The cabin was small, but quaint. It was only one room, with a fireplace, kitchen area, a bed in the corner, and a small table that I assumed was used for dining. Enola led us to the rug beside the fire where she sat and motioned us to sit. I sat next to Chenoa quietly, trying to rid myself of the smell of dust and damp wood.

"Adeline, do you know who you are?" Enola began while continuing to stare at me.

I was confused. I was Adeline Jasely, the girl whose life had become more of a fairy tale than anything else.

"I meant, do you know what other people in the tribe think you are?" Enola tried again.

I nodded, my eyes not meeting hers. Enola took my hands and made me look into her eyes. She was smiling widely, like a child that had found a new toy.

"You are just like her. Algoma I mean. I miss her."

"Who's Algoma?" My palms were sweating and I was sure she could feel it.

"Cole's mother. She was such a good person. They thought she was you," she explained.

"Who are 'they'?"

"The tribe. They thought she was the reincarnation. I miss her," She repeated again.

Enola dropped my hands and covered her face while shaking her head. I turned to Chenoa for help, but she just shook her head also.

"Give her a minute," Chenoa whispered.

I turned back to Enola and saw that she had lifted her head from her hands was staring at me again.

"What do you wish to know, Adeline?" she asked as she took my hands again.

"Um, well, about the tribe and the Chosen. Why am I in danger?" I stuttered. I felt silly for being here. I was going to go home and be in even more trouble with Emma than I already was. I was getting answers to questions that didn't matter. This was all a fantasy or a dream I would wake up from. None of it mattered. I looked toward the fire as she began.

"Now, the Chosen, as you know, are the ones that protect the tribe from the rebels. They are shape shifters, spirit warriors. They have two main goals. Protect the tribe and find the reincarnation and protect her. The heavenly being, from the legend, was a beautiful creature. But she was cursed because she fell in love with a mortal man. That man, Heluka, was cursed for loving the being in return.

"She had great power. Power that caused many from the rebel tribe to come looking for her. Unlike the Chosen, the rebels are unable to take the form of an eagle, but rather can only train them and then take their bodies. But with the power of the heavenly being, they could have the same gift as the Chosen, being able to turn into their eagle partner with no consequences.

"You see, when someone takes the body of an animal, they steal its soul. It's a sin to commit such an act, but the rebels only did this when it was absolutely necessary. That doesn't make it right, but they knew that they were cursed. They only did it so that they could somehow find the power of the heavenly being and be cursed no more.

"Now, Algoma, Cole's mother, was just like you. After Dena had left Paco, he was lonely and didn't really know how to raise two children on his own. One day, he met Algoma, and over time, they fell in love. It was much like the legend of the heavenly being and Heluka, and that made the tribe very anxious.

"They were afraid of the rebels, and they knew that if word got to the Turtle Mountain Tribe that Paco, leader of the Chosen, had fallen in love with a white woman, well, war would have begun."

"So the tribe only thinks I'm the reincarnation because of my skin color and what I look like?" I spoke softly, completely absorbed in Enola's tale.

"No, Adeline," she replied patiently, "they believe you are her because of Cole."

I gaped at her as she continued. Cole had said it before, but now it seemed more real, more concrete.

"It's not right for someone from our tribe to let an outsider in without approval. Paco broke all of the rules for Algoma, and I'm sure he would do it again if given the chance.

"You see, Cole has done the same with you from what Chenoa has told me. He has let an outsider in without hesitation. The Delsin, leader of the Chosen, will be drawn to the reincarnation, like Heluka was drawn to the heavenly being. Paco was drawn to Algoma, and Cole is drawn to you. Like a moth to a flame…" Her eyes gazed into the fire. I was afraid she forgot Chenoa and I were still there.

"What happened to Algoma?" I whispered, afraid to speak any louder.

"The rebels came. The Chosen were unable to save her, and Paco was devastated, as was I. About a month after she was taken, Cole was found on Paco's doorstep with a letter tied to his hand. It said that Algoma was not the reincarnation, but that the rebels would keep looking, once every generation. When Algoma had been taken, she was pregnant with Cole.

"She had died while giving birth, or so they say. I believe that she is still alive, but that's why the tribe calls me crazy," She whispered the last bit, and I sat, unmoving, as I tried to absorb everything that I had heard.

"But I saw her grave. Cole took me to it," I was still so confused. They must have found her body.

"That grave holds no being," Enola explained. "It is merely a memorial. No one knows where Algoma truly is."

Silence descended as I took this in. So no one really even knew if Cole's mother was alive or dead. I wasn't sure if that information should comfort me or not.

"Does that answer your questions?" Enola asked while taking my hand again.

"What about Cole? He doesn't believe all of this, does he?"

"He doesn't want to because he is afraid that you will get hurt," Enola answered while holding my hand tightly. "He is afraid you will meet the same fate his mother did."

"Will I?"

"I can't answer that."

"Is Cole Chosen?" I asked, looking Enola straight in the eye, but still afraid of the answer.

"Yes. He is the next Delsin. He is still in the first phase of the transformation though."

"First phase?"

"Yes. There are phases. The gift to shape shift is a powerful thing, and the body must prepare for such a drastic change. Once he has shifted into his second half, his human body will have to be able to handle such an alteration."

"What will happen to him?"

"He will protect the tribe and you."

"What now? What am I supposed to do?" I asked, feeling desperate. It seemed that there was nothing I could do. Cole could get hurt, and there was nothing I could do to save him.

"Everything will happen as it should. All you need to do is stay safe," Enola said while cupping my face with her hand. "You have extraordinary power like no other. You will know what to do with it when it is time." I searched her ancient face for a clue of what she meant.

"I'm not powerful or special."

"Ah, that's where you are mistaken. You hold much," she then placed her hand on my chest, above my heart. "Here is where your power will arise when the time comes."

I tried to shrug out of her grip as I looked to Chenoa.

"Thank you for your help, Enola. We'll leave you now," Chenoa said gently as she helped me out and led me to the door. Enola stayed seated on the floor next to the fireplace.

"Come again, Adeline. I will miss you," she reflected wistfully as I walked out the door to the truck. I didn't stop, not even for the rain, until I was safe in the cab. Chenoa was in the driver's side in a heartbeat.

"What's wrong, Adeline? You had your questions answered," Chenoa snapped as she pulled out of the clearing and onto the dirt road. She seemed annoyed.

I stayed silent, unsure of what to do or say. For some reason, I was angry. Angry at the answers I was given. I wanted to be told that everything would be all right, that there was no hidden war or legend coming to life.

"Adeline? What's wrong?" Chenoa demanded, her temper rising with the car's speed.

"I just don't know what to think."

"Do you believe it? Are you finally understanding?"

"I don't know."

The car ride back to the Dyami residence was tense and quiet. I could tell that Chenoa was frustrated that I didn't believe everything as quickly as she would have liked. She truly believed that Cole was Chosen and that I was the reincarnation. That alone was hard to swallow. We had pulled into the garage when I finally noticed the massive, black GMC truck was back in its original place.

"Crap," Chenoa muttered under her breath.

"What?" I asked, afraid of her tone.

"Cole is not going to be happy."

I opened my door after Chenoa and followed her into the house.

"Chenoa," I heard a deep, familiar voice bellow from the kitchen.

"Yes?" she asked as she walked into the grand kitchen. I followed behind quickly. I stopped in the doorway when I saw Elsu, Paco, and Cole all standing in a circle waiting for Chenoa and me. The sight of the whole Dyami family caused a course of shivers to quiver up and down my spine. Never in my whole life had I seen such beautiful people all standing together. They really looked like copper-skinned angels.

"Adeline," Cole sighed with relief as he took two large strides toward me.

I was suddenly enveloped in a pair of warm, rusty arms. I melted into him, glad to be out of the cold rain and away from the old cabin with the strange woman.

"Where were you?" he asked, pulling me away to look into my eyes. I tried to look past him to Chenoa, but he was too tall.

"Adeline," Cole repeated, this time slower.

"I just went to visit someone with Chenoa. She said she would answer my questions," I replied quietly, blushing under everyone's gaze.

"And were they answered?" Paco asked stepping toward me. Cole moved to the side, but kept his hand firmly on my waist. I felt safe.

"Yes, I think so."

"What were you thinking Chenoa?" Elsu roared at Chenoa, causing me to flinch at his tone.

"Oh, be quiet, Elsu. She was going to find out the truth sooner or later," Chenoa replied, untouched by Elsu's temper.

"So you thought taking her to Enola was the right thing to do?" Elsu yelled. His whole body tensed and he seemed to shake as he squeezed his fists together. Cole's hold on me tightened.

"You took her to Enola?" Cole asked, blue eyes widening.

"You never said I couldn't do that," Chenoa reasoned while leaning against the counter.

Paco sighed, "You can't do that Chenoa. You knew what Cole meant. He is the Delsin and you know that."

Both Elsu and Cole cringed at the word "Delsin."

"Please stop calling me that," Cole whispered to Paco. I almost didn't catch it.

"She already knows, Cole," Paco whispered back, "There's nothing we can do about it now."

"We could always take her to Meda," Elsu smirked, his eyes creasing into a smile. I shuttered when I glanced at his scar.

"That's not an option," Cole growled. Elsu only smiled wider at Cole's disfavor.

"There are always options little brother."

"Shut up, Elsu."

"What? Are you going to make me? I know you won't do it in front of her," Elsu smirked even more, brown eyes shinning in victory.

"Do what?" I asked, tired of everyone talking about me as if I wasn't there.

"Nothing," Cole answered quickly, eyes still glued on Elsu's every move. "It's time to take you home."

"What about what the elders said? What about my safety?" I asked, replaying what happened this morning over again in my head. I saw Chenoa shutter from the corner of my eye.

"You will be safe. I won't let anyone get near you," Cole whispered as he took my hand in his. I looked past Cole's face and toward the rest of the Dyami family. Elsu continued to glare at Cole and me. Chenoa tried to smile when my eyes fell on her, but I could tell something was bothering her, and Paco was just as he always was, emotionless. I looked back up to Cole when he said, "I promise."

I nodded as he took my hand and led me to his truck. I paid one last glance toward the Dyami family and found them looking around the kitchen aimlessly, but all with the same expression, discontentment, because of me.

Chapter Twelve

Cole had me home in record time and with a good excuse for Emma when she started to yell at me, talking about my "irresponsible behavior."

"This is my fault, Miss Jasely," Cole had said smoothly. "I had forgotten about the project Adeline and I had due this Monday, and we needed to get it done. I knew she was grounded, but all of the materials were at my home." Emma had nodded, speechless. Most people reacted that way when Cole unleashed his breathtaking dark blue gaze.

"Well, if it was for school, then I guess it's okay. Just call me before you leave, Adeline," Emma had replied. Of course, our project had been due last week and we were already done. But Emma wouldn't remember that.

Cole turned to leave, but before he left, he pulled me into an embrace and whispered in my ear, "Keep your window unlocked tonight." I blushed at his words, but nodded without Emma taking notice. Cole then left, and I was alone with Emma and her continuous lecturing.

"What has gotten into you lately? You know to call me if you want to leave the house with someone! And what's this school project for anyway?" Emma asked while following me around the kitchen as I prepared dinner. I instantly stopped what I was doing as I thought up an excuse. I could hear her fold her arms across her chest. I could practically feel her questionable gaze burning a hole through the back of my head.

"Oh, it's for English," I replied lamely as I washed the peas. Emma was quiet for a time, thinking over my response.

"Whatever you say, Adeline," Emma rolled her eyes as she left the kitchen and walked toward her office.

I sighed when I knew she was out of hearing range. I didn't know how much more of this lying thing I could take. It wouldn't be long before Emma would see through it, and I would be dead for sure.

Physically, I was in my kitchen, safe as I prepared dinner. Mentally, I was back at the reservation with Cole, possibly in danger.

None of this made sense. Why would a tribe so old want me for my so-called power? It wasn't too hard to believe that Cole was Chosen. He always had an air of magic about him. He seemed too good to be human. An angel was my original thought; now he may possibly be a shape shifter, someone who could become an eagle.

It was especially hard to believe in all of this mythical talk when Cole himself didn't really believe it. He seemed absolutely positive that he was not Chosen, let alone the Delsin. But he did seem to believe in Jacy and that I was in danger. He must believe in it to an extent. If all of this really didn't exist then he wouldn't be so obsessed with protecting me. Maybe, just maybe, all of this talk of men who turn into eagles and rebellious tribe members did exist in my world. Maybe I was the heavenly being reborn.

The sound of the oven beeping and the smell of smoke hitting my nose brought me out of my thoughts and back to reality. I quickly turned the oven off and pulled out the almost burnt chicken. I began to set the table and pour drinks when Emma walked in.

"I smelled something burning. Is everything okay?" she asked, nose wrinkling.

"Everything's fine. I saved dinner," I continued to prepare the table for Henry and Emma.

"Oh okay," she said quietly, "Henry will be here in about ten minutes."

"Kay."

I heard the sound of her footsteps retreat to her office, and I sighed relieved. I was afraid she would continue to question what happened today, and I didn't think I could continue to make up excuses. She would catch on.

Just as Emma had said, Henry rang the doorbell ten minutes later and dinner began. I didn't eat much, just pushed the food around my plate while I tried to not look at Emma, Henry, and their continuous kissing and such. I was pretty sure that Emma was able to feed herself without Henry's help. So much for being Miss Independent.

"You feeling okay, darlin'?" Henry asked, his southern accent sounding even more irritating than usual.

"Yeah, I'm fine."

"Well, you sure don't look like it. Are you and that boy on the rocks, Hun?" he asked, laughing at his own personal joke. I looked up from my plate and glared at him from across the table.

"No. We're just friends."

"Sure, sure. You keep thinking that," he laughed before he stuffed his face with more chicken. What did Emma see in him?

"Don't you have a tractor to go fix or something?" I muttered under my breath.

Luckily, neither of them noticed my comment. They just continued to talk between themselves and that was fine with me. Finally, dinner was over, and I excused myself to my room for the remainder of the evening.

I fell onto my bed, too exhausted to take a shower. My mind was becoming hazy, and I could feel sleep approaching, but what

Cole said before he left made me shoot up from my comfortable position, causing a painful headache.

Keep your window unlocked tonight...

I walked to my window and unlatched it and let the cold wind brush against my face, swirling my hair around. The moon was full and shining brightly. There was hardly a cloud in the sky. I breathed deeply, trying to calm myself. Cole would be here soon and that was something to look forward to.

I walked back to my bed and lay down. It was becoming difficult to stay awake. I remembered falling asleep, hoping Cole would tap on my window like he had done the night before.

"Adeline," a smooth, silk-like voice whispered, "Adeline." I smiled in my sleep. I was sure I was dreaming.

"Cole…"

"Yeah, it's me. Are you awake?" he asked gently, his warm breath caressing my cheeks and eyelids.

"No." He chuckled at my answer.

"All right, sleep. You are safe. I won't leave, I promise."

"Okay," I yawned, my eyes still closed.

There were a few more moments of silence before I asked, "Cole?"

"Yes?"

"Are you a birdman?" I felt his body shake from beside the bed as he tried to control his laughter.

"Goodnight, Adeline."

"Answer the question," I demanded sleepily. I would at least get my answers in my dreams.

He sighed heavily, "Other people think so."

"What about what you think?"

My speech was becoming slurred, as I got closer to complete dreamless slumber.

"I'm not sure what I believe. I know something is changing. I can feel it. I'm just not sure if it is for good or bad." I sighed in my almost slumber.

"I'm sure you'll figure it out." I then fell into a dreamless sleep. The last thing I heard was Cole chuckle and the sound of my window closing.

*

It had been one week since I saw Enola with Chenoa. It had been one week since I saw anyone, other than Cole, from the Dyami family. I sat in my fourth period class, trying to listen to Mr. Jackson's explanation of the Industrial Revolution. I was having a hard time concentrating and I didn't have to look far to find the answer.

Cole had not been to school. His truck had not been waiting in my driveway as usual. Instead, there had been my yellow bus, waiting impatiently. I wasn't sure of what to make of his absence. I was definitely surprised and a little hurt. But I was sure that there was a reason for his absence. There had to be.

The rest of my classes went by, and I was still trying to figure out what could have kept Cole away. Was there something wrong at the reservation? Were Chenoa and Elsu and Paco okay? Was Cole okay?

It wasn't until I was half way home on my bus did the thought occur to me that Cole could be sick or in trouble. I glanced around the bus and found everyone minding his or her own business. Sasha and Brittany were gossiping, Joanne was flirting with a poor guy that clearly wasn't interested, Matt and his football buddies were laughing at the expense of a freshman, and I was sitting quietly, listening to my iPod and internally worrying about a boy that none of them cared about.

I quickly exited the bus when it came to my stop and ran to my door. Emma was home early and was busily working in her office by the sound of her fingers hitting the keys on her keyboard. I half ran into her office, my breath shagged.

"Can I borrow the Jeep?" I asked as I threw my bag to the floor. She finished the sentence she was on and turned in her chair to look at me.

"Why?"

"I need to visit someone," I replied hastily. I felt like I was running out of time.

"Is it Cole?" she asked, her left eyebrow arched.

I rolled my eyes, "Yeah."

"Isn't there a rule about no visitors?"

I hadn't thought of that, but Cole wouldn't mind. I knew he wouldn't.

"I can go. I promise." She sighed, her eyes scanning me.

"Fine," she agreed, "but be home before seven." I smiled as I ran to the kitchen to get the keys.

"Thanks, Em," I yelled as I ran out the door. I unlocked the door to the Jeep and jumped in. I drove out of the driveway and headed toward the Little Shell Reservation. It wasn't until I came to the "No Visitors" sign did I notice my hands shaking.

I took a deep breath as I drove down the road and looked for his house. I pulled to the side of the road when I found his beautiful home. I was happy to see his truck in the driveway. I jumped out of my Jeep and practically ran to the front door. I rang the doorbell and took another deep breath.

The door opened and I found myself face to face with an older version of Cole, Paco Dyami. He was staring at me, questions in his ancient, blue eyes.

"Can I help you?" he asked, folding his arms across his chest. He looked intimidating.

"Is Cole home?" I stuttered as I bit the inside of my lip. He shifted his weight from his right foot to his left. I gulped and looked into his eyes again.

"Nope. Just missed him."

I was taken aback. I knew he was there.

"But his truck," I replied, pointing to his truck in his driveway. "He's here."

"He and Elsu went out," he retorted, "in Elsu's truck." Cole and Elsu went out? As in they were hanging out? That was very strange.

"Oh," I replied dumbly, "okay. Thanks." I turned to walk away, when Paco stopped me.

"But you can wait for him in the kitchen if you would like. Chenoa should be home soon as well."

I turned around and nodded, "Okay. If you don't mind."

He led me into the kitchen and asked if I wanted anything, but I declined. I sat down at the large oak table. Paco sat in front of me, watching me warily.

"How are you, Adeline?" he asked, folding his hands on top of the table.

I gulped, "I'm fine. How are you?"

"I am well. Thank you."

It was obvious where Cole received his good manners. Although Paco said all the right, polite things, his voice did not echo it. It was cold and distant, the very opposite of Cole.

"There is something I wish to speak with you about, Adeline," he began. My pulse accelerated. This wasn't going to be good.

"Do you remember the day when you came to the reservation and heard the legend about the two tribes?" he asked, his face unreadable.

How could I forget? My life seemed to revolve around that legend.

"Yeah," I replied in a small voice.

"Well, there is more to it, if you would like to hear it," he said, instantly drawing me in.

"Of course," I responded excitedly. I was shocked that Paco would be the one to share secrets with me. I thought he wanted me as far away from his tribe as possible.

"Well, according to the legend, there's said to be men with strange talents throughout the tribe. They are also descendants of Chief Heluka. I'm sure you know by now that our family is part of the direct line of the great chief. It is said that men descended from his direct bloodline have inherited his spiritual ability to shape shift. You know that they are called the Chosen. Chenoa has explained that already. Instead of the Chosen being chosen by their eagle partners, they inherit their eagle partners from their ancestors. The Delsin would then inherit Onida, Heluka's eagle partner.

"In the legend that my father told me and his father told him, it says that the Chosen will arise against the rebels, those who are descendants of the original rebels who sided with Tama against Heluka. The legend also speaks of a great power that the two tribes are fighting over. The Chosen wish to banish the power, so that no more war will ensue. The rebels wish to harness it and cause more destruction. Do you know what that power is?"

I nodded my head numbly, "The heavenly being." My voice was barely audible.

He nodded, impressed, "Yes, the power is the reincarnation of the heavenly being. You know more than I gave you credit for."

He stood and walked toward the archway connecting the kitchen and living room. He turned to me, "Not to frighten you, but I think it would be best if you would stay away from the tribe and my family."

I was shocked. I didn't understand. Why would he tell me all of that and then tell me to stay away? Nothing was making sense. He walked away, out of sight. I heard the front door close and the sound of a car drive away down the road.

I sat at the large oak table, not really seeing or doing anything. Everything was sinking in. I had come here to check on Cole, and I received an ominous warning in return. The sound of a car pulling into the driveway and two car doors slamming shook me out of my hazy thoughts. The front door slammed open.

"I can't believe you! All this time you never once believed, and now you think you own the place!" someone yelled. It sounded like Elsu.

"This isn't my fault! I didn't ask for this!" I recognized that voice immediately, although it sounded much deeper and much more intimidating. The two Dyami boys walked in and stopped when they saw me.

"What are you doing here?" Elsu ordered, his tone demanding and certainly not welcoming.

"Elsu," Cole said, a new edge to his voice, "Not now. I'll handle this."

"Adeline," Cole spoke, his voice instantly gentle, "what are you doing here? Is everything okay?"

Elsu huffed and then ran upstairs, slamming his door once he made it to his room.

I nodded numbly, staring up at the boy who seemed to be changing before my very eyes.

"Cole?" I asked standing up. "Have you grown?" He was taller, much taller.

"And your hair, has it grown?" His hair was shaggier and longer. Something was happening that he wasn't telling me. Cole shifted his weight from one foot to the other, nervously.

"You didn't answer my question. What are you doing here?" he asked again, this time more severe. I was shocked. He had never used that tone with me before. It wasn't like him.

"I came to check on you," I replied in a small voice, "You haven't been to school and I was worried." His expression softened.

"I'm sorry I made you worry," he said, his voice finally softening. "I had some things to take care of. You didn't need to worry."

"I'm always going to worry, Cole. I care," I whispered, not completely sure on what I meant. I cared for him like a friend. That was it. His eyes fell to the ground. He was hiding something.

"Cole?"

"They're right," he smirked. "Why me?"

"Who's right Cole?" He looked to me, his expression pained.

"No one. Don't worry about it. I should get you home."

"That's okay. I drove here," I replied as he led me outside to the driveway. He walked me to Emma's Jeep and opened the door for me.

"Cole?" I asked as he shut my door.

"Yeah?" His eyes looked tired. His whole body looked weaker.

"Are you sure everything is okay? You look awful." He laughed causing my heart to jump immensely.

"Thanks, but really, I'm fine."

"You don't seem fine. You know that you can tell me anything, right?"

He sighed, "I know."

I looked into his deep blue orbs again, "Then why won't you?"

Cole tucked a stray hair behind my ear, replying, "Because I won't do that to you. You deserve to live a happy, normal life."

"That doesn't make sense. I'm the happiest when I am with you!" I exclaimed. I didn't like the way he was talking.

"Calm down. Everything's okay," he caressed my cheek in an attempt to calm me. It was working. My face melted into this palm. It was scorching, but the heat was welcomed.

"I care about you, Cole. I always will."

He gulped, his eyes holding something back.

"And I care about you, Adeline Connor Jasely," he choked, "More than you will ever know."

And I believed him. But there was more to his words than he was letting on. I drove home, fighting back the tears that were threatening to spill over. I had a horrible feeling that something terrible was going to happen, and there was nothing I could do to stop it.

The next week had flown by. Before I knew it, it was Friday, April the fourth. My birthday. Luckily for me, Friday was a teacher workday, which meant no school.

Although the week had gone by so fast, I did notice subtle, strange changes in Cole. Cole had returned to school the next day, but he was different. He seemed so preoccupied, like his mind was somewhere else. Whenever we talked, he seemed distant. He no longer brought up the reservation or the tribes or the legends. It was as if that weekend was a strange dream, and I was grateful. Maybe it was just a dream.

Another thing had changed. Chandler was gone. There were rumors about him, saying that Cole had scared him off at the dance. Truthfully, I was grateful. Maybe things were returning to normal.

Yet, every day, as the days grew closer to my birthday, a seed of inexplicable doubt and fear had rooted itself within me. It was the same feeling when watching a horror movie and being unable to save the protagonist. The only difference was that I was the stupid girl opening the dark closet and I couldn't save myself.

Some sort of knot was forming in the pit of my stomach, always making its way to my chest. The small tug in my chest still pulled, but more painfully. The small candle was burning down, flickering away. I tried to ignore the feeling, but it was there when I fell asleep and when I woke up. I never in my whole life wanted my birthday to begin and then end, so that this feeling would leave.

I woke up Friday morning to the smell of something burning. I shot up in my bed, but banged my head on my headboard.

"Ouch."

I rubbed my head as I ran to the kitchen to find the source of the burning.

"What's happening?" I asked sleepily.

"Oh, well good morning, sugar! How'd ya sleep?" Henry asked obnoxiously as he fanned the area above the oven, trying to make the smoke disappear.

"What are you doing here?" I demanded while searching for a clock.

"I'm here to make breakfast. You and Emma work too hard, so I came over to help ya out. Consider me your servant for the day," he replied happily as he continued to scramble the burnt eggs. My nose wrinkled at the smell and at the situation. I looked at the clock. It was nine thirty. Too early for Henry. I lazily walked back to my room to get ready for the day. I unsuccessfully tried to avoid Emma.

"Hey, birthday girl. Did you say hi to Henry?" she asked as she skipped from her room in her new, light blue dress.

"More or less. What's with the dress?" I asked, leaning against the wall yawning.

"Oh! Henry didn't tell you? He's taking me out for the day. Isn't that so sweet?" Emma asked while continuing to skip to the kitchen. "I hope you don't mind. I promise we will celebrate tonight and tomorrow!"

I rolled my eyes as I walked into my room. At least Henry was getting her mind off of me and my birthday surprise. I could only imagine what she had in store this year. I stumbled into my bathroom and took a shower. The hot water was able to wake me up to an extent, but I was still yawning as I dried my hair. I brushed my teeth and dressed. As I made my way to the kitchen, the phone rang.

"I got it, Hun!" Henry yelled as he picked up the phone. "Hello?"

I walked into the kitchen and poured myself some orange juice. Henry's cooking didn't seem very appetizing. Emma was trying to force it down, but I could tell that she was hiding some of it in her napkin.

"Oh sure! She's right here. One moment," Henry smiled widely. "It's for you, Adeline."

I almost choked on my juice. Who would call me? Henry handed me the phone with what looked like a sparkle in his eye.

"It's that boy."

My heart jumped, and I smiled, "Hello?"

I walked to my room for some privacy as I waited for a response.

"Happy Birthday," the deep voice replied.

My smile disappeared, "Chandler."

"Did you miss me?"

I gulped as adrenaline kicked in. I felt like he was so close. Apparently, my nightmare was real.

"What do you want?" I demanded, trying to sound forceful. Instead, my voice cracked. Not very intimidating.

He chuckled, "Why, you should know this by now. I want you." I closed my eyes, trying to calm myself.

"I'm going to hang up now."

"I'll be watching, Adeline. Don't ever forget that."

The line went dead, and I stood there, numbed by fear and the unknown. Cole was right. Something was changing and I was sure it was for the worse. I dropped the phone on my bed and slid to the floor. I held my knees to my chest and gently rocked myself. I didn't think I could handle all of this. Everything was happening so fast, and I was afraid. Afraid of what Chandler meant when he said he would be watching.

But I knew one thing that Chandler wouldn't have to worry about. I don't think I would ever forget that he would be watching. I could feel his eyes on me even in that moment. I took in a deep breath to try to control myself. The phone rang again, and I threw it across the room. It left a small dent on the cream colored wall.

"Adeline! Phone!" Emma yelled.

I slowly walked to the phone that was now lying helplessly on the floor next to my closet. I picked it up carefully.

"Hello?" I asked shakily.

"Hey Adeline. It's Cole. Are you okay?" Tears of relief filled my eyes. Even his voice made me feel safe.

"Yeah," I choked, "I'm fine."

"You don't sound fine. What happened?" He sounded so worried, so afraid, but still distant.

"Chandler called, and I just got scared. He said he would be watching me, always." There was silence on the other end.

"Stay where you are. I'm coming over."

Then the line was cut off, and I stood, completely relieved. But fearful once again because I could no longer hear Cole's reassuring voice. I walked into the kitchen, just in time to catch Henry and Emma leaving.

"Cole's coming over, okay?" I stated as I hung up the phone. Henry was helping Emma into her jacket.

"Um, sure. Be good," Emma said as she walked toward the front door.

"Oh, and happy birthday!" Henry yelled before he shut the door behind himself. I had actually forgotten my birthday for a few moments. I wondered why Cole hadn't said anything.

Several minutes passed before I heard someone knock on the door furiously. I rushed to the door.

"Cole," I sighed, comforted.

"Adeline," he said with equal passion as he enveloped me into one of his warming embraces. His heart was beating erratically like mine.

"Are you okay?" he asked into my hair.

I nodded against his chest, unable to say anything. I was afraid that my voice would give me away. He pulled away to close the door. I stayed still as he looked through the window in the living room and then while he closed the curtains. He turned back to face me and tried to force a smile. I could tell something was wrong. He was different. His body language was very serious and remote.

"What's going on, Cole?"

"It seems that things are changing, Adeline."

"What sort of things?" He sighed as he ran his hand through his hair. It had grown again since I last saw him.

"I can't explain it."

"Can't or won't?" I asked, folding my arms over my chest.

"Both," he replied, eyes narrowed.

"Why?"

"Because it's not safe for you."

"Wake up, Cole! I'm already in danger! I think it would help if I knew what I was up against." Cole shook his head and began pacing the room.

"I'm trying to do what's best for you."

"What's best for me is to tell me what's happening."

"No, Adeline!" he bellowed vigorously.

I stared at him, wide eyed. He'd never been that harsh before. He looked back at me, eyes filled with guilt. I felt a huge knot in my stomach. The same feeling that I had been experiencing this whole week was back.

"Adeline, I'm going to do what's best for you." I shook my head, afraid of where he was going with his words.

"No…"

"I'm leaving with my family to go to North Dakota."

"And you'll be back," I interrupted, "You'll come back."

He lifted his head to look me in the eye. His eyes were colder than they were before. He seemed even more distant than he had ever been.

"We're not coming back, Adeline."

My heart was pounding. Tears hit the back of my eyes, blurring my vision. My stomach fell to my feet.

"What about the tribe and school…and me?" I asked as silent tears began to fall down my cheeks. My throat was burning, and I felt dizzy.

"You'll be safer this way. The other tribe will follow us. They have to protect their homeland," he smirked. He looked more like Elsu than the Cole I knew.

"No," I shook my head, "you promised." He took one step toward me.

"You can't just leave!" I almost screamed. "This soon. You just got here and I need you…"

"You don't need me. I only cause you more trouble." His face was emotionless, just like Paco. Nothing like my Cole. I licked my lips, trying to find my voice.

"What about the reservation?"

"The other elders will protect it."

"What caused this? Why are you leaving now?" he owed me that much.

He sighed, "Things have changed. I understand the situation better now."

I looked him over. His hair was longer and shaggier than usual. His copper skin seemed darker and his blue eyes were cold. He wasn't my Cole anymore.

"What did I do?" I whispered, tears flowing freely.

He swallowed and closed his eyes. He began to shake, but quickly recovered.

"I'm not the same anymore."

I gulped afraid that my nausea would become apparent.

"And that is?"

"It's better that I leave you. Better for me and better for you. We both win." I closed my eyes and tried to steady my breathing.

"You don't want to be with me. You don't want to be my friend." It wasn't a question. It was fact.

"That's right."

It was then that I understood. I knew why I had been feeling so anxious about my birthday. A part of me knew that this would happen, and I was trying to prepare myself. But nothing could have prepared me for this hurt. He seemed so confident, so sure. I knew he was serious and content with leaving. He wasn't at all bothered by never seeing me again. I only wished that I could feel the same as he did.

"If that's what you want."

"It is," he replied quickly.

I opened my eyes to look at him. Tears blurred his face, but he was still beautiful, like a watercolor painting. I knew this would happen. Why would someone like him, so stunning, so perfect, want to be my friend?

"Okay," I said weakly. "I won't keep you."

I knew he didn't need nor want my approval, but I gave it anyway. He walked toward the door, his scent brushing against me. I ached for him. He walked out the door, and in an attempt to save him and a part of me, I ran after him. It was pouring rain.

I stopped when I saw his truck already on the road. I watched helplessly as his red taillights disappeared. I fell to my knees, letting the rain soak me. I wished that I could melt away with it. I felt like my world had shattered in a matter of minutes. Everything that I ever cared about just drove away, and I did nothing to stop it. It was sort of ironic. On the day of my birth, a part of me, the most important and crucial part of my existence, had died.

ALLISON BLANCHARD

PART II

"Love does not begin and end the way we seem to think it does. Love is a battle, love is a war; love is a growing up."

~ *James A. Baldwin*

ALLISON BLANCHARD

Chapter Thirteen

Drip, drop. Drip, drop.

My face was wet with tears and rain as I sat on the cold cement. I merely sat there in total exhaustion. Emotional, physical, and mental exhaustion. I slowly stood, numb and cold. I somehow managed to make it to my bedroom. I fell to my knees again, clutching my stomach as the numb and cold turned to excruciating pain.

The pain shot through my body in waves and slowly started to devour me. Each time I felt my blood pulse through my veins, another fire-like ache would throb through my body, leaving me breathless.

"No…" I mumbled to myself as a fresh wave of tears made an appearance. My throat burned from breathing in the cold air. I brought my knees to my chest to try to warm myself, or to keep myself from falling apart. I began to sob louder and harder to the point that I could no longer breathe. I wanted something to end the pain, anything.

I saw bright headlights pull into the driveway through my window. A flicker of hope burned in my heart, but was easily extinguished when I saw the two people leave the car.

I heard the door open and the sound of footsteps come to my door. I was still breathing heavily, trying to calm myself. But the hole in my chest was raw, gaping, bleeding.

"Emma! I think something is wrong with Adeline!" Henry yelled as he stopped at my door. Emma quickly ran into my room, getting on her knees in front of me. My sobbing continued no matter how hard I tried to stop it.

"What's happened, Addie? What's wrong?" Emma asked, violet-hazel eyes panicked. My sobs continued as I tried to choke out a response.

"He…I…. gone…never…coming…"

"Who?" Emma asked as Henry left the room quickly.

I stared at Emma, not really seeing. Henry entered the room again, placing a blanket around me. My sobs settled a bit, and I tried to focus on breathing.

"Who?" someone asked again. The voices were becoming fuzzy. My vision was blacking out.

"Cole. He's never coming back," I whispered as I fell into my personal darkness.

*

I woke up with a numbing sort of feeling. My breathing was even and my heart was beating, but it didn't feel right. Something wasn't right. I could feel my blood pulse through my veins. Physically, I was sound. Mentally and emotionally, I was broken. I kept my eyes closed, hoping I would drift away. I was safe when I was unconscious; the pain was easily numbed then. I heard the sound of voices. Emma and Henry.

"I can't believe this! I knew he was no good! She should have listened to me!"

"Now, darlin', we don't know if he really meant to hurt her. We'll have to wait until she wakes up to tell us more."

"I want to kill him!"

I flinched at the harshness of her words. It took me a moment to realize whom they were talking about. My breathing became shallow and my head throbbed. I squeezed my knees to my chest, trying to stop the achy, hollow feeling in my chest. I faintly heard the sound of footsteps coming toward me.

"Adeline?" Emma asked as she brushed the fresh tears from my cheeks. I opened my eyes and found Emma closer than I thought. She didn't seem angry like I thought she would be. She was sad too. I embraced her roughly and she held me close.

"Oh it's okay, baby. I'm here now," she whispered into my hair. I continued to sob into her light blue dress for a long time, and she never once tried to make me move. For that, I was grateful. When my tears had finally dried, Emma mumbled something to Henry that I couldn't understand. Suddenly, another wave of pain knocked the breath out of me, and I desperately tried to get air back into my lungs.

"I think she's having an asthma attack," Henry whispered to Emma as he leaned against my doorframe. Emma sat on the edge of my bed and began to rub my back gently.

"She'll be okay."

My breathing gradually slowed and then Emma and Henry quietly left the room. To make a phone call I assumed. Emma's words echoed in my head.

She'll be okay...

She was wrong. I would never be the same ever again. I buried my head into my pillow and tried to muffle my sobs. It was unsuccessful. I tried to remember what I had done to cause myself this pain. Maybe luck or fate decided that I had enough good in my life. Something bad needed to happen, but this was the absolute worst thing. I fell asleep, crying to myself and trying to mend the broken pieces of my heart. I didn't think they would heal anytime soon, or ever.

*

Weeks had passed and I remained the same. The pain was still strong and potent, but it numbed itself during school and work, at least enough to keep me from falling apart in front of people. As for my birthday surprise, and a way to keep my mind busy, Emma had gotten me a job at the *Great Falls Tribune*. Just something after school. I mostly made coffee and ran errands. It was good for a while, but when I went home and tried to sleep, the dull ache in the pit of my stomach would spread throughout my whole body. I gently rocked myself every night, trying to keep Emma from hearing my cries.

"What about you, Joanne? Who are you taking to prom?" Sasha giggled as she flipped her hair and sat down.

"Oh, Evan is taking me! He asked me yesterday," Joanne gushed.

"Really? You two will make such a cute couple," Sasha replied while taking out her makeup mirror.

Their voices soon faded away. I wasn't listening anymore and I no longer tried to. The last thing I needed on my mind was prom. I continued to skim over the English assignment, not really absorbing the words. I didn't have the heart to.

"So, who are you taking to the prom, Adeline?" Brittany questioned as she turned in her desk to face me.

The whole class became silent and glanced back at me. I thought they forgot I existed.

I looked up to Brittany's smirk and tried to ignore the splitting pain that was shooting from my chest to every other part of my body.

"No one," I whispered, "I'm not going."

"Isn't it funny how not even three weeks ago, you had both Cole and Chandler chasing after you and now no one?" Brittany exclaimed, watching me carefully to see if I would break. I breathed in sharply. Had it really been three weeks? It felt like three years.

I glared at her, "Hilarious." Soon enough, the bell rang and everyone scattered. I slowly walked to my locker.

"Hey, Adeline!" Lily greeted as she met me at my locker. I slowly pulled my books out, trying to keep my voice even.

"Hey."

"How are you today?" she asked gently. I closed my locker and walked with her to English.

"All right."

It was quite obvious that I wasn't "all right", but it was the only thing I could say. No one really wanted to know how I was doing. Lily seemed to understand my words, but she never asked for more.

We sat down in our usual seats, and I waited for class to start. It was only then when people would stop whispering, at least for a while. The bell rang and Ms. Cook began her lesson.

"Take your notebooks out. We will begin our discussion on *Jane Eyre*. I trust that you all did your assigned reading."

The class moaned in unison. I stayed silent, hoping this discussion would not include me. Not because I didn't do the assignment, but because of my current condition. What Brittany had said stung, and I was afraid that if I talked, I would fall to pieces in front of everyone.

"Now, Mr. Danner, what happens after Jane leaves Mr. Rochester?" Ms. Cook asked, catching an off-guard Josh Danner. I thought I saw him texting on his cell phone. He quickly put it away, discretely, and looked up to Ms. Cook.

"Um, she cries…and stuff," he answered slowly. The class erupted into giggles and snickers and Josh smiled widely at Ms. Cook. Apparently, she didn't catch the joke.

"Could you be more specific? What do you think is the reason behind her misery and sadness? Did she place this heartache on herself?" Ms. Cook went on.

Josh stammered, "Well, she left him because he was married to a crazy lady, right?"

Ms. Cook rolled her eyes. "Yes, Mr. Danner. Could you explain that for us?"

"So, Jane finds out and then leaves because she doesn't want to be his mistress, but she probably should have stayed cause now she's homeless and stuff."

I rolled my eyes this time. Was it really possible for someone to be that incompetent?

"Anyone else have more to add to that?" Ms. Cook asked. It seemed that her class wasn't as excited about the lesson plan as she had been.

I heard someone answer Ms. Cook's question, but I was too deep in thought to notice. My eyes were watching the window. The clouds were gray, hiding the sun. I had a feeling that it was going to rain.

The raw, gaping hole in my chest stung slightly at today's topic. I only knew too well the heartache Jane was experiencing. Of course, I had already read the book and knew she had a happy ending - her very own happily ever after. Where was mine? What did I do to deserve this misery, this hell?

I looked back out the window, trying to change the direction of my thoughts. What I noticed next almost made me fall out of my seat. There was an eagle. The same eagle I had seen from the reservation over a month ago. It was flying over the school parking lot, the same way it had when I was at the reservation. It screamed and its massive body continued to fly over the school. I gulped as my pulse sped up.

We already have Jacy watching over your house when Cole can't be there.

A flicker of hope ignited in my chest and I tried to keep my breathing even. I was so consumed with watching what could be Jacy, a shape shifter, that I didn't even hear the bell ring.

"Hello! Adeline? You there?" Lily asked, waving a hand in front of my face.

"I've got to go," I paid one last glance at the eagle before rushing out of the room and toward the parking lot.

"Where are you going? We have French!" Lily called following me closely.

"Just say I felt sick and had to go home. I'll talk to you later," I dismissed as I ran out the door and into the parking lot. Lily didn't follow, but I had a feeling that I would have a lot to explain when I talked to her next.

I looked up to the sky, searching for the eagle. I almost missed him. He was flying down the road and, from what I could tell, back to the reservation. I ran down the highway, trying to keep up with the eagle. Maybe he would lead me back to...

I stopped in my tracks and let my breathing slow to its normal pace. What was I doing? He had made it very clear that he wanted nothing to do with me. I was too much trouble. How could I run back to the reservation? He wouldn't even be there. I sighed as I let the pain that I had briefly numbed overwhelm me. The aching was much stronger this time and that was my own fault.

The sky began to rain, just like the first day the throbbing had consumed me. I decided to walk home and deal with Emma when I got there. She would not be happy with my leaving school and missing work. The rain was cold, soaking through my clothes to my skin. I continued to shiver as I walked home, alone.

Maybe I had imagined the eagle, something my subconscious was trying to bring to life.

I unlocked the door to my house and I dropped my bag to the floor. I made my way to my room, finally falling onto my bed and burying my head into my pillow. I wasn't sure how long I lay there, wishing I would disappear, but soon enough, I heard Emma drive up into the driveway. I looked my digital clock. It was only half past noon.

She probably came for lunch.

"Adeline?" I heard her ask as she walked into the house. She must have seen my bag.

"Yeah?" my voice cracked. I heard her footsteps hurry to my room.

"Oh, Adeline," she whispered as she sat on the side of my bed.

I looked up to her face and saw the disappointment and sadness.

"I didn't feel good, so I came home," I replied, trying to keep my voice even. I failed.

"Okay."

I laid my head back on my pillow and waited for her to leave. Emma finally stood and walked out the door, closing it quietly. I squeezed my eyes, trying to stop the tears. It was useless. I turned over onto my back and stared at my ceiling. The tears were sliding down my cheeks onto my pillow and hair.

I heard something screech and I shot up in my bed. I ran to my window and saw something that almost caused me to pass out cold. Outside my house, sitting perched on the only tree in my backyard was an eagle. He was even more massive than I thought. His cold, brown, humanlike eyes were staring right at me.

It was then that I understood. Jacy, a shape shifting eagle, was watching me and possibly trying to warn me.

Chapter Fourteen

"Adeline, did you hear me?"

I looked up from my half eaten dinner. "What?"

My mind was somewhere else. More specifically, with the eagle that was sitting in my back yard.

"I said that Aunt Cassie is coming tomorrow and is staying here while I am on my business trip," Emma repeated while taking another bite.

"What business trip?" I asked, surprised. Wouldn't she have told me before now?

"The one I have been talking about for a week. Goodness, Adeline, where have you been?" Emma sighed while continuing her dinner.

That was a good question. I'm pretty sure I was in my own personal hell.

"When will Aunt Cassie arrive?"

I didn't remember much about Aunt Cassie. I only knew that she helped take care of Emma and me when our parents died. Emma was only fifteen, but when she turned eighteen, she took me and moved out. I remembered that Aunt Cassie wasn't too thrilled with Emma's decisions.

"She'll be here when you get home from school," Emma replied as she placed her plate in the dishwasher.

"Oh, okay."

"It'll only be a few weeks, Adeline. You won't even have time to miss me," she smiled while walking out the kitchen toward her room. I nodded while taking my plate to the sink. I walked to my room and fell onto my bed.

All that had happened had left me exhausted. Even though my body craved sleep, I walked to my window, pulling my curtains back. He was still there. The massive eagle was still perched on the tree, human-like eyes staring at my window.

If the legends and myths were true and there really was a hidden war going on, then there was a very strong chance that I was somehow the heavenly being, or could possibly be mistaken for her. It was also true that I was in danger, no matter who left. I went to bed, understanding a bit more due to the presence outside my window. Whether I liked it or not, I was in danger and the way I saw it, it was up to me to keep myself out of it.

The next day went by without trouble. When I woke up and went to my window, there was no eagle perched on my tree. Part of me thought I had dreamed it, but when lunch came around, I saw the same eagle, Jacy, flying over the school parking lot. It was sort of comforting, but painful at the same time. A strange mixture of emotions, but I knew that I would take the slight comfort over the pain any day.

When I saw Jacy, then I knew that *he* was still around, alive somewhere. I knew that he wasn't just a figment of my imagination, but a real person that affected my life. And no matter how he affected it, good or bad, I never once regretted it.

When I arrived home, I remembered what Emma had said about Aunt Cassie being there when I came home from school. I mentally prepared myself for the worst, yet nothing could have prepared me for what I found when I walked into my kitchen. There was no brunette, gray-streaked fifty-year-old woman like I had been expecting. No baggy, ill-fitting jogging suit and tennis shoes or wrinkles hidden beneath large glasses. No glares of disproval of my older sister's life choices.

Instead, there was a beautiful blonde with piercing blue eyes and creamy pale skin. She couldn't have been any older than forty, at most. She looked like a model for high fashion magazines with her designer clothes.

"Um, who are you?" I asked as I stood in the doorframe of my kitchen. She was preparing spaghetti dinner. She quickly wiped her hands on her apron, smiling as she took me in.

"Oh, you must be Adeline! Your Aunt Cassie couldn't make it. Her husband, your Uncle Tony, was sick so she sent me. My name is Alexia Hamilton." She shook my hand. It was warm and a little clammy. Maybe she was just as nervous as me.

"Hello, Miss Hamilton," I greeted unsure of what else to say.

"Oh, please call me Alexia," she insisted as she continued to prepare her salad. "I hope you like spaghetti and salad." I took my jacket off and nodded as I went to place my bag in my room.

Dinner was silent, but Alexia continually tried to keep the conversation going. She had told me that she was a friend of Aunt Cassie's for a long time. I felt guilty for not remembering her, but she never questioned me. I was surprised to find out that Alexia was an archeologist. She found and studied Native American artifacts throughout the Midwest. She immediately changed the subject when I asked if she had been to the reservation down the road. I was surprised that I even mentioned it without really thinking about it, like it was natural to talk about it.

"So, I hear that you have a job," she spoke awkwardly, taking a roll and dipping it in her spaghetti sauce.

"Yeah, it's only Mondays, Wednesdays, and Fridays," I replied quietly, still surprised that she changed the subject so quickly.

"Sounds fun. Isn't Emma on a business trip?"

"Yeah, she has a story to cover in Mississippi. You know, with all the flooding and stuff," I replied trying to sound polite. I was never good with people I didn't know very well.

"I see."

After a while I excused myself to my room and retreated happily. I did my homework and began to get ready for bed. I felt accomplished. The numbing and the pain hadn't bothered me all day. Maybe I was staring to turn a corner.

My accomplished feeling faded away faster than I could blink. Once my head hit the pillow, the pain came in waves like it had every night before. The throbbing surged through my body, starting in my head and making its way to my chest. Tears painfully hit the back of my eyes and I had to muffle my sobs in my pillow. Apparently, no one had told Alexia about my condition. There was a light knock on my door, followed by Alexia's concerned voice.

"Adeline? Are you all right?"

I heard the door crack open and felt the light from the hall hit my eyes. She was taken aback by my tears, but carefully made her way over to my bed. She sat on the edge and pulled my hair out of my face.

"Adeline?"

"I'm fine," I snapped. I didn't need people staring at me like I was crazy.

"That's a lie."

She surprised me. She didn't seem like the type of person that would try to talk something like this out.

"Well, you don't need to worry about it."

"But I do. Are you going to tell me?" I could tell by her tone that she wasn't going to leave until I told her something. I sat up in my bed reluctantly.

"I...I'm just going through a tough time right now," I whispered hesitantly. I had never talked about any of this. Not even with Emma.

"What happened to cause you this much hurt? I heard you whispering someone's name when I came in. Cole, was it?"

Even the sound of his name caused a tight tug in my chest. I had been very careful to never speak or think his name. I hadn't realized that I was whispering it.

"Yeah."

"What happened?"

"I don't want to talk about it."

"It will help, I promise."

I glanced over to her and found honest concern in her pale blue eyes.

I sighed, "He left."

"Why?"

"I'm not exactly sure. To get away from me I suppose," I sniffled. The tears slowed their pace, but didn't completely stop. The sharp pain in my chest was still throbbing with every beat.

"I highly doubt that. Who would want to leave you?"

"He would."

She sighed and looked down to the floor. She tilted her head and her eyes widened. Alexia bent down and grabbed something from under my bed. I breathed in sharply. She was holding his jacket, the one he gave me after the campfire ceremony. The night everything changed.

She folded it in her lap, "This is his, right?"

I nodded. I was holding my breath trying to keep myself from falling apart. Alexia surprised me by wrapping it around me.

"There," she said while patting my back. "Now you will feel closer to him."

All the emotion and heartbreak that I had been holding in for the past three weeks finally burst through my wall. A wall I had been so careful in building. I broke down in the arms of my Aunt Cassie's friend, a complete stranger. The tears came in strong waves, never ceasing. I never knew I could cry this hard and long.

She continually hummed a soothing song and held me close. I finally felt closer to him, something I hadn't felt in a long time. Even though the pain was terrible, it felt nice to feel so close to him, like he was the one holding me. The last thing I remembered was Alexia's humming, the smell of Cole's jacket, and my head hitting the pillow.

*

The next day I woke to the smell of pancakes and coffee. I stumbled into the kitchen and found Alexia fixing breakfast.

"Good morning! How'd you sleep?" she asked cheerfully.

I sat down at the kitchen table, still disoriented. "Fine. What about you?"

"Wonderfully. That mattress is so soft."

The meal went by without a problem. Thankfully, Alexia didn't mention anything about last night or Cole for the remainder of the morning. It became easier to talk to her too. Conversation was no longer forced, but welcomed. She wasn't the kind of person that wanted to talk to ease her own curiosity, but she truly wanted me to feel better and more comfortable. She reminded me of a mother. I wondered if she had any children, but when I asked, she froze up.

"Oh, children. Well, I had one once, but I miscarried," she replied quickly, looking everywhere, but at me.

"Oh, I'm sorry," I mumbled in response, dropping the subject.

Instead of taking the bus, Alexia offered to take me in her rental car, and I gratefully took her up on the offer. Usually, I would prefer to ride the bus only because I could drown in my music. But being with Alexia numbed the pain, at least for a while.

It wasn't until I was in homeroom that I noticed I had taken Cole's jacket with me. It was in my school bag. I wasn't sure if I had put it there or if Alexia had. My heart stopped when my eyes fell on it. I was waiting for the empty hollow feeling to overtake me, but nothing happened. I carefully took it out of my bag and laid it on my lap. No one was looking my way, and I was thankful. I didn't know how I would be able to explain it.

It was light brown and soft to the touch. There was fleece on the inside and the arms were amazingly long. I smiled at the small hole in the sleeve. The jacket even smelled like him. I took a deep breath and placed the jacket back in my bag. I didn't want anyone to see it and question me. I didn't think I could handle that today.

Lunch came soon enough and with it, questions from Lily. I was walking to my usual seat in the corner with Lily not far behind.

"What happened the other day?" Lily demanded.

I sat in my chair and took another deep breath.

"I thought I saw someone. Sorry, it won't happen again."

"Who, Adeline?

"No one. Don't worry about it."

"Was it Cole? I swear, Adeline, I know you, like, loved him, but you seriously need to move on. There are more important things," Lily muttered coldly before walking to her table where Eric was waiting.

My mouth fell open and the sharp pain in my chest came back. I looked down to my tray and tried to keep myself from crying. I would not cry in front of these people. Maybe the only reason Lily wanted to be my friend was because of him and the popularity he had. I shouldn't be too surprised. Lily had appearances to keep up. Besides, she had left me once before. It wasn't too hard for her to do it again.

I gulped and tried to stop the stinging behind my eyes. It was becoming difficult to control myself. I glanced out the window and found that it was raining. Thunder erupted, but I didn't really hear it. My eyes were fixed on the migration of eagles in the sky. I counted nine in all. I also saw a familiar eagle with them. Jacy.

My mind was going a mile a second. Pieces of a puzzle that I had been trying to solve were suddenly connecting together. The leader of the huge migration of eagles was pure black with lines of lighter brown and white swirling from the head to the tail. They were too far away for me to catch a glimpse of their eyes. The one thing that all of them had in common was their size. All of them were massive, too large to be the regular eagles someone would see on the *Discovery Channel* or in *National Geographic*. These weren't ordinary birds.

I watched in awe, completely unaware of anyone else in the cafeteria. I was too busy watching the huge flock and their flight pattern. They were so in tune with one another, completely absorbed in each other's actions. They all flew over the school for about ten more minutes then suddenly flew away. It was like they disappeared into the sky.

The rest of the day went by in a haze. I wasn't completely aware of what was going on around me. The only thing I was paying attention to was the sky and the things in it.

I didn't even realize I was in Alexia's car until she said something.

"Adeline? How was school?"

"Huh?"

"Are you all right, honey? You seem distracted."

"I'm fine. I'm just stressed," I replied, finally tearing my eyes from the window.

"Are you sure you can go to work today?" Alexia asked as she pulled into the parking lot of the *Great Falls Tribune* office.

"Yeah, and don't worry about dinner. I'll cook tonight," I replied as I got out of the car.

"If you're sure?"

"Yeah. I'm sure."

"Well okay. I'll pick you up around six."

"Sounds good," I said as I shut the car door and ran inside the building.

"Hello, Adeline," Mrs. Farmer, the secretary, greeted unenthusiastically as I walked through the door. The office was just as I last saw it. Gloomy and busy.

"Hey, Mrs. Farmer. Need anything?" I asked while hanging my raincoat on the hook beside the door.

"Some coffee would be lovely," she replied while continuing to type.

I walked to the small lounge area where the coffee maker sat. I knew the coffee would be old, but I didn't have time to make a new pot. I had some research to do. I quickly poured Mrs. Farmer's cup, added her sugar and cream, and hastily stirred it. I carefully placed it on her desk as she was finishing a phone conversation.

"Thanks, Adeline," she whispered while she placed her hand on the phone's speaker. "That's it for now. I'll call you if I need anything else."

I walked to Emma's office and sat at her desk. No one took much notice. They were too busy getting stories in for tomorrow's issue. I turned the computer on and impatiently waited it for it to boot up. I clicked on the search engine and typed in "eagles." A lot of ads for zoo tickets and stuffed animals popped up, but I soon found what I was looking for.

I skimmed the page and found out that the flock that I had seen today was very unusual. Not only in individual size, but also in flock size. Eagles usually traveled alone for hunting purposes and only came together to mate. That would usually only be two eagles.

Also, the color of their feathers was unheard of as well. There had never been reports of solid black eagles, and if there were, they were very rare and in a place more exotic. Not in Great Falls, Montana.

I sat back in my chair and stared at the computer screen. Maybe I had just imagined what I had seen. That was unlikely, but still a possibility. I then typed in "Little Shell legends." I had done this once before, but this time was different. I now had more of a purpose. Last time was for curiosity's sake. Now it was for information that I needed.

Once again, there was not much useful information, nothing about the legend of the split or the Chosen. I again felt like I had dreamed everything that had happened. Maybe there was no legend and no mystical creatures flying around.

Part of me felt that way, but the other part knew that was wrong. I was tired of doubting and not knowing enough. I needed more information and there was only one person that I knew who could give it to me—Enola.

*

Alexia picked me up around six, and I had dinner on the table by seven. I was not completely sure of what I had made. I wasn't really paying attention.

"The dinner is really good, Adeline," Alexia said while taking another sip of her water.

"Thanks." My mind was a good fifteen to twenty miles away, in a small cabin hidden in the woods.

"So how was work?" Alexia asked, trying to gain my attention again.

"It was okay. I just made copies of faxes and got coffee," I replied quietly, my eyes still glued to the window.

"Are you all right, Adeline? You still seem distracted. Is there anything you want to talk about?"

I thought for a moment. Would Alexia understand my situation? She did have experience with Native American legends.

"Alexia, have you ever had trouble believing something? All the evidence pointed to something, but what if that something was hard to believe?" I glanced up from my plate to look into her eyes. I wondered if she thought I had lost my mind.

"It depends on what that something is. If it feels right and the evidence seems to be correct, then I suppose it would be believable," she replied honestly.

"Okay, thanks," I stood and placed my plate in the dishwasher.

"Adeline?" she asked just as I was about to walk to my room.

"Yeah?"

"Is there anything else you need to tell me?"

I could see the real concern in her eyes, but what could I tell her? Yeah, well, I think I may be in danger with some shape-shifting eagles that may want my so-called power. You know, the usual teen drama.

"No," I replied quietly before escaping to my room.

The next week, I spent most of my time in the library reading anything and everything about eagles and any other bird, from parrots to falcons. I wanted to know anything that could possibly help me. I studied things from behavior to hunting styles. If I knew what I was up against, then I had a better chance of protecting myself.

The next week was almost enjoyable. Alexia was the perfect person to talk to. Of course I didn't tell her what was really going on. If this war really was occurring then I needed less people involved.

Alexia was also the kind of person that didn't try to get into other people's business. She left me to my room and my "studies" and never questioned me. She also made the pain disappear for a while. But obviously when I went to bed, that was a different story. Just because the pain and fear left me alone when I was conscious, that didn't mean I was free in my sleep.

Every night for the past week, I would have the same dream. More like a dream gone wrong. It always started the same. I was in a vacant field, no trees or roads; only dead grass that came up to my hip. I would always run around, looking for him. I would continue to call his name, hoping he would appear soon. After about the twentieth time I called, he would appear behind me, his warm breath causing the skin on my neck to rise.

"Adeline. I missed you."

I would whip around and look up to find deep blue eyes staring at me. He would hold his arms out to me and I would gladly fall into them. He would hold me for a long moment, continually whispering sweet nothings in my ear. Then, just as his head would lean into mine, like he was going to kiss me, Jacy would come screeching and flying over us. Trouble was near. Cole's handsome, angel-like face would fall into a frown and his eyes would reflect anger and sadness. Just before I would wake screaming, Chandler and a group of other Native Americans, who I assumed were of the rebel tribe, would surround us.

"It's time," Chandler would whisper, eyes on me.

The dream would always leave me with an empty feeling in my chest. It was like I found something that I had been desperately looking for and then had it ripped away from me. I would sit in my bed, trying to gain control of my sobbing and breathing again. The nightmare usually woke me around three and I stayed awake until it was time for school.

It was Monday, and as usual, the nightmare woke me around three and I sat in my bed, trying to gain control of my thoughts. For the past week, Jacy followed me home and always sit perched on my tree while I slept. I found this out when I would check my window at three in the morning. I had wondered if the neighbors had seen him yet.

I dressed around seven and ate breakfast with Alexia ten minutes later. I had been meaning to ask her if I could borrow her car to visit a friend. I had tried several times, but always chickened out. I knew she would ask where this friend was, and I would either have to lie or tell the truth, telling her I was going to the reservation. I'm sure she knew about the "No Visitors" rule and would question me about it.

"So, Alexia, I was wondering, is there any possible way I could borrow your car to visit a friend?" I asked into my cereal bowl.

"I guess so," Alexia said, surprising me while taking a seat in the chair across from me. "Where is this friend?"

"Oh, well. She lives outside of town," I stuttered.

"Where?"

"Uh, about fifteen miles into the Little Shell Reservation," I mumbled, hoping for the best. Alexia's face fell and her eyes widened.

"Why would you go back there?"

She was referring to what I was going through. I had told her little things about him; like that he lived on the reservation.

"To visit my friend," I replied, trying to sound innocent. She shook her head, but didn't directly say no.

"I don't know, Adeline."

"I promise I'll be home before curfew. I already have the day off from work. I just really need to see her today," I pleaded.

Alexia sighed while looking at me. "Fine, just be home by ten, okay?"

I jumped out of the chair happily and gave Alexia a hug. "Thank you so much!"

Alexia seemed shocked, like myself, at my outburst of emotion. I hadn't really been very excited for the past few weeks. She returned the embrace and then took me to school, a smile lingering on her lips.

"I'll pick you up from school and you can just take me back to the house," Alexia said before I got out of the car to get to class.

"Okay," I replied as I opened the door.

I watched as Alexia drove away, but soon hurried to the library. Luckily, I was able to go to the school library during homeroom and lunch to conduct my research. I logged onto the school's computer and continued my research on birds. I read articles ranging from birds in zoos, to the wild, to household pets. Every time, I came to the same conclusion. No one else in the entire world had ever heard of humans shape shifting into birds. I truly felt like an idiot.

Soon the bell rang and I went to my normal classes, still convinced that I would lose my mind trying to figure everything out. I hoped that Enola would be able to answer my questions. School seemed to move by slower than any other day. But soon enough, the final bell rang and I was free to drive Alexia home and then make my way to the reservation.

I drove extra slowly and carefully, making sure that I wouldn't fall apart at the site of the reservation sign. Hopefully, I wouldn't even notice it. I continued to drive until I came to the turn in the road. About five more minutes past, and I came to the dreaded sign. I held my breath as I passed the welcome sign along with the "No Visitors Allowed" sign posted next to it.

I drove down the road and involuntarily stopped in the street. I put the car in park, but didn't look to my right. I already knew what I would find, so what was the point? Was my subconscious trying to kill me? I glanced to the right and exhaled.

There it was. The red brick house with the two large bay windows and the large oak tree with the tire swing. It looked about the same since the last time I saw it.

It didn't look like anyone was home, but it didn't look vacant either. Maybe they had come home? I immediately dismissed the silly notion. There was no way they came back.

I threw the car in drive and sped down the road, as fast as I could to get away from that house.

I continued to drive until I came to the old dirt road to the right. There was nothing but woods and the sky began to drizzle; yet the sun was still visible. The ride to this point took much longer than I imagined it would. I guess I wasn't that fast of a driver. I turned onto the road and followed it until I came to the small cabin hidden in the woods.

The cabin looked the same. The wood was the same dark color and the flower boxes were still hung below the small windows. I did notice smoke coming from the chimney. So she hadn't left. Part of me was thrilled she was still here and the other part was terrified.

I pulled up to the side of the house and parked. I slowly walked toward the porch. I stood in front of the door, not moving. Once I knocked on this door, everything would change; but it was too late for that anyway. Now, I was about to learn everything and there was nothing, and no one, holding me back.

Just as I was about to knock on the door, the sound of an eagle screeching stopped me. I turned and found Jacy sitting on the branch of a tree in Enola's front yard. He was about ten feet away from me and even more breathtaking. I stared into his brown eyes, trying to understand what he was doing. He nodded his head toward the cabin and I almost fell over. This was the first time he had ever tried to communicate with me. I turned around and took a deep breath.

"You can do this, Adeline. You can do this," I told myself as I knocked on the door.

I turned one last time and found Jacy still sitting on the tree branch, staring at me. His eyes were distant, but showed intelligence. The door swung open, startling me. Enola was wearing the same white gown that I first met her in and her gray hair was in two long braids. She still wore no shoes, and I began to think she never wore any.

"Hi, Enola. It's me, Adeline. We met a while ago," I said, trying to keep my voice from trembling. Her ancient brown eyes looked me up and down and suddenly her face broke into a childlike grin.

"Adeline…" she whispered lovingly.

"Yes. I was hoping you could help me again. I have more questions."

"I know and don't worry about him," she said, nodding her head toward Jacy. "He's just following his orders."

"His orders?"

"Come inside and I'll explain," Enola smiled while stepping to the side, allowing me entrance. I walked in and sat down on the rug next to the fireplace, like the first time I visited. The sharp pain in my chest was starting to come back again, but I fought it back. I couldn't lose myself here.

"You are strong, Adeline," Enola said sitting across from me, "I don't know if it helps, but he feels just as lonely."

I was taken aback. "Who?"

"You know who, but I won't say his name. I know that must hurt."

I ignored what my mind was screaming. I wasn't here for him, but for me.

"Anyway, what did you mean by his orders? The eagle outside, I mean," I asked, changing the subject.

"Jacy was ordered to keep an eye on you. To protect you if need be"

"And how do you know this?"

"Because Chenoa told me. She tells me a lot," Enola replied, as if it was obvious. Even her name caused the sharp pain to take its toll. The voice in my head was screaming again. Telling me to ask her to take me to him.

"H-how?" I stammered.

"She visits me when she can."

I nodded trying to absorb everything and stop the pain in the process.

"What were Jacy's orders exactly? And who ordered them?" I asked, with new resolve in my voice. It wasn't trembling like before.

"Jacy was ordered to make sure no one from the rebel tribe touched you. Although part of the orders were to keep you off the reservation, in case any rebels came back. I suppose he thought the Delsin wouldn't notice," she explained.

"The Delsin. He's the one who ordered Jacy, right?" I asked, looking for clarity.

"Correct."

"And I suppose I already know who that is."

"You do."

I sighed, working up the courage to speak his name. "Cole..." I whispered. His name felt like water on my parched lips. I needed him more than I originally thought.

"You miss him."

Saying I missed him hardly covered it.

"You could say that," I whispered again.

"I'm glad you have accepted it - your connection," she smiled widely. Her teeth were very white, a deep contrast to her dark, copper skin. I tried to smile, but failed miserably.

"What else do you wish to know?" Enola asked, her smile now faded away.

"Everything, sparing nothing."

She nodded, "All right."

"Now," she began, "the rebels know who you may be and where you live. At the same time it seemed the Delsin realized his power and responsibility. The Chosen have risen and are able to train for the war."

"What war?"

"The war over the heavenly being." I gulped, knowing she meant me.

"Now, they are training, and Jacy, being already so experienced, was ordered to protect you."

"Tell me more about Jacy." Enola sighed and looked longingly into the fire.

"It's a sad story. There is no happily ever after," she explained.

"I know a lot about no happily ever afters."

She looked sadly from me back to the fire before starting her story.

"A long time ago, about a hundred and twenty years ago, Jacy was a man with a family. He had a beautiful wife and an adorable little girl. He was Chosen as well, but the tribe hadn't had any trouble for some time. The tribe fell into a false sense of security.

"The rebels attacked early one morning, while the Chosen were up on the mountain training. There wasn't much left when they came back. Jacy looked frantically for his family. When he came to his home, it was in ruins. His wife and child had been killed in the attack.

"Jacy was filled with much grief and begged the chief to let him to die. The chief refused to do so. Jacy was Chosen and was needed in the tribe. Jacy was tired of his human emotions, so he transformed into his eagle self and has stayed that way ever since. When one who is Chosen shifts into their eagle self, they are given completely over to their animal instincts. Jacy's human emotions were easily contained, numbed. It made it easier for him to live."

I sat, unmoving, while I tried to absorb everything I heard. I wish I were so lucky.

"Why hasn't he…well how can he be over a hundred and forty years old?"

"Chosen don't age while in their eagle forms. Their human bodies stay exactly the same from the last time they transformed. I suppose if Jacy transformed back to his human self, he would look the age of twenty, the age he was last human."

I sat still, staring at Enola.

"Do you understand?"

"Yes, but why does the rebel tribe want me?" I changed the subject, trying to understand the whole concept. It was very difficult.

"You have been told the legend, haven't you? With your power, the rebels will be able to be shape shifters like the Chosen," Enola explained patiently.

"But I don't have any powers," I replied exasperated, "I'm just an ordinary girl."

"Ah, but that's where you are wrong! Your power still lies within you. It hasn't revealed itself yet."

"But haven't you and your tribe gotten it wrong before?" I was almost on the verge of anger. "You thought Cole's mom was the reincarnation and looked what happened to her!"

"I never said I believed she was the heavenly being, only that the tribe was suspicious," Enola corrected.

I felt the blood leave my face. "So, you truly believe I am this being?"

Enola nodded, "Without a doubt."

"Okay, so if I just give the rebels what they want, they'll leave your tribe alone, right?" I reasoned. If they got what they wanted, then there would be no more war. It was a rather simple solution. Enola's expression and tone was grave.

"To get that power, Adeline, you must be killed."

I felt my stomach drop to the floor. Part of me knew that my solution wasn't going to be that easy.

"Isn't there any other way?" I whispered. My newfound determination and bravery just went down the drain. I was terrified now.

"When the heavenly being died, her power was given to Heluka and the other Chosen. That power is the shape-shifting ability. She also gave them the ability to have the shape-shifting gift passed down from generation to generation. They only shared the body before, now the Chosen and the eagle partners are one, in body and mind. That power is what enables the Chosen to do what they are able to," Enola explained. "Heluka unsuccessfully tried to banish it from this world. Power like that doesn't die. It simply takes another shape. The Chosen's abilities rely on nature and the heavenly being."

"But I thought that Heluka's eagle partner, Onida, died alongside him."

"The eagle partners die mortally, alongside one another, but when the time comes for the next generation, they are reborn."

I nodded numbly. An idea hit me, and I wondered why I hadn't thought of it before.

"But if the rebels did get the power, would they leave your tribe alone?" I asked, now with new excitement. Enola looked at me curiously.

"I'm not sure. It's possible. Why do ask?"

I realized that now that I didn't have Cole as a friend or anything else, then why not make it easier on his tribe? Without him, I didn't really have anything else in life to look forward to. Nothing in life would be able to give me the same happiness that he did. Enola's eyes widened. She had probably figured out the plan I was forming.

"No," she whispered, fear etched across her ancient features. "No!" Her tone surprised me. She was yelling now. "I will not let you do something so foolish!"

I immediately stood as she jumped from the floor. She was becoming hysterical.

"No! You can't do that! You can't do that to me or to him! He wouldn't be able to live with himself!" she continued to sob.

"Who?" I asked as I slowly walked toward the door.

"Cole! You are not the only one who is suffering because of your separation!" she replied harshly. My eyes widened. There was no way he would miss me. He made it clear he was done with me.

"Thank you for your help, Enola," I said after she had calmed down a bit. "I'm going now."

"Please, Adeline, stay safe, if not for your sake, for his," Enola pleaded as I opened the door.

I nodded, "Okay."

She relaxed and sat back down on the rug. I took my cue, walked out the door, closing it behind me. When I looked toward the tree in the front yard, Jacy was still perched. The look in Jacy's eyes almost caused me to trip down the steps. He looked so angry and betrayed.

There was something that I was absolutely sure of as I drove back to my house with an eagle following in the air above me. I was positive that there really was a war happening; that there were shape-shifting eagle-humans flying around, that I was in danger, and finally, that Cole Dyami missed me. Maybe not as much as I missed him, but he still missed me. And I was also sure that a part of me had fallen for him without even knowing it.

Chapter Fifteen

I parked the car in the driveway and walked quickly into the house to get out of the drizzling rain. I stopped short at the door when I saw who was in my living room. There, sitting on my couch, making small talk with Alexia was Elsu Dyami. The small tug in my chest pulled aggressively, fearfully.

His eyes were the same fierce brown that popped against his dark, copper skin. His scar jaggedly made a path from the corner of his eye to his mouth, but it seemed less apparent and certainly did not take away from his beauty. His black hair was pulled back into a ponytail at the base of his neck, just like all the other times I had seen him. But his hair was shaggier and longer than I remembered.

"Hey, Adeline. Elsu came to talk to you for a few minutes," Alexia explained, obviously charmed. Who wouldn't be charmed by such a handsome man? Even with his scar, Elsu still looked like he belonged on a runway or in a magazine. He stood and looked to Alexia, "Thank you, Miss Hamilton. I enjoyed your dinner, and I only wished Adeline could have been here to enjoy it as well."

I was completely shocked. I had never heard Elsu sound so polite and charming. Was this some trick? I was pretty sure that

Elsu hated people from the city, especially me. Alexia blushed while saying goodbye before excusing herself to the kitchen. Elsu turned to me, and all remains of his politeness had disappeared.

"What are you doing?" he demanded. His tone caused me to take a step back.

"What?"

"I thought my brother made it clear to you. You need to stay away from the reservation. You need to forget we ever existed." His eyes were staring me down, and I made the mistake of looking into them. I couldn't respond.

He rolled his eyes, "I swear everything would be better if you just disappeared. No more bloodshed or war." His words cut deep and tears stung the back of my eyes.

"I'm sorry, but I want to help. I can do something..." I stuttered, trying to defend myself.

"No you can't," he replied harshly. "All you need to do is to leave our family and tribe alone. He doesn't love you." The last four words left me speechless. I stood unmoving, not seeing. I think Elsu left because I faintly heard the front door close. The only thing I was focusing on was breathing. In and out. In and out.

This time, I felt no sharp pain or waves of hurt course through my body like before. The tug in my chest seemed to have given up. The flickering flame had been extinguished. This time, something much worse took effect. I felt nothing. A numbing sense of hopelessness was the best way to describe it. A feeling of utter despair took over all of my senses. I didn't even cry. There weren't any tears left to shed.

I walked to my bedroom and fell onto my bed. I was breathing, and my heart was beating, but I wasn't really living. I fell asleep and hoped I would never wake. This was the worst pain I had ever endured. I thought I would die of it.

*

I woke to the sound of birds chirping outside my window. The cold numbing sensation still clutched my heart in a tight grip. I was in my own cage of ice within my body. I ate breakfast in silence, only nodding and speaking when I was expected to. Alexia drove me to school without trying to keep up conversation anymore. She knew to leave me alone.

I walked to homeroom completely unaware of anyone else around me. I think Brittany said something sarcastic about me, but I didn't hear her. Classes came and went, and I remained alone, oblivious to everything around me. I sat in my usual seat at lunch, but didn't eat. I just sat there pretending to read my book. It was obvious that everyone had forgotten about him. Everyone but me.

The final bell of the day rang, and I was grateful. I walked to the parking lot, but stopped in my tracks when I saw who was waiting on the other side of the lot. Chandler Phalcon and three other Native Americans that I didn't know were leaning against Chandler's car. All of them were staring at me.

My stomach fell to my feet, fear and adrenaline pumped through my veins. I tried to calculate how far and fast I could run before they could catch me when a scream from above caught my attention. It was Jacy, and he seemed frantic. He was flying around us, crying repeatedly. When I looked back over to Chandler and his group, they all seemed just as nervous as I did. They were staring at Jacy as well, fear evident on their faces. Chandler said something, and then they all piled into his car and sped away. Jacy still refused to calm down, and now, other people in the parking lot were beginning to notice him as well.

"What is that?" I heard Katie Newberry ask Maggie Harron.

"It looks like a bird, but it's so big," Maggie responded, obviously stunned.

I looked around the parking lot and saw everyone staring at the sky; just as unsettled and astounded as I was the first time I had seen Jacy. I became frantic. I didn't know the rules about the Chosen, but I was pretty sure that it went without saying that no one outside the tribe should know about them. Jacy continued to fly around recklessly, and I began to understand what he wanted. He was trying to get my attention.

Jacy was ordered to make sure no one from the rebel tribe touched you...

He was doing as he was told. He scared the rebels away, and now he was trying to protect me. And here I was, endangering him by keeping him out in public. I looked around the parking lot, but I didn't find Alexia or her rental car. A heart-wrenching panic hit me hard. I almost fell to my knees at the thought. I looked around the parking lot again, this time desperate. I still didn't see Alexia, and I only began to feel worse.

Adrenaline kicked in, and I ran past all of the dumbfounded people in the parking lot, down the road toward my house. My house was a good two miles away so I wasn't sure how long I could run and how long it would take me to get there. It was strange, this adrenaline rush and my fear for the strange woman in my home. I felt like it was my duty to make sure she was all right. I continued to run, without stopping, and found Jacy flying above me, almost directing me, and possibly trying to encourage me.

I heard my blood pulsing in my ears. My mind was going a million miles a second. Visions of what I would possibly find at home only made me run faster. I'm not exactly sure how long it took me, but I was surprised when I turned onto my street and ran up my driveway. I stopped in my tracks, breathing heavily, when I saw that the door to my house had been ripped off its hinges. I continued to breathe deeply, trying to keep the stinging tears behind my eyes from falling.

I looked to the driveway, but didn't find Alexia's rental car. A flicker of hope burned in my chest as I made my way into my broken in home. I walked through the front door and slowly into the living room. The couch had been turned over and books were spread everywhere. All of the electronics were still in place, so I knew that this wasn't a robbery. My mind was not put to rest. I stepped on bits of broken glass as I made my way to the kitchen.

There was no blood or broken body lying next to the sink like I had imagined. There were broken plates and chairs from the table that had been turned over.

I glanced to the refrigerator and found a note taped to it. I ripped it off and found it was from Alexia. Apparently, she hadn't been home since breakfast this morning. She assumed that I would have taken the bus home when I found she wasn't there to pick me up. She had gone into town to meet a friend. I sighed, relieved, knowing she wasn't here when someone or something broke into my house.

I heard another screeching sound and knew Jacy was outside. But I didn't feel comfort or safety. My skin rose instead. I walked to my room with the strange foreboding feeling again, like the boogey man was going to jump out of my closet when I walked in. I turned the knob and carefully walked into my room. Unlike all the other rooms in my house, my room hadn't been touched. There were no tables turned over or papers thrown on the floor. In fact, it looked like someone had cleaned it up. My dirty clothes were no longer piled on the floor next to my bed, but in my hamper. My bed was no longer a tangled mess of sheets, but was made without a wrinkle in sight.

I felt my heart race and terror swept through my body. I heard the sound of my door clicking shut. I jumped, turned around, and found someone's back to me. He was wearing a leather jacket and torn jeans with black boots. I wanted to scream, but nothing came out. My mouth was dry as a desert. I felt like those girls in horror movies. No matter how loud I screamed at the television, they just remained motionless, almost hypnotized by their fate.

He kept his back facing me, and I gulped, trying to figure out an escape plan. My window was about a foot away from me. I could jump through it like the cops on that law show Emma watched. Of course, my glass wasn't stunt proof, so I would probably be knocked unconscious. I trembled as the man in the leather jacket turned to face me. My fears were realized when I came face to face with Chandler Phalcon. I wondered where his companions were. I wondered if they were hiding somewhere in my room, waiting to jump out.

"You are a hard person to find, Adeline," Chandler said huskily, taking a step toward me. "Harder still to get in touch with." I took a step back, not responding. "You know, when Cole led us to North Dakota, I really thought that he was dumb enough to take you with him. I'm surprised he was able to stay away from you this long." I backed up to my window next to my bed. I was trapped. "What? You have nothing to say?"

"Where's Cole?"

He smirked, obviously pleased with my question.

"So, you are still clueless, huh?" he smiled, white teeth showing.

I decided to play dumb, just as Chandler thought. He didn't know that I knew everything.

"What are you talking about? Where's Cole?"

He looked me up and down, trying to figure out if I was lying. He took a couple more steps toward me, and before I knew it, he had me pinned to the wall. He held my wrists by my side and stared into my eyes for the longest time. I tried to shrug out of his grip, but it was useless.

He put his lips to my ear, "I killed him." My eyes widened and my heart stopped beating. My breathing became shallow as I took this in.

"You're lying," I said. Cole was stronger than that.

"And how do you know? When was the last time you saw him?" he teased. I flinched at his grip on my wrists.

An image of a black eagle with lines of lighter brown and white swirling from the head to the tail ran across my mind. Part of me knew that was Cole all along. I had just been too blind to the truth to recognize it.

He chuckled again, and I looked up to him, still scared and unsure of what he was going to do. But then, I suddenly knew what

I was going to do, what I had to do. The idea that Cole may possibly be dead, that I was living in a world where he didn't laugh, cry, or live was unthinkable. I couldn't live like that. I wouldn't live like that.

"I'll make you a deal," I said, shocked at the resolve in my voice.

Chandler raised his eyebrow and his grip on me loosened. He stepped back, but kept his eyes on me.

"I'm listening."

"If I come," I continued, "you leave Great Falls and don't ever come back. You leave the tribe alone. Forever."

Several moments of silence passed as Chandler took this in.

"You're willing to die for him, for his tribe?" he asked, surprised.

My answer was immediate, "Yes."

"Well," Chandler's arms relaxed, "that changes things."

"Do we have a deal?" My voice shook as I held my hand out and he shook it roughly.

He laughed, elated, "Deal."

After Chandler felt he was safe, he dragged me to his Jeep. None of his companions said a word as he lifted me in. They only stared at me with an emotion I couldn't place. Possible triumph? No, it was too soon for celebration. I was still shaking as Chandler buckled me in. He jumped into the driver's seat and pulled out of my driveway as if he had just stolen money from a bank.

I was sitting in between two Native American men. The one on my left looked about twenty-two and the one on my right couldn't have been any older than fourteen, only a few years younger than me. I did notice that the one to my right never really looked me in the eye. Mostly at my hair or hands. I could tell he was trying to seem brave. He looked terrified. Of me or possible shape-shifters in the sky, I wasn't sure. I looked out the windshield and noticed the sky was becoming gray.

"Did anyone follow her?" the man in the passenger's seat asked Chandler. His voice was deep, and husky. I couldn't see his face, but he sounded like he was in his late twenties or early thirties. His arm was lying on the armrest and that was when I noticed his jagged scar. It started at his elbow and continued to his pointer finger. I shuttered at the thought of how he must have received it.

"The old one, Jacy, followed her to her house, but disappeared," Chandler explained. His eyes glanced back to me. "She came willingly."

The man in the passenger's seat shifted uncomfortably.

"On what conditions?"

"That we leave this precious town alone," Chandler laughed. The others, besides the boy to my right, joined in.

"Does your little Delsin know about this?" The man in the passenger seat turned to me, his eyes mocking.

I swallowed my fear, "No." It came out in a whisper.

"I wonder how he's gonna handle this when he finds out," the man continued, shaking his head.

"But he's still in the mountains training, right?" the boy to my right asked. His voice was shaking.

The man to my left glared his way, "Whatever happens, we will fight."

"The last I heard, the Delsin was training the Chosen in the Northern Mountains. It'll take them awhile to get to us. By the time they figure out she's gone, we'll be half way to North Dakota," the man in the passenger's seat said to Chandler, ignoring the boy.

"I'm surprised. I really thought the new Delsin would give us more of a challenge. He only sent one Chosen to watch her. And even then, who knew she would be so willing," the man to my left chuckled while glancing at me. I shuddered. Chandler smiled, but the man in the passenger's seat thought otherwise.

"No need to get overconfident. We don't know what they are planning."

"Oh come on, Tom. It's obvious the kid doesn't know what he's doing. If he was careful, he wouldn't let us touch her."

Tom sighed, "Be careful of what you say in front of her."

The man to my left tensed. The boy on my right was staring out the window, clutching his hands together tightly. His knuckles were becoming white. Conversation ceased.

Throughout this conversation I became sure of a few things. Number one, Cole was alive. Chandler had lied, most likely to scare me. Number two, the rebels had been planning and training just as long as the Chosen had. How long that was and how prepared they were, I had no idea.

It was strange, this feeling of resolve I had. I didn't wake up that morning thinking I was going to die. But now that it came, so much regret filled my heart. Regret for not telling Emma I loved her, for not allowing anyone past my wall of distrust. Regret for not ever realizing I had fallen in love, for not acting on that love. But I was acting on that love now. This was to be my first and last act of love. Sacrifice. And it was worth it.

Suddenly, the whole Jeep tilted to the right, almost as if someone hit us, causing Chandler to almost drive into a ditch.

"What's happening?" the boy asked. He was trembling.

The man to my left looked out the back window, "We've got company."

I tried to look behind me, but the man grabbed my head and pulled it forward. I thought he was going to break my neck.

"Don't move," he threatened, teeth clenched.

"How did they catch up so quickly?" Chandler asked, continually looking at his mirrors.

"I told you that they would have a plan," Tom said, shaking his head. He was the only one that seemed calm. The man to my left finally let me have control of my head. I stared at the floor, afraid of what would happen if I looked behind me again. Another hit to the Jeep almost sent it on its side. Chandler never slowed down, but continued to drive faster.

"What's happening?" my voice was shaking.

"They've found us…" the boy whispered, more to himself than to me.

"Shut up, Tyler! Be a man and get ready to battle," the man to my left ordered as he threw a black bag to Tyler. Tyler caught it and opened it slowly. He took out a mask. It was black and only had holes for the eyes and mouth. He put it on quickly, and before I knew it, everyone else in the jeep was wearing one similar to it. I was utterly confused. What was the point of masks? Some tribal tradition?

I was literally knocked out of my thoughts as the Jeep took another hit from some unknown force. It was then that I heard the sound of nine eagles crying and screeching. My mouth fell open at the thought of what was outside, attacking the Jeep.

I didn't have much time to make sense of anything because the Jeep took another hit and began to flip. Everything was a blur, and I was trying to keep myself calm. I think we flipped about four times before the Jeep slammed against a tree on the side of the road.

My head throbbed, and my back ached. I tried to stretch out my body, to see if I had broken anything. Thankfully, all of my bones were intact, but I was pretty sure my head was bleeding. My fears were realized when I saw warm, red liquid drip from my head to my hands.

No one in the Jeep moved, and for a moment, and I thought they were dead. Suddenly, I heard Chandler moving around. He kicked the glass out of the windshield and climbed out. Tom followed him, telling the others in the back with me, "Get her and start running. Don't let her out of your sight."

The man to my left nodded and began to unbuckle me. Tyler remained motionless, as if he was in a trance.

"Tyler, help me out here," the man ordered. Tyler suddenly looked to me and to the man.

"The others are coming. They'll be here in about thirty minutes," Tyler said quickly.

"What? Who are the others?" I asked.

No one answered me. The man dragged me through the broken glass of the windshield. Tyler followed behind me, still shaking.

I looked around my surroundings, and I only saw the highway and a vacant field. There was a forest on one side of the road, where the Jeep had crashed. I looked around, but saw no Chandler or Tom. I didn't see any eagles either. The man tightened his grip on my arm and began to run, dragging me behind him. Tyler was running as well, not far behind me. After about five minutes of silence and constant running, I thought we were away from the battle that was about to begin back at the Jeep. It wasn't until I saw a flock of eagles flying above us that I realized the battle had followed us.

"Tyler! Take her into the woods. They won't be able to see you," the man ordered Tyler as he threw me to him. Tyler caught me easily. I hadn't realized how tall and muscular he really was. It was his face that gave his age away, and that was covered by his mask. I would have mistaken him for twenty-five.

Tyler nodded and grabbed my hand, leading me through the woods. As we entered the woods, I heard the sound of three thunderous explosions and eagles screeching behind me.

"Come on. Keep moving," Tyler begged as he continued to drag me along. We had been running for about ten minutes, but it felt like an hour to me.

"Can we take a break?" I asked, breathless. I pleaded with my eyes, and even though I couldn't see his face, I could tell he was considering it.

He sighed, "Only for a few minutes."

I smiled, grateful, as I sat down at the base of one of the many trees that surrounded us. I looked up, but couldn't see the sky. It was covered by shades of green and brown. I looked over to Tyler and saw him leaning against a tree, about a yard from me. He was staring at his boots, which were making designs in the dirt.

"So," I said, trying to sound calm, "what's with the masks?"

His head shot up.

"They didn't tell you?"

I shook my head slowly.

He looked up to the sky and paused before finally saying something.

"It's to keep our identities a secret."

"From who?"

He scoffed, "The Chosen and people like you."

"But I've seen your face, Tyler."

"I said people like you. You're not normal if you haven't noticed."

"Yeah," I whispered, "I've noticed."

A silence followed and I strained my ears to hear anything. A screech. An eagle flapping its wings. Anything.

"Let's go," Tyler said all of a sudden.

He offered me his hand, but I simply looked at it, as I got up on my own. He brought his hand back to his side and began to walk through the forest again.

"Who are the others?" I asked.

He stopped and stood without replying. "The rest of the rebels."

I'm not exactly sure what surprised me more. His answer or the way he answered it. His voice seemed distant and heartrending.

"How did you know they were coming?"

He sighed. I didn't think he was going to respond, but he said, "It's my gift. I see visions of what is to come."

"Like the future?"

"Yeah, sort of. Not many people in my tribe have abilities," he said, almost smug.

"Who else has abilities like you?" I asked carefully. Even if I didn't make it, maybe I could give someone some kind of warning of what the rebels were capable of.

"There's no point in telling you all of this," he said quickly. "You won't live long enough to see or understand what we can do." Regret and guilt seeped through his voice, almost as if he was sad about my impending death. I didn't get the chance to voice my thoughts because the sound of people running toward Tyler and me captured our attention.

"Let's go," he demanded with more force.

I stood motionless. I wasn't sure what I was doing. If Tyler was afraid of who was coming, then I shouldn't move. It could be him. The thought caused chills and goose bumps to rise on the back of my neck.

Tyler was done being patient as he grabbed my arm and began to drag me through the forest. Branches and twigs continued to cut at my face and leaves became entangled in my hair. My head was still throbbing and blood continued to drip down my face.

I suddenly felt someone grab me from behind and lift me bridal style. Tyler turned around, shocked. I looked up to who was holding me and was both disappointed and terrified to come face to face with Elsu Dyami. He was shirtless, wearing jeans, but no shoes. I blushed furiously, not really aware of Tyler and some other people fighting. I was too focused on not fainting from embarrassment and loss of blood.

Elsu began to carry me briskly away from the scene. There were at least three others fighting Tyler, and he was about to surrender. There were one man and two girls. The girls were wearing tank tops and shorts. The other man was in the same attire as Elsu, and once again, I blushed. I looked up to Elsu's face. He was staring straight ahead, eyes on where he was going.

"Don't hurt him," I whispered.

"Who?" he asked, still not looking at me.

"Tyler. He's just a boy," I pleaded, trying to look past Elsu's broad shoulders. Elsu shifted me in his arms, to keep me from looking past him.

"If he surrenders, then the Delsin will decide what to do with him," he replied, seeming bitter. I nodded numbly.

"Can I walk?"

"No. I was strictly ordered to carry you back," he replied, smirking. I fumed as he continued to carry me.

Suddenly, I heard the sound of running footsteps approaching us from behind. I began to panic, but Elsu remained calm. He continued at his own pace, not acting aware of anything. Like he was taking a walk in the park.

"Is she okay?" a female asked as she appeared next to Elsu.

"I think she may have a concussion. Her head is bleeding," he answered solemnly.

The others appeared, with Tyler on a rope. One of the men was leading him. Tyler's mask was gone and his expression was one that I would never forget. I hoped whomever he had to deal with would give him mercy.

"That didn't take long," Elsu commented to the girl to his right.

"He surrendered when he saw that he was outnumbered," she replied.

"How are the others doing?"

"Not so good." My heart sank. "The rebels retreated. The Delsin doesn't know yet."

Elsu remained silent as he continued to carry me through the forest. I tried to look at where we were going, but I only saw trees and bushes. No direct path. Everyone remained silent and I kept the questions that were buzzing around my head to myself. I was just grateful that I wasn't going to North Dakota, at least not today.

I was wondering where we were going, and it wasn't until I heard the sound of water that I realized. It sounded like a waterfall. Like the one Cole told me about so long ago. I never thought I would actually see it. My heart began to pound and tears stung my eyes. I fought them back. I couldn't break down now.

The sound of water became louder, and with it, the pounding of my heart. It finally came into sight. A beautiful, magnificent waterfall. The one I had been trying to imagine ever since he told me. I stumbled out of Elsu's hold and pushed the tree branches out of my way. I walked over to the tree next to the river. His tree.

I took a deep breath and took in the scent of mist and trees. The achy, hollow feeling in my chest came back again. The small tug in my chest, that had been dormant for so long, pulled tightly; the small candle began to burn once more.

"Adeline…"

My imagination was even better now. I thought I heard him call my name.

"Adeline," he said again his deep, rough voice seeming desperate.

"Yeah?" I asked aloud, not caring if I was talking to myself. I heard someone walk up behind me, and I quickly turned around, afraid of whom it would be.

What I saw knocked me breathless, just like the first day I had ever laid eyes on him. His black hair was a mess, with a few leaves mixed in. His bangs were longer, but his eyes were still visible and just as dark blue. He, like the other men I had seen, was shirtless with only a pair of jeans. His skin was the same rich copper. And his expression…it made me think he missed me too.

He took another step toward me while he lifted his arms out to welcome me to him. I ran into him, hard. I wrapped my arms around him, but found him too tall and muscular. He wrapped his arms around my waist, holding me close. My head was on his chest, sobbing. His heart was beating fitfully, like mine. I breathed in his warm scent, trying to memorize it. If this was a dream, then I wanted my memory to give it justice.

"Adeline," he whispered into my hair. He breathed deeply and held me tightly.

"Shh, don't say anything," I said in between sobs. "I'm not ready to wake up yet."

He smirked, "You're not sleeping. This is real. I'm real."

I shook my head, "No, but I'll enjoy this while I can."

He sighed heavily, making me look him in the eyes.

"I'm so sorry I caused you this much pain."

I stared numbly back up at him. He cupped one hand on my face and left the other holding me at my waist. Pain. It was almost funny how the word suddenly meant nothing to me. There was no empty hollow ache in my chest. I couldn't even remember what it felt like. My heart felt whole again. All of the tiny pieces managed to glue themselves back together again. I don't even think my heart had a scar. It was as if Cole Dyami never left in the first place. My breathing finally slowed to its normal pace, but the tears continued their steady flow. He brushed the tears away with his thumb, and I gulped.

"What do I have to do to make you believe that you are not dreaming?" he whispered.

Dreaming? That was right. I thought I was dreaming. The dull ache was threatening to come back again. The tiny pieces of my heart were beginning to come undone. His blue eyes searched mine, and I remained silent. I didn't know what to say.

He leaned in closer to me and tilted his head. My dreams had always stopped here. I was supposed to wake up now. We both closed our eyes. I felt raindrops land on my cheeks and eyelids as his lips lovingly, gently met mine.

It was in that moment that everything made sense. The puzzle pieces fit perfectly. He was Chosen. The Delsin, to be exact. There were rebels chasing me. There was an ancient war, taking place in modern times.

And most importantly, I loved and was loved in return.

PART III

"Love is patient, love is kind. It does not envy, it does not boast, it is not proud. It is not rude, it is not self-seeking, it is not easily angered, it keeps no record of wrongs. Love does not delight in evil but rejoices in the truth. It always protects, always trusts, always hopes, always perseveres. Love never fails."

~ 1 Corinthians 13:4-8

ALLISON BLANCHARD

Chapter Sixteen

The only sound that was able to reach my ears and process in my brain was Cole's breathing and my erratically beating heart. I kept my eyes closed, still afraid that this was all a dream that I would wake up from. It didn't feel like a dream. I could feel the blood rushing in my ears, and I could feel the heat that Cole's embrace was giving off, the pressure of his lips on mine. I smiled slightly when I felt Cole rest his forehead against mine.

"Adeline?"

"Yeah?"

I peeked through my eyelids, afraid I would come face to face with my room. I was happily surprised when I looked up into Cole's deep, blue eyes. He caressed my cheek with his thumb, his blue eyes shining. We were instantly taken back to reality when I heard someone's deep voice.

"We have to go, Cole. It's not safe," Elsu said, his eyes glancing uncomfortably at the sky and at us. Reality slowly began to sink in. I was in Cole's arms, Elsu had witnessed our first kiss, there was a battle taking place not far from where we were, and I could possibly not live to see tomorrow.

No matter how I looked at the current situation, I couldn't bring myself to regret anything that had happened. I couldn't be angry with Cole for leaving or for the fact that I was in danger. I was just grateful that life had granted me this blessing.

Cole nodded in Elsu's direction and took my hand. He began to lead me to the edge of the woods where Elsu had been standing. The others had left already. Cole picked something up off the ground on the way through the woods. It looked like a leather pouch. He threw it over his shoulders. I noticed that Elsu was wearing one as well.

"Where are we going?" I asked. My voice was very quiet, almost afraid to give away our location by even breathing.

"Taking you somewhere safe," Cole replied glancing toward me.

"What's gonna happen?" Neither answered and neither made an attempt to look to me.

"Cole?"

He looked toward me regretfully. He was about to answer when Elsu interrupted him.

"There will be war."

*

I wasn't completely aware of everything that was happening around me. My eyes were on Cole only. He seemed so much more confident and strong. He continued to hold my hand while he told Elsu what to do as we made our way to a clearing. Six people stood in the middle of the field.

I immediately recognized Chenoa, standing by Cole's truck, even through the pouring rain. Her beautiful face broke into a grin as she came running toward us. She grabbed me in a loving embrace, but Cole still refused to let go of my hand, not even for a second.

I blushed when everyone else turned to notice me. They were all staring at me, with very different emotions in each of their eyes. Some were relieved, others frustrated. My eyes darted to the ground, trying to escape their stare.

"Don't worry, Adeline. They are just happy you are all right," Chenoa whispered in my ear. "How's your head? Elsu said that you might have a concussion."

"It's okay. Just hurts a little." Thankfully, the bleeding had stopped, but the throbbing hadn't. I knew Chenoa saw through my charade, but I didn't want to complain. I was just thankful to be alive. She released me and stood on the other side of me.

"Where did they go?" Cole asked the group. His eyes searched each one of their faces. I immediately recognized Elan, Dylan, and Ella. So, they were a part of this craziness too.

Everyone's mood and attitude changed as they looked to the ground, sky, and trees. Anywhere that Cole wasn't.

"What happened?" he demanded, deep voice booming.

I was taken aback by the urgency and command in his voice. I looked over everyone and saw the answer without anyone even speaking. Chandler and the others had gotten away. I noticed that Tyler was nowhere to be seen.

"Where's Tyler?" I asked Chenoa.

As soon as the words left my mouth, everyone, including Cole, stopped to stare at me. My face flushed. Elan stepped up. He was taller, but still lean. His black hair was in a bun, a few strands going astray. He, like the other men, was shirtless. He was also wearing the same leather pouch as Elsu and Cole. Everyone was.

"The rebels surprised us and took him back. I…we think they have learned how to transform, like us…"

Cole's face fell, and I knew that trouble was near. My head began to swirl, and my thoughts were hazy.

"How is this possible?" he asked. No one answered. I lightly tugged on Cole's hand. His eyes gradually drifted toward mine. Despair and guilt stared back at me.

"What does this mean?"

He licked his lips and gulped. Not a good sign.

"Things have changed," he answered slowly, "but you have nothing to worry about."

He turned his attention back to Elan. "What else has happened, Elan? Do we know where they are heading?" Cole asked, his voice strong and determined.

I glanced from face to face, looking for some sort of clue as to how much trouble I was in. Everyone was staring at Cole, giving him his or her full attention.

"They seem to be returning to North Dakota to regroup. We're not sure how they came into their new power," Chenoa replied, her voice fading as she finished.

"This isn't good," he whispered to Chenoa. "How could they obtain that power? Don't they need…"

"Me?" I finished for him.

Cole's eyes focused on me. He was confused, wondering how much I knew.

"I know a lot," I informed him. Cole glanced to Chenoa. She mouthed "Enola." He rolled his eyes muttering, "Figures."

"So what are we going to do?" I regretted speaking when I saw seven other people staring at me intensely.

"You are not going to do anything. I'm taking you home," Cole said unwavering. He wasn't even going to consider anything else.

"That's not a good idea," Chenoa replied steadfast. She, too, wasn't going to budge.

"What do you mean?" He was irritated. Everyone was looking from Cole to Chenoa, watching to see who would win. My money was on Chenoa.

"They've been to her home. She would be safe on the reservation."

"We'll be watching her home twenty four hours a day. They wouldn't think about returning."

"She's coming home with us, whether you like it or not," Chenoa commanded, firmness overtaking her usual sweetness. Cole didn't speak, but glared, blue eyes on fire. Chenoa stood unmoved by him. A few minutes of silence passed before Cole sighed heavily. Chenoa broke into a grin. She won. Cole turned his attention back to the group. Everyone suddenly straightened up and looked to Cole.

"Adeline will be coming home with me. The rest of you return home and rest. We will begin training here at five. Don't be late. We have a lot of work to do." And with those final words, Cole led me to his truck with Chenoa right behind.

I tried not to look at the people around me, but it was a bit difficult. Out of the nine Chosen, there were four girls and five boys, including Jacy. They were all inhumanly striking and muscular. Whenever I caught a glance from one of them, they would either smile encouragingly or blankly stare back. I learned to keep my eyes on Cole's hand holding mine. Cole opened the back door of his GMC truck and pulled out a t-shirt. He quickly threw it on, and I immediately ached for his hand.

He quickly took my hand and smiled warmly to me. My smile. My heart fluttered in response. Cole opened the passenger's door and lifted me in. Normally, I would protest, but now I was just elated to have him near me.

Chenoa jumped into the back seat as Cole got into the driver's seat. Suddenly, I heard six thunderous explosions. Fear swept through me at the thought of Chandler and the rest of the rebels returning. When I looked out the window, I jumped in surprise. There were no longer any people in the clearing, but seven large and terrifying eagles. My hands started to shake as fear took hold of me. All seven of them took flight and, with beauty and grace, flew out of sight.

"What?" I asked aloud, more to myself than to anyone else.

Chenoa giggled, "It's part of their training. They have to fly home." Flying. I was going to have to get used to that.

"Oh…" I mumbled, looking out the windshield. I suddenly felt someone's warm hand grasp mine. I looked to my left and found Cole driving, but his eyes glued to me. I blushed, but didn't look away. For the first time in several weeks, I was home.

Chenoa talked the whole ride, but I can honestly say that I didn't have the slightest idea what she was talking about.

Cole pulled into his driveway and it wasn't until I heard Chenoa shut the car door, did I notice we were parked. I looked over to where Cole had been sitting and found an empty seat. A deep, empty feeling hit me in the pit of my stomach. Had he really been a dream? I sighed, relieved, when Cole opened my door and lifted me from my seat. He set me down on my feet and we stood there, staring at each other.

"Are you okay? You didn't say much," he whispered as he tucked a stray hair behind my ear.

I gulped, "I'm fine." My head was even starting to feel better. He grinned, white teeth shinning.

"We better get you inside. Chenoa is making dinner as we speak."

Cole then took my hand and led me into his home. We stopped in the doorway to the kitchen when we heard the sound of angry voices.

"What do you mean they got away?" Paco yelled as Chenoa continued to prepare dinner. She had changed into jeans and a t-shirt.

"They retreated. We are going to get them, Dad. Don't worry."

Cole stepped up, leaving me in the doorway.

"It's my fault, but I'll take care of everything."

Paco turned sharply to see who had spoken. He looked worried and tired. His eyes suddenly darted to me. I blushed out of embarrassment.

Paco sighed, "Be careful." He was talking to Cole. Paco walked by me and out the front door.

"Don't worry about him," Chenoa said. "He's just worried about the tribe." I nodded, looking to the floor.

It seemed that Paco still hadn't accepted me. My heart longed for him to understand. Now that I knew I couldn't be without Cole, Paco and Elsu would have to deal with me. I wouldn't survive another day without Cole. Because that was all I did when he was gone. I merely survived, existed. No one could call that living.

I was taken out of my thoughts when I felt a pair of warm arms envelop me. My pulse raced, and my heart felt like it was going to burst out of my chest. This was the feeling that I had missed terribly. The raw, gaping hole in my heart was healed. No more shooting pain. The weeks of my life without Cole were days I never wanted to revisit. I leaned into Cole willingly. I was whole again, and I was never going to give that up.

"So, she's staying the night, right?" I heard Chenoa ask from behind Cole.

I buried my head in Cole's chest. His t-shirt smelled like trees and rain. I breathed it in, trying to memorize it.

"Yes," he replied into my hair, "she's staying." I smiled, looking up to Cole's face. He caught me off guard. He wasn't smiling like I had pictured. He had a very serious expression, like he was deep in thought.

"Is something wrong?"

"What about Emma?" he asked, holding me closer to him.

"She's in Mississippi covering a story." He looked puzzled.

"She left you alone? Jacy said someone was with you."

"That was my Aunt Cassie's friend, Alexia Hamilton."

Both Cole and I turned in surprise when we heard a clatter and the shattering of glass. I was shocked to find Chenoa leaning over the sink with broken measuring cup pieces everywhere.

"Chenoa?" Cole asked, letting go of me and walking toward his sister. "What's wrong?" Her mouth hung open and her eyes were wide. She looked as if she had seen a ghost. She quickly recovered, shaking her head.

"I'm fine. The cup slipped."

Cole looked at her warily. "Are you sure?"

"Yeah," she snapped, "I'm fine."

"Wait," realization hit me, "I have to go back home." Both Chenoa and Cole looked to me cautiously.

"No. You are staying here," Cole demanded, taking a step toward me.

"When the rebels came, they left my house in a mess. If Alexia comes home to that, I'm gonna be dead," I groaned. The last thing I needed was an irate Alexia. Both Chenoa and Cole chuckled and then it grew to all-out laughter. I stared dumbly at them.

"How is this funny?"

"Don't worry about your house. We've taken care of it," Chenoa replied, picking up the broken pieces of glass and throwing them away.

"How?"

"We have our ways," she winked.

After Chenoa checked out my injuries and bandaged my head, we sat down for dinner. Chenoa had made chicken for dinner. I hadn't realized how hungry I was until I was asking for thirds.

"Are you hungry?" I asked Cole.

"I'll eat something later," he replied. "I'm enjoying myself right now."

"Doing what?" I was confused. He was just watching me be a pig. It couldn't be that entertaining.

"Watching you. I can't believe you're sitting next to me," he brought his hand to my face, gently caressing my cheek. "I have to keep reminding myself that I'm not dreaming."

"Me too," I agreed.

Chenoa excused herself and left Cole and me alone.

"I'm sorry I left," he whispered, his eyes staring at our interwoven fingers.

"Me too," I repeated, "Don't ever do that again."

He looked up, a smile tugging at his lips, "Never."

I nodded, "Good."

"Can you tell me something?" he asked as I pushed my empty plate away.

"Of course."

"How did Chandler get to you?" His eyes went cold at the mention of Chandler's name. "What exactly happened?"

I swallowed hard, "I made a deal with him."

Cole slammed his fist on the table, "You did what?"

Tears stung my eyes, "I thought it would be best. You know, you said you didn't want to be my friend, so maybe if I just ended it, gave them what they wanted, you and your tribe could live in peace." My head began to throb again.

"Adeline," his voice was much softer now. I looked up and found his face crumbled in guilt. "I didn't mean that, you know, what I said when I left. I was trying to protect you the best way I knew how. Guess it failed…"

"You could say that."

"But don't ever do that again," his voice was severe again. "Don't ever give up like that. I won't live without you, Adeline. I can't."

I nodded, a few stray tears falling down my cheeks, "Okay. I promise."

Too soon, Cole had to leave to meet up with the rest of the Chosen. Luckily, Chenoa was staying behind with me.

"I'll be back soon," he whispered into my ear while holding me close. We stood on his front porch saying our goodbyes. I was being utterly ridiculous. I was so afraid to let Cole go. I almost started crying again. He tried to pull away, but I held him closer. I suppose he could have easily pushed me away, but didn't.

"I promise I'll be back as soon as I can," he whispered. "I am so sorry."

I felt guilty for making him feel remorseful, but I couldn't help it. He pulled away to look at me. I glanced up and was appalled to find my eyes watery. I couldn't believe I was crying. I was only hurting Cole more.

"Oh, Adeline," he whispered. His face crumbled in pain. I was causing him agony.

"I'm fine," I croaked, "I'm just gonna miss you."

I was pleasantly surprised when Cole's lips crashed onto mine. It was a desperate kiss, not like the first. Desperate in the way he seemed to be trying to convince me he would return. When we broke apart, we were both gasping for air.

"I'll be back. I love you, Adeline," he said as he placed one last kiss on my forehead.

"I love you too," I whispered as he turned to go. My heart almost burst. He loved me. I watched as he ran into the woods. I wondered why he didn't take his truck, but understood when I heard a thunderous explosion. I looked up and found an eagle flying above the house. Chenoa came up behind me and placed her arm around my shoulder.

"He'll be back. Don't worry."

I looked to Chenoa and found her smiling. I tried to smile back, but I was sure it looked more like a grimace.

"Let's get you inside. You probably want a shower," Chenoa said as she led me inside and upstairs to her room. A shower sounded nice. I must have looked pretty rough.

Chenoa brought me a towel and some clothes to change into. I walked into her pink bathroom and was shocked to find my bag of toiletries sitting next to the sink. When did Chenoa get my things?

I took a long shower, washing the leaves and dried blood out of my hair. As soon as I was done, I changed and towel dried my hair. I winced when I brushed the tender spot on my head. A bruise was slowly forming. Chenoa was sitting on her bed, waiting for me.

"When did you get my things?" I asked, holding up my bag.

"When Olivia and Ava went to your house to clean up the mess. I had them bring some clothes too," Chenoa replied, pointing to my overnight bag that was sitting on her desk.

"Oh, thanks. Who are Ava and Olivia?"

"Two of the Chosen. Ella and I are the other girls," she replied with a smile. "I hope you don't mind borrowing my pajamas. Ava and Olivia seem to have forgotten yours."

"Oh, I don't mind," I replied looking down to Chenoa's pink tank top and matching shorts. "Thank you." Silence ensued as Chenoa took a brush from her bedside and began brushing and playing with my hair after she had bandaged my head again.

"You know Elsu came to me," I whispered. The memories, all of the memories from that dark place in my life, were very vague, slowly fading. But the memory of Elsu in my living room, telling me to stay away still stung. It threatened to rip open the hole in my chest again.

"I don't know if you've noticed, Adeline, but Elsu is extremely envious of Cole. He doesn't understand why a mixed blood like Cole is the leader of the Chosen. He doesn't understand why someone like you would be interested in Cole over him either," Chenoa explained.

"Wait, why would Elsu be interested in me?" I was flabbergasted. I was pretty sure Elsu hated me.

"Elsu doesn't like you like that, Adeline. He is just so used to being the best, being better than Cole. In every way."

Suddenly, Elsu was beginning to make more sense to me. I now understood why he had such hatred toward his younger brother. He was supposed to be the Delsin and his father's favorite. Elsu was a pureblooded Native while Cole had the blood of his white mother running through his veins. But the love Paco had for Cole's mother transferred to his youngest son, leaving Elsu in the dark. I suddenly felt pity for the eldest son of the Dyami family.

"Well, I'm sure you're exhausted and want to get to bed," Chenoa said, breaking the silence.

"Wait. I have a few more questions."

Chenoa continued to brush through my hair, "Go on."

"Why do the rebels wear those masks? Tyler said something about it protecting their identities."

Chenoa's hands hesitated. Apparently, it wasn't good. "We are not exactly sure but we have reason to believe that the masks are designed to keep the wearer's identity a secret, like what Tyler told you. We also believe that the masks hold the power to help them transform like us. We're not sure how they were able to do it. It has something to do with black magic."

I nodded, taking it all in. "Where did you all go? You know, when Cole said he was leaving," I whispered the last couple of words. The memory of Cole leaving was still too raw and fresh in my mind.

"We trained in the mountains for a while and led the rebels on a false trail back to North Dakota. We came back when Jacy told us the rebels had returned."

"Wait, how did Jacy tell you?" From what Enola told me, Jacy had been in his eagle form for over a hundred and twenty years.

"When we shift into our eagle partners, we are able to talk to each other through our thoughts. Some of us are having trouble controlling what we mean for everyone to hear and what is to remain private," Chenoa smirked.

"So, you can read each other's minds, but only when you want to?"

"Sort of," Chenoa sighed. "It's hard to explain, but the communication is very useful when we are in flight."

I nodded in agreement. There was so much I wanted to know, but I felt drowsy. "What about those leather pouches?" I asked suddenly when I saw Chenoa's lying on the floor. "Why do you all wear them?"

"Well, when we shift we don't exactly transform with clothes on. We have to bring these pouches because they contain shorts and tops. We wear them when we fly too. It doesn't weigh much."

I blushed at her explanation. I should have known that. I looked to Chenoa's digital clock, unhappy with how late it was. Cole still wasn't back yet.

"Don't worry about him," Chenoa said, noticing my constant turning to look at the clock. "He'll be back soon."

I nodded in agreement, but the hollow feeling in my chest was threatening to return.

"He's pretty much the same way when he is without you," Chenoa continued, trying to comfort me. "You were in his thoughts only. I don't think anything or anyone else ever crossed his mind."

"Really?"

"Really."

I was taken out of my thoughts when I heard the front door slam open. The house shook with the force.

"This is ridiculous!" I heard Elsu yell as he stomped his way up the stairs and into his room, slamming the door when he made it there. I heard another set of footsteps slowly make their way toward Chenoa's room. There was a light knock on the door.

"Come in, Cole!" Chenoa greeted. My face broke into a grin as my personal cherub entered the room.

"Cole!" I yelped as he walked over to me in two long strides and pulled me into him, lifting my feet off of the ground.

He breathed into my hair, "I missed you."

"I missed you too," I mumbled into his t-shirt.

"I'll give you two some privacy," Chenoa giggled as she skipped out of her room.

"So, how was training?" I asked as Cole sat down on Chenoa's bed, still holding me.

"We've had better. It was mainly to talk strategy," Cole explained, "Not everyone is thrilled with my course of action."

"Is one of them Elsu?"

Cole rolled his eyes, "How could you tell?"

"Well, the door slamming was a good clue."

Cole laughed causing my head to bob up and down with his chest. I pulled away to look into Cole's eyes. He looked to me, his smile fading slightly. "How are you?"

"Better now," I replied honestly, "You can't leave me ever again."

"I know, and I never will. I need you, Adeline," he whispered while pressing his forehead against mine.

"I know. Chenoa told me."

"Of course she did," he replied sarcastically.

"It's okay. I'm glad."

"Yes, but I would have liked to have been the one to tell you how much you mean to me," he explained, his blue eyes shining love and adoration back at me. I was taken aback by the passion in his voice and the love in his eyes.

"It's never too late to do it yourself," I replied breathlessly.

He smiled while taking my face in both of his large, warm, calloused hands.

"Adeline Connor Jasely," he spoke with a tone of seriousness and endearment, "I love you, and I don't ever want to be away from you from this day on."

My heart felt as if it was about to explode. I gulped, "Ditto."

He laughed, his eyes creasing.

"So, what course of action are you taking that Elsu is not happy with?" I asked, trying to calm my furiously beating heart.

"Well, Elsu and some of the others wish that I would go after the rebels. But that would mean me leaving you, and I refuse to go through that again. So I ordered that we wait for the rebels to come back to us. It is a risk, but so is leaving our land and people vulnerable," Cole explained.

I nodded, " I see. So what do we do now?"

He shrugged, "We wait. They will try to contact us one way or another."

"Oh."

"Don't worry. They won't come near you."

"I know," I replied, leaning into Cole while stifling a yawn.

"It's time for someone to go to sleep," Cole smirked.

"No," I whispered as Cole tucked me into Chenoa's bed. It was so warm, and I was tired.

"Yes," Cole murmured as he turned off the lamp on the bed stand. "Goodnight Adeline."

Just before I drifted into deep sleep, I felt Cole place a kiss on my forehead and then quietly leave Chenoa's room.

ALLISON BLANCHARD

Chapter Seventeen

After spending the weekend with Cole and Chenoa, Cole took me back to my house and Alexia. Luckily for me, the house was clean and Alexia was clueless as to what had occurred. She was even unaware of the still healing wound I had received. Luckily, my hair covered it.

I explained that my absence that weekend was due to Chenoa and Cole moving back. Alexia seemed concerned, but let it go when she saw how genuinely happy I was.

I was elated to have Cole pick me up for school like he had done so many times before. It was as if he had never left, as if there had never been a hole in my chest to begin with. It was even more exciting when he kissed me after I opened the door. It was only a peck, but it left me dizzy and desperate for air.

That Monday I went to school no longer trying to hold myself together, no longer trying to keep the bleeding at bay. I was no longer afraid of the whispers or stares. I no longer cared what other people thought of me. The news of the Dyami family's return to Great Falls had spread like wild fire. Many of the students at Great Falls High welcomed Cole back with open arms. Others had spread rumors on the reason for their return. Most rumors included me.

As quickly as I had become invisible after he left, my sudden popularity grew now that he was back. The first time he came to the school, we were friends. Now it was safe to say we were much more than that. The gossip was hard to take, but having Cole beside me made everything worth it.

Cole pulled into the parking lot and walked me to class before he went to the office for his new class schedule. He held my hand tightly, sometimes placing his arm around my waist protectively. People stared, but I didn't care. I was whole again, finally complete. Cole walked me into my homeroom and pulled the chair out for me to sit in. Brittany's mouth fell open. Joanne looked as if she was going to pass out. I tried to suppress a smirk and turned my attention back to Cole. My Cole.

"I'll be back," he whispered.

He kissed my cheek and left. The air definitely dropped a few degrees after he walked out of the room. The class was speechless, and no one made a move to talk to me or about me. Just as Cole had said, he returned five minutes later and was by my side. I felt incredibly safe with him near. He would protect me.

Days passed and I remained in my blissful, oblivious state. I almost forgot about the impending war. Almost. When Cole drove me home one day, I found Chenoa waiting in the kitchen talking to Alexia. The way Chenoa was staring at Alexia was strange, as if she was seeing a ghost.

"Well hello, Cole, Adeline! Are any of you hungry?" Alexia asked, smiling widely. She was just as happy about Cole being back as I was. She was happy that I was happy.

"No, thank you, Miss Hamilton," Cole replied politely.

"What are you doing here, Chenoa?" I asked as I sat down at the kitchen table. Cole followed suit, sitting next to me.

"I just had an interesting conversation with someone and thought you two should know," she replied as she sat in the seat across from Cole and me.

Cole's face fell, and anxiety filled me. I knew these past few days were going too well to stay that way. Alexia noticed that she didn't have enough ingredients for dinner. Thankfully for us, she had to go to the supermarket.

"Will Chenoa and Cole be joining us for dinner?" Alexia asked as she began to leave, grabbing her jacket and keys.

"Oh no, thank you. We'll be leaving soon," Chenoa replied, smiling.

"Okay. I'll see you all later." Alexia left. A few moments of silence passed and no one moved.

"What's happened?" Cole asked slowly.

"They contacted us. They want to make a deal."

"What sort of deal?" His eyes narrowed. My heart was hammering against my ribcage. My grip on Cole's hand tightened when Chenoa shifted uncomfortably in her seat.

"They said they would leave us alone, no more war if..."

"If what?"

"If we give them Adeline and let them see if she truly is the reincarnation."

Cole slammed his fists on the table. I thought the wood would break under the force.

"Absolutely not!" he yelled.

"Calm down," Chenoa sighed, "Obviously, that isn't an option."

Cole and Chenoa continued to talk after Cole had calmed somewhat and sat back down. To be honest, I wasn't listening. The deal wasn't so bad. If it meant keeping Cole and the others safe, then it would be worth it. One life for a whole tribe. Jacy flashed across my mind. All the unnecessary deaths caused by this war could stop if I just gave the rebels what they wanted.

I felt sick at the thought of never seeing Cole again. We had only been together for a few days, and now I was on the verge of losing him again. I loved him, but did I love him enough to sacrifice myself for his tribe?

I didn't need to think twice. Of course I did, and of course I would. If I went with the rebels then there would be no more war. Finally, this tribe would be at peace. It was selfish of me to think that I deserved more time with Cole. Life had given me more than I could have ever dreamed possible. So I should have expected it would need a trade. Nothing lasts forever. So I should be grateful for the time and for the love I was given. Even if it would all be over so much sooner than I would have liked.

Faster than I would have liked, Alexia was back to prepare dinner. Cole and Chenoa stood to leave.

"I'll be back in the morning," Cole whispered in my ear, causing chills to course through my body. He kissed my cheek, then he and Chenoa left. I walked into the kitchen in a daze.

"So, how was school?" Alexia asked while stirring some soup.

"Okay," I replied as I grabbed my bag and headed to my room. "I'm gonna do some homework."

"Dinner will be ready in a few," Alexia called back.

I threw my bag onto my bed and sat on my comforter. My phone was sitting on my bedside table, mocking me. If I called, I would be signing my own death wish. If I didn't call, other innocent people, Cole included, could die.

I walked over to my desk and grabbed the school directory. He had to be in there somewhere. When I found his name and number, I began to tremble. I grabbed my phone and slowly dialed the number, praying that it had been disconnected.

"Hello, Adeline." His voice was deep and husky, much more intimidating than I remembered.

"Chandler?"

"Yes, is there something I can do for you?"

I should have hung up the phone. I should have forgotten my stupid plan. I should have tried to protect myself. I should have called Cole and asked him to stay with me. But I didn't.

"Um, I want to talk to you about that deal. The one you offered earlier," I gulped as he laughed on the other end.

"They told you about that?"

"Yes."

"Well, what would you like to talk about?"

"I'm willing if you promise me something."

"What are your demands?" He was smiling into the receiver. I could feel it. "The same as before?"

"Yes. No more war."

"Deal, but only if you promise you will come willingly. No one can save you at the last minute."

I gulped, "Okay."

"Adeline! Time for dinner!" Alexia called from the kitchen.

"I'll make this short," Chandler replied. He gave me the address to a place where he wanted to meet. "I need you to find a way to get there alone. Do you understand?"

My eyes widened and tears threatened to fall, "Yes."

"No one can know. That would end badly for your friends."

"Yes." Tears stung my eyes.

"Well, I'll see you soon."

The line went dead, as did my future.

*

Word had gotten to the Chosen about Chandler's plan. I didn't know how. Maybe Chandler wanted Cole to know. Maybe he wanted to see the look of horror on Cole's face when I ran from his safe embrace into the arms of death.

Of course, Cole was blissfully unaware of my plan to end my own life. It was even harder to be around Chenoa, so I avoided her whenever I could. There was nothing I wanted more than to tell them. I wanted to tell them what was going to happen and save myself in the process, but that would be selfish. I loved Cole. I loved his tribe. So I was going to prove that love. I refused to be greedy and keep my life to myself. I had opened my heart, let myself be vulnerable, and I was going to have to pay the price.

The battle was going to take place soon, in the same open field where the Chosen usually trained. Cole knew they would be coming back to fight. He said that he and the others were ready. Cole knew how worried I was, so he decided to take me to prom so that I could get my mind on normal things and not worry so much about him. It was then I decided I would go to Chandler, during prom. I would sneak away when Cole least expected. My heart was breaking at the thought, but I had to do this. I had to end this war once and for all. Cole deserved to live, deserved my sacrifice.

*

The pink and white streamers were hung around the gym in an attempt to cover up the dark wood paneling that covered the walls. The balloons were on the floor and tied to the chairs on the stage set for the Prom King and Queen. The gym was decorated according to this year's theme, which I didn't care enough to remember. Everyone was listening and dancing to the loud, vulgar music, smiling to their dates, happy that all the days in preparation had been worth it. The ladies' hair was done by professionals and all of the styles were well worth the money. The manicures and pedicures went perfectly with the colors of the dresses and the limos managed to arrive on time.

All of the normal teenage planning and desires seemed trivial to me. Instead of being carefree like the other girls surrounding me, I was, in a way, fighting for my life and for the lives of nine other people. For the lives of an entire tribe.

We walked through the fake ivy archway into the gym and stopped, only to have our picture taken. I don't remember if I was smiling or not. Cole held my hand the entire car ride to the gym and throughout the night. Cole and I danced a little, but my mind was somewhere else.

"Adeline," Cole whispered into my ear as we continued to dance, his arms protectively holding me close to him.

"Yeah?" I asked, my eyes still scanning the gym door with the prom posters taped on.

"Don't worry," he kissed my forehead, causing the butterflies in my stomach to flutter. "Enjoy this night. No one is going to hurt you."

To be perfectly honest, it wasn't my safety that I was entirely concerned about. I felt so guilty for what I was about to do. I was breaking my promise, leaving Cole in order to save him. It was hard knowing that tonight would be the last night I would ever see him again.

Any normal person would have run away by now. She would have left Cole and would have a normal life, with no angry Native American tribes looking for revenge. She wouldn't care about what would happen to Cole or to the other eight Chosen who lived their lives to protect her and would give them up in an instant if need be. This was one of the first moments that I was thankful for not being normal. The other eight people that I had slowly begun to accept were watching out for me, had become my second family. If anything happened to them, I would never forgive myself.

After our seventh dance, Cole asked if I wanted anything to drink. "Yes," I replied hastily. This was my chance to run, to get away before he knew.

He laughed, "Okay. I'll be right back."

"Cole!" I grabbed his arm. Fear had taken hold of me again.

"Yes?"

I looked up to find his beautiful face confused. I almost gave myself away then, almost broke down in sobs. I almost told him what I was about to do, but I didn't.

"I'm gonna go to the restroom," I said quickly, before I lost my nerve.

He smiled again. I tried to commit it to memory.

"Okay. See you soon."

I looked up to his blue eyes, looking for reassurance. I was taken aback when his lips crashed onto mine. He kissed me roughly, but lovingly at the same time. It was like he knew we didn't have much time left. Guilt washed over me again. This was really going to hurt him. He smiled before walking toward the drinks. I turned and ran out the door, never looking back.

*

"You look beautiful," Chandler said as he took my hand and kissed it. I flinched in response, fighting back the tears.

I had made it to the location Chandler told me about. It was an abandoned shop downtown. Chandler had been waiting patiently.

"Anyone follow you?" I shook my head, trying to stop the stinging of tears that were threatening to fall.

"You ready to go?" he smiled, pulling a brown sack out of his jacket. I nodded, unable to find my voice.

"That's a good girl," Chandler smiled as he took my face with his hand. He brushed my cheek with his thumb. Suddenly, the bag was pulled over my head, and Chandler quickly tied my hands together.

"This may hurt, darling, but it's just a precaution," he whispered. Something hard and cold hit the back of my head. Then everything went black.

I woke to a throbbing headache and a bump on the back of my head. The bag was still over my head, so I couldn't see anything. All I could gather was that I was no longer in the old shop, but tied to a chair. I thought I was outside because of the chill in the air. My breathing became shallow as I heard footsteps echo toward me. Someone ripped the bag off my head. I looked around and found myself in a warehouse with large crates surrounding me. Then I saw Chandler standing in front of me, smiling.

"How was your sleep? Good, I hope," he said, walking in a circle around me.

My mind was spinning, and I was trying to remember exactly what was happening. I groaned aloud when I remembered. I was going to die.

"Well, darling," Chandler whispered in my ear as he wrapped his arms around me from behind, "I have been waiting a long time for this moment."

My skin rose, and my body began to quiver. Tears steadily flowed down my cheeks, staining my light blue dress.

"Well get on with it," someone said from the shadows. I noticed that all of the other rebels were hiding themselves in the shadows of the crates. One by one, they all walked into sight. Shudders coursed through my body as I stared at them. There were many more than I remembered. There had to be at least fifteen, maybe even twenty. There was no way that Cole and the others could fight all of these men off.

One of the men was eyeing me, his whole body shaking with excitement. He was tall and muscular. He reminded me of Elsu, only more menacing.

"Let me at her," he whispered to Chandler. My eyes widened in horror. What were these men going to do to me? I struggled with the ropes that were tying me to the chair. My hands were chafing against the ropes as I tried to struggle free. The men watched, amused.

"Let's enjoy this while we can," Chandler said to everyone.

Everyone began to laugh except for one. I noticed Tyler was standing behind the others with what looked like guilt and sorrow etched across his face. He was looking at me with pity and remorse. A flicker of hope burned in my chest. Maybe he would help me. The hope burned out when he turned his back to me and walked into the shadows. My head fell, as did my hope of living. What was I expecting? That Chandler would honor my sacrifice and possibly give me mercy?

I felt someone's hand grab my chin and lift my head up. Chandler was looking me in the eye, joy and victory evident in his brown orbs.

"Look at me. I want to see your face when I take you away from this world. I want to be able to recall it perfectly so I can tell

Cole exactly how it happened." Tears blurred my vision. I only hoped Cole would forgive me.

"Untie her," Chandler ordered, letting my face go. I felt someone come behind me and untie the ropes that had cut the circulation to my hands. I fell out of the chair onto the cement floor. I caught myself with my hands, but the impact caused me to flinch back in pain.

"Ouch," I muttered as I rubbed my wrists, trying to get the blood flowing.

"Now can I have her?" the same man from before asked, this time shaking even more. Chandler held his palm up to him.

"No. She's mine."

I stared at him as he took another step toward me. I was shocked when he slapped me across the face. I felt warm liquid cascading down my cheeks. It took me a moment to realize that he had caused a gash.

Chandler walked toward me, and I tried to crawl away. I was too slow, and he was inhumanly fast. He grabbed my neck with one hand and held me up. Oxygen was no longer reaching my lungs as the grip around my neck was becoming tighter by the second. It wouldn't be long now. I tried to be patient and not focus on the pain my lungs and heart were enduring.

Chandler stared at me with frustration written across his features. He squeezed harder, and I continued to gasp. I tried to dig my nails into his hand, but it was like he was made of stone. I didn't even make a scratch.

"What's wrong?" I heard someone ask. The voices were becoming fuzzy. I recognized the voice and face of Tom. He walked up to Chandler, seemingly unaware of the fact that I was being strangled.

"Isn't she supposed to do something?" Chandler asked exasperated. Tom finally took notice of me and sighed.

"What?" Chandler asked angrily. His hold on my neck became loose and I took in a much-needed breath.

"You should have known this would happen."

"Known what would happen?"

"She came willingly. She came to sacrifice herself so that the Chosen wouldn't have to fight. She gave up the will to live. She doesn't want to survive," Tom explained while shaking his head in disappointment at Chandler.

Chandler growled angrily and threw me to the ground. I hit the cement with a loud thud. Pain shot through my body from where I hit the ground. I closed my eyes, trying to keep myself from crying out in pain.

"What do you mean she gave up the will to live? How do we fix that?" Chandler asked Tom, obviously unhappy. I opened my eyes slightly and saw Tom staring at me intently.

"We give her a reason. Get the masks." Everyone took out something from their pockets. Chandler was the last to pull something out.

The masks are designed to keep the wearer's identity a secret. We have reason to believe that the masks hold the power to help them transform, like us. We're not sure how they were able to do it. It has something to do with black magic...

I looked quickly to every covered face around me. Fear and panic swept through me. I stood up and tried to look for an exit, any way to wake up from this nightmare. Suddenly, all of the men disappeared into thin air after several thunder-like explosions. I blinked a couple of times trying to understand what happened. It was then that I heard a loud hawk cry.

I looked up, and found twenty hawks perched on the beams and crates, their human-like eyes watching my every move. They were large and intimidating. I immediately noticed one circling the air above me. I realized he was Chandler, and he was marking me as his prey. I did the only thing I knew to do. I ran as fast as I could, through the cracks between the crates. I ran fast and hard. It was hard to do wearing heels, but I didn't care. I heard the sound of wings flapping above me, all around me. They all cried in unison.

My breathing became hard and shallow. My muscles ached, but I couldn't stop. I had to get away. My heart fell when I ran into a dead end. Nothing but crates. Tears stung the back of my eyes as I tried to push the crates out of my way. It was useless, but I tried anyway.

"Oh, come now, Adeline. I thought you came willingly. Isn't that what you said on the phone?"

I turned around sharply and found Chandler walking toward me. I was completely pushed up against the crates, my back to them. He continued to take steps toward me, enjoying the fear he saw in me. My heart hammered against my ribs; adrenaline pumped through my veins. I wanted it to end soon. I wanted to wake up from this nightmare.

Chandler was on me. He had his hand wrapped around my neck like before. The sound of the hawks crying faded as I stared at Chandler.

"What?" he asked mockingly, "You aren't gonna fight back?"

He squeezed harder. My windpipe was completely blocked, and for some reason, my body wasn't struggling in pain. Maybe this was what it felt like to pass from this world in to the next because I no longer felt Chandler's hard, calloused hand wrapped around my neck. I no longer saw the warehouse I was in or the other rebels. All I saw was a bright light. It felt like I was floating. The air around me was warm and inviting. It smelled like flowers and ocean water.

I saw someone walking toward me, her long blonde hair flowing to her feet. She was very tall and lean. Her skin was pale, almost translucent, and her eyes were the palest gray I had ever seen. Her skin and hair sparkled in the light, and she was smiling, her white teeth shinning. I had never in my whole life seen someone so beautiful. It was unearthly.

"Wh-who are you?" I asked. My voice echoed, like I was in a cave. I looked around, but saw nothing but light and the woman in front of me.

"I am Ogin," her voice was smooth and pleasant, "and you are Adeline."

"How do you know that?" I stuttered. My knees were shaking.

"I know a lot about you. Everything about you. All of your thoughts, hopes, and dreams."

"How?"

"Well, I am a part of you," she replied as if it was obvious. I was confused. I thought I was dead and here I was talking to an angel who apparently knew me. She laughed and it sounded like bells.

"Oh no. You are not dead."

I took in my surroundings with my eyebrows raised, "No, I'm pretty sure I'm dead. Isn't this heaven?"

"No."

Oh.

"No, you are not in hell, either. You are not dead," she sounded exasperated, yet lovely at the same time.

"Then where am I?"

"That's difficult to explain."

"I think I have plenty of time."

"You really don't," she replied, taking a step toward me. Her scent almost knocked me over. She smelled like wet flowers and honey. Everything smelled sweet. She laid her hand on my shoulder.

"You are inside of yourself," she explained slowly, "Your time has come, although it wasn't supposed to be this way. No matter, you are now ready."

"Ready for what?"

She smiled warmly. Suddenly, I felt myself being pulled downward and the warm air around me disappeared. The angel, Ogin, was fading away. I felt myself hit something solid and cold. My body suddenly throbbed with pain. My eyes were too weak to open, but I heard everything loud and clear.

"Where is she?" someone yelled angrily. I knew that voice.

"I don't know," someone else replied. I knew her too.

The sounds of eagles crying and screeching filled the air. I lay on the cement floor motionless, trying to stop the throbbing of my head. I moaned as I tried to stretch my legs and arms out to see if I had any broken bones. I yelped when I tried to twist my left ankle. It felt like it was shattered.

"I hear something over here," a deep voice yelled.

Footsteps echoed, coming closer and closer. I only hoped that it wasn't Chandler coming to finish me off.

"Oh, my!" someone gasped. I probably looked as bad as I felt. "Adeline!" he yelled passionately.

My eyes shot open at the sound of his voice. "Cole?" I croaked. My throat was dry. I felt warm arms lift me carefully. He held me against his chest and gently kissed my cheeks. I was safe. I was home.

"I am so sorry," he sobbed as he held me tightly, but without causing pain.

"Cole. I'm sorry I lied…"

"Shh, you have nothing to apologize for," he whispered. I felt him wrap something around me, but I wasn't sure. Probably his jacket, but I was too busy trying to stay awake.

"Cole," someone said, obviously stressed, "we have to get her out of here now. They can only keep this up for so long."

"Chenoa?" I muttered.

Cole stood up, easily carrying me from where I had been laying.

"Don't worry about anything. You are going to be okay," Chenoa whispered as she gently stroked my hair.

"Close your eyes. When you wake up, you'll be away from here and safe," Cole said, his voice comforting, causing my eyelids to feel heavy.

"I want to help," I muttered incoherently.

The sounds of fighting were even louder than before, but they steadily faded as I focused on Cole's breathing and heartbeat, my own personal lullaby.

He smirked, "You have already helped. You've done so much. Thank you."

I fell into a dreamless slumber, completely unaware of the battle that was taking place around me.

*

The sound of rain beating against a window woke me from my sleep. My body ached with pain and my mind felt numb. I felt something heavy on my left ankle. I tried to move it, but winced in pain.

"She's awake." The voice was soft and familiar, but it was hard to place.

I opened my eyes, but closed them when I saw the burning light. I tried again, this time more carefully. I succeeded in opening my eyes and found myself in my bed at home. I looked to my right and found Alexia and Emma sitting next to me. Alexia was calm and smiling. Emma's eyes were swollen from tears. Guilt swept over me, slightly numbing the pain.

"Emma?" I asked. It came out in a whisper. I wasn't even sure if she heard me.

"I'm here, baby," she said, taking my bandaged hand in hers. "How are you feeling?"

I nodded. It was the only move I could make without my body throbbing. I suddenly became aware of a third person in the small, cramped room. He was standing on the other side of the wall, next to my computer. He wasn't moving, only watching. He looked like a statue made of pure bronze. We locked eyes, and all of the pain suddenly disappeared. I was lost in blue orbs, completely unaware of anyone else in the room. It was just the two of us. Someone coughed, possibly to get my attention. I ignored them, but they coughed again, this time saying my name as well.

"Yeah?" I croaked.

Alexia was staring at me, as well as Emma.

"Maybe we should call the doctor again," Alexia said to Emma, "so he can give us her prescription." Emma nodded and slowly stood from her chair. Alexia followed her out of the room and closed the door quietly.

My heart hammered against my ribcage, painfully, as he walked toward me. He moved the chairs out of the way and got on his knees next to my bed. His eyes were watering and his hands were shaking as he took my hand. He carefully kissed it. He rested his head on my hand, being careful not to cause any pain. The warmth his body gave off felt nice, much better than the pile of blankets.

"I am so sorry, Adeline," he whispered into my hand, "I am so sorry."

"You didn't do anything wrong. You saved me."

"I put you in danger."

He lifted his head, and I was surprised when I saw tears flowing down his face. It was a crime to make an angel cry.

"Please don't cry," I begged, "Please."

"I almost lost you," he said, his voice very quiet. "I almost lost the one thing that I live for. Adeline, I'm not sure if you truly know how much I need you. How much I love you."

I smiled and he noticed.

"What?" he asked, seeming confused.

"You love me."

He smiled, "I have always loved you. I always will. I am yours, Adeline." He kissed my hand again, "I am yours until you don't want me anymore." I shook my head furiously, causing another headache.

"I will always want you. I need you too."

He smiled again, white teeth showing, causing my heart to flutter.

"How long have I been asleep?" I asked, trying to keep myself from blushing. I was not sure if it worked.

"About a day and a half. The meds the doctor gave you were pretty strong," he replied, gently stroking my hair.

"So, what happened?" I asked. My memory was still hazy. All I could remember were bits and pieces.

"Well, we told them that you fell off of Chenoa's balcony. Doesn't seem that farfetched," he smirked.

I rolled my eyes, causing another wave of pain.

"But what really happened?"

His smile faded and he looked to my hand again. He caressed it gently.

"Cole?"

"The others tried to entice the power out of you. They tried to put you in a life-or-death situation, something that would trigger your power and cause you to save yourself. But you didn't. You blacked out."

"What happened to the rebels?"

"We destroyed most of them. However, several got away. Chandler was one of them, but Tyler surrendered. He is being debriefed as we speak. You know, if it wasn't for him, I don't think we would have made it in time."

"What do you mean?" I asked, perplexed.

"Tyler led us to you."

The words took a moment to sink in. So Tyler had helped me after all.

"I owe him my life," Cole added.

"How?"

"Because he saved yours. You are my life, my everything. Don't forget that," he kissed my forehead. My pulse raced, and I tried to steady my breathing.

"What now?"

Cole sighed, his warm breath intoxicating me.

"We wait. We wait for them to make their next move. They won't give up, Adeline."

I nodded, my mind and body slowly succumbing to sleep again. I tried to fight it. I wanted to talk to Cole more. I wanted to hear his voice.

"Cole," I said, my words slurred, "I love you."

I heard him chuckle, "I love you too. Now sleep. I'll be here when you wake."

I closed my eyes, satisfied with my life. So I had a few bumps and bruises, but I was alive. I was alive, and Cole was by my side. No matter what happened, no matter who came after us, I knew that Cole would protect me. Even if I was this heavenly being, which I still wasn't positive about, I had Cole, my best friend. I had a reason to live, to fight, to believe.

EPILOGUE

The car ride was peaceful. The sounds of her breathing and her heartbeat were music to my ears. Never in my whole life did something sound so beautiful. I glanced over to her again, trying to suppress my smile. She was beautiful, even with her neon green cast and crutches. Her hair was down, flowing and framing her face. Her eyes were watching the world outside the window, carefully memorizing anything that she saw.

She brought the bouquet of flowers to her nose and took a deep breath. Personally, the scent of the blue forget-me-nots paled in comparison to the woman beside me. She was indeed a work of art. I turned into the graveyard carefully and drove until the voice of an angel stopped me.

"Stop here. This is it," she said, smiling as she pointed to a spot to park.

I carefully parked the car and jumped out. I ran to her side and opened the door, her scent almost knocking me over. I grabbed her crutches from the backseat and leaned them against the truck. I gently picked her up and held her as I closed the door and handed her the crutches. She smiled her thank you and began leading the way. I walked beside her, while carrying the bouquet she had picked this morning.

She stopped when she came to two graves nestled under a tree, the leaves shielding the graves from the morning sun. She handed me her crutches, and I grabbed her waist.

"I've got it, Cole," she whispered.

I loosened the hold on her waist, but didn't completely let go. She got on her knees and reached for the flowers in my hands. I handed them to her as I sat down on my knees. She placed them in the pot between the two graves. It was all very serene. The air felt warmer, more at peace. The graves read:

Samuel Jasely and Nicole Jasely
Beloved Parents
"The Lord is my Shepard. I shall not want." ~ Psalm 23

"Mom, Dad, this is Cole Dyami. He's my best friend," Adeline whispered, breaking my thoughts. I smiled at the woman beside me. Her heart was so pure and her intentions good.

"Hello, Mr. and Mrs. Jasely. It's nice to finally meet you."

My mind went back to the time when I first introduced Adeline to my mother. How vulnerable I felt. I suddenly felt humbled by her. How she was willing to let me see her in her most helpless state. Adeline sighed deeply, her head hanging.

"What's wrong?" I asked, suddenly worried.

"I miss them," she croaked, her tears falling down her cheeks. I pulled her into me, gently wiping away the tears, wishing I could mend her broken heart.

"I'm sorry," I whispered. I didn't know what else to say.

She lifted her head and, once again, her eyes took my breath away. They were the windows to her soul, and I wanted nothing more than to drown in them. To know how she felt, to feel a part of her. To understand how this amazing creature could love a monster like me.

"I love you," she whispered, as if she was trying to clear away my doubts.

"I love you more than anything," I replied, holding her closer to me.

She rested her head against my chest, closing her eyes. My heart jumped, and my face broke into a grin. I felt at home with her. She was the missing piece to a puzzle that I didn't even know I was trying to solve. I swore that I would protect her, and I would. I would with every fiber of my being.

I knew our peace would not last forever. I knew the rebels would return, but with her, I didn't care. She was worth fighting for, worth dying for. She was my best friend, my everything.

We sat under the tree next to her parents' graves. We laughed and cried. We stayed like that, in our own state of being, until the sun began to set. And as we got ready to leave, as we watched another day end, I looked down to the girl beside me. Our life together was just beginning, just starting to mold and take shape. I smiled to myself, and thanked God for the chance to love one of His angels.

ABOUT THE AUTHOR

Allison Blanchard is currently a student at Georgia College and State University in Milledgeville, Georgia where she is pursuing her bachelor degrees in English Creative Writing and French. She is an active sister in Sigma Alpha Omega where she continues to grow as a woman in Christ. She writes every day, drinks too much coffee, and is looking forward to the next adventure her characters will take her.

Made in the USA
Charleston, SC
29 October 2012